Dear Little Black Dress Reader,

Thanks for picking up this Little Black Dress book, one of the great new titles from our series of fun, page-turning romance novels. Lucky you – you're about to have a fantastic romantic read that we know you won't be able to put down!

Why don't you make your Little Black Dress experience even better by logging on to

www.littleblackdressbooks.com

where you can:

- Enter our **monthly competitions** to win **gorgeous** prizes
- Get **hot-off-the-press** news about our latest titles
- Read **exclusive** preview chapters both from your **favourite** authors and from brilliant new writing talent
- Buy **up-and-coming** books online
- Sign up for an essential slice of romance via our **fortnightly email** newsletter

We love nothing more than to curl up and indulge in an addictive romance, and so we're delighted to welcome you into the Little Black Dress club!

With love from,

The *little black dress* team

A graduate of New York University, Karen Yampolsky has spent the past eighteen years working as an executive/personal assistant to high-profile executives in the media and entertainment industries, including a nine-year stint at *Jane* magazine as the right-hand woman to the founder and editor-in-chief, Jane Pratt. She lives in Westchester County, New York, with her husband and two children.

Falling out of Fashion

Karen Yampolsky

little black dress

First published in 2007
by KENSINGTON BOOKS

First published in Great Britain in hardback in 2007
by LITTLE BLACK DRESS
An imprint of HEADLINE PUBLISHING GROUP

First published in Great Britain in paperback in 2007
by LITTLE BLACK DRESS
An imprint of HEADLINE PUBLISHING GROUP

A LITTLE BLACK DRESS paperback
1

Cataloguing in Publication Data is available from the British Library

ISBN 978 0 7553 3954 9

Typeset in Transit511BT by Avon DataSet Ltd,
Bidford-on-Avon, Warwickshire

Printed and bound in Great Britain by Clays Ltd, St Ives plc

HEADLINE PUBLISHING GROUP
A division of Hachette Livre UK Ltd
338 Euston Road
London NW1 3BH

www.littleblackdressbooks.co.uk
www.headline.co.uk

For Steven, Ben, and Lily

Acknowledgments

This book could not have been completed without the help and support of my closest friends and family. They know who they are but I want their names here anyway. So thank you so, so much, Squid, for all of your help, direction, and genius imagination. Roger Cohen for being my dad, my friend, and my lawyer. My mom, Audrey Cohen, who is a constant source of support. Marilyn Yampolsky for always being there, just a phone call away. Sharon, Dalita, and Geri for not only your input and your humor, but for being the best kind of women a girl could call friends. My extended Cohen and Yampolsky families – Nancy, Andrew, Paige, Max, Stephen, Michelle, Phillip, Daniel, Yetta, Gail, Jackie, David, Leah, Danielle, Mark, Terry, Rachel, Aaron, and Hannah – I love every one of you more than I can say.

Big thanks to John Scognamiglio at Kensington for your excitement and your patience.

Thank you to my agent, Frank Weimann, and everyone at The Literary Group, for your hard work on my behalf, and for believing in the potential for a first-time author and the story I wanted to tell.

Thanks and love to Jane Pratt for being a great boss and friend and an inspiration to me and a million other women.

And, finally, thanks to Steven, Ben, and Lily, who were

even more excited than I was by the idea of this project and, with their love, support, and beautiful faces, helped me believe I could do it.

1

Jill's Ad Pages Suffer 10% Decline

— AdAge, October 2004

It started like any typical workday. At about ten minutes past noon, I chugged the last drops of my Diet Coke just as the elevators opened onto the eighth floor. I had forgotten my ID and had already been subjected to everything but a cavity search by building security. So I was relieved to see that the usual box of copy paper was propping the glass door open. The eighth floor didn't have a receptionist, so if the box of copy paper wasn't there, I'd have to call someone to let me in. Not a big deal, but I liked to keep my arrival into the office as inconspicuous as possible. Which, in actuality, was impossible. It was impossible due to 'the walk.'

Because of the layout of the floor, there was no way for me to get to my office without being accosted by nearly every staffer along the way. Not that I had anything against my staffers – most of them I really liked. But 'the walk' was just a ritual that made the act of getting to my office and, then, actually getting some work done, an even longer, more drawnout time-consuming process than it already was.

I suppose I could avoid the problem by getting into the office before anyone else. Which meant before 9 A.M. Which was completely, absolutely out of the question. It's not that I was a total diva about early mornings; it's just that after benefits, parties, and late-night live television interviews – all to keep the magazine's PR profile up – combined with my lovely insomnia problem – I needed a few extra hours of sleep in the morning.

So to deal with 'the walk' as graciously as possible, I sometimes liked to picture it as a 'red-carpet' kind of walk. Celebrities who arrive at the Oscars, for example, don't stop and chat with every person waiting on the sidelines. Otherwise they would never make it into the ceremony. But they oh so nicely blow them off, cheerfully waving and smiling, stopping only to offer a brief pose or sound bite.

So I put on my best red-carpet smile, pulled open the glass door, and started 'the walk.' As I approached the sea of cubicles, I imagined the alt-funk blaring from a staffer's radio to be sweeping orchestra strings. I pictured the unflattering fluorescents to be bright spotlights. And instead of must, dust, and rotting lunches, I tricked my nose into believing that the stench in my trail was some A-lister's expensive French *parfum*. The cluttered stacks of CDs, books, and back issues became ivory pillars, lining the way. But the Sharpie-defiled Britney Spears poster plastered near the conference room . . . that always stayed in the picture, ensuring that my red-carpet smile stayed in place.

I know it's all a terribly egotistical fantasy, but the illusion amused me. And it gave me my game face – the jeez-Jill-is-so-pleasant-and-cool-and-in-control visage behind the smile. I needed it so much more now, since our managing editor recently had jumped ship. Without her, I had a lot more work and . . . one less barrier from the accosters.

Their barrage began.

'Jill! Will you be able to look at my copy today?'

'Jill! What do you think of this as a "Hoax" for the March issue?'

'Jill! Do you think I'll be able to get your approval on this layout? It ships tonight.'

I sailed on, smiling, responding in rapid fire. 'Heeeeey. Hi. Leave the copy with Casey. Yeah, good "Hoax." Later, I promise.' I practiced my Queen Elizabeth wave. The fantasy was especially useful in making the utter crappiness of the floor melt away. When Nestrom Media first bought us, we moved to the fifteenth floor, sharing it with *Fashionista* magazine. But that didn't last long. I could tell by the fashionistas' consistently disgusted scowls that they couldn't bear our tattoos; piercings; cheap, multihued haircuts; and general slovenliness for long. Before I knew it, we were being kicked downstairs, shoved in a corner behind the cafeteria, between the supply guy and the check-cashing lady. Now it couldn't be any clearer where *Jill* fit into the hierarchy of the Nestrom magazine empire.

Just a few more feet to go. And the onslaught continued. 'Jill! Do you *really* want me to call back Katy Hanson's people and tell her we're not interested in having her on a cover? Really?!'

That one stopped me in my tracks, snapping me right into reality. It came from Rosario, the entertainment editor. 'Yes, really!' I snapped.

'But her album just hit number one,' she halfheartedly pleaded. 'And you said we had to start thinking a little bit more mass appeal for the covers.'

I looked at Rosario, her blue hair matted in all directions. She of all people should know better, I thought. She was a downtown girl – a dj, for crying out loud. I guess she misunderstood me in last week's meeting. 'I meant someone more along the lines of a . . . Jennifer Aniston,' I explained. 'Definitely *not* a cheesy reality show winner. The only way that Katy Hanson would end up on one of our covers would be via a cover line reading 10 REASONS WHY KATY HANSON BLOWS.'

With that, I continued making my way to my office when I felt a furry presence brush my ankle. I stopped again and stooped to pick up Ruggles, Kyra the photo editor's dog. I had no choice but to make Ruggles the office mascot since Kyra brought her in every day, despite more than a few threatening letters from HR. I held the Yorkie to my face, expecting a kiss. But she just yipped at me. I sighed before I tossed her back on the floor. No matter how hard I tried, that dog just didn't like me.

Casey, my assistant, perked up when she saw me approach. I gave her my best don't-let-*anybody*-in look when I reached my office. She knew better than to join the conga line from hell trailing after me, and she usually waited for me to get settled before she confronted me with anything, no matter how urgent. I could tell by her exasperated expression, though, that she had some really pressing, and probably unpleasant, news.

Within a second, Casey was in my office looking me up

and down with her big brown doe eyes. She shook her head. 'Of all days for you to arrive looking like Mary-Kate Olsen dressed you,' she said, referring to my ratty jeans and my stretched-out, extremely vintage yet very comfortable V-neck sweater. 'Get to the fashion closet and the beauty closet, now.'

'Oh, shit,' I said.

'Yeah,' Casey confirmed. 'Liz's been calling all morning. She – *and* Ellen – want to see you right away. Like, half an hour ago.'

I trusted Casey's urgency. She was always looking out for me. Even though she was a few years my junior, in her early thirties, she had a wise, motherly way about her, which contradicted her hip, petite, girlish looks. The best thing about Casey was that she was extremely grounded. She worried for me, put out fires, cleaned up messes, played my 'bad cop,' and only occasionally broke a sweat. She was also one of my few confidants, and her sardonic sense of humor never failed to cheer me up, even on the most dire occasion. Somehow, she was even able to juggle raising two kids in addition to taking care of me. And sometimes I thought she could read me at least as well as my husband.

My phone rang insistently. Casey picked it up. 'Yes, Liz, she'll be there in just a few minutes,' she said, rolling her eyes. 'She's already on her way,' she added, giving me a gentle push toward the door.

'Any important messages?' I asked as I headed off.

'Richard Ruiz,' she called after me. 'He wants to have dinner. Oh, and did I mention that Liz and Ellen want to see you *now*?'

I picked up the pace, fully aware I was most likely facing

another ass chewing. I'd been getting at least one a week since the incredibly brief honeymoon period with Nestrom Media had ended. The postcoital glow hadn't even lasted a month before my new bosses began to lay into me about 'making some changes' and 'getting those ad numbers up.' At first, they were all spirit – 'rah-rah, we're a team; we're the best and we're going to get better.' They threw money at me like they were printing it themselves. I had a budget for clothing, primping, dining, and entertainment that seemed near impossible to spend. Even my staff members were allowed to expense 'twelve working lunches' per month, when they would binge on everything from sushi to porterhouse steaks. If someone on staff was having a birthday, corks from the finest champagne would pop and cake would be delivered from the city's finest bakery. If it was someone senior enough, or someone like Casey, I'd be able to expense a very nice gift, like a Prada wallet. My office looking a little drab? They allowed me to hire an interior decorator to spruce it up, and I put a feng shui expert on the tab while I was at it. If I received a lot of swag at Christmas, I could hire three cars to take it all home. They were only eighty dollars an hour, after all. Did a Nestrom editor need to hop to Paris for a meeting? 'Take the Concorde, for Christ's sake!' T.J. Oldham, the company's chairman would say. Nestrom editors never, ever, ever flew coach.

But of course, there were enormous puppet-like strings attached to all of it. Soon that team spirit and devil-may-care attitude with money devolved into a far less subtle, 'make us more money already, bitch' attitude. When the ad numbers weren't breaking world records, every other day I was subjected to a new mandate, budget cut, or system to implement. If I wanted to reshoot a cover, for example, I now had to beg for it, or use mediocre shots because Nestrom wouldn't want to spend the money. Long gone were the days of adding bells and whistles to an issue – like releasing two different covers, or including a flashy fold-out cover. I now had to fight for such 'extravagance,' as they would call it, while *Fashionista* never seemed to have to fret about any expenditure. (Sometimes I even suspected that cutbacks were made to *Jill* to compensate for Fashionista's elaborate spending.) But I took it all in stride, curbing my habits a bit, too, being a little more conscientious about my spending, when expenses for the whole magazine – and staff – were suddenly scrutinized. I listened patiently, letting the suits feel that they were contributing something, then did what I pleased. After all, my name was on the cover, not theirs.

Nostalgia for the careless, decadent 'old days' still plagued me as I dodged two dozen verbal bullets before I finally hit the fashion closet. Full of cast-off freebies and fashion shoot leftovers, these closets were godsends in emergencies like this. Stepping inside and closing the door behind me, I ripped off my Pumas, jeans, and sweater, leaving them in a heap on the ground. I rifled through the racks, coming upon a navy blue Marc Jacobs skirt in my size. That would do, I thought. As I began to pull it on, the closet door swung open. Sven the art director stood in the doorway. 'We have to talk about the December fashion layout,' he said. 'And if it ends up that Rosario can't get anyone better, I think I can do something with Katy Hanson.'

I defiantly put my hands on my hips, standing there with

nothing on except my lacey pink bra and the Marc Jacobs skirt. 'Later, Sven,' I said, in my best I'm-in-charge-here voice, despite my scanty attire. The minutes were ticking away, and I didn't want to give Liz and Ellen any more reasons to get riled up. 'I promise. And drop the Katy Hanson thing,' I added, giving him a pleading look. I loved him dearly but I had bigger issues to deal with at the moment than our next cover model.

Sven still lingered, turning on his European charm. 'What if we did something completely against her image?' he pressed. 'A tasteful nude, perhaps, with her hands obscuring her breasts. I could light it like a Mapplethorpe. What do you say?'

'No,' I insisted. 'I'm not putting Katy Hanson on the cover just because you want to see her boobs. Plus, we've already got a ton of letters complaining about the abundance of breasts in the last few issues.' Sven definitely appreciated the female physique. A little too much, I'd say. I didn't mind skin in the magazine, but it was my opinion that most women don't want to see perfect 34Cs on every other page.

With that he gave up, yet he still lingered in the doorway. 'Suit yourself,' he said, shrugging.

I quickly pulled on a cranberry and pink, spiral-patterned Anna Sui blouse; found an appropriate pair of D&G shoes; and pushed past Sven's tall, blond frame to get next door into the beauty closet. There, I combed out my hair, which was looking like a wet golden retriever's pelt; grimaced at my dark roots; made a mental note to ask Casey to get me in with my colorist; and put on some lipstick and a swift paint of mascara. I checked myself in the mirror. Almost decent. I was ready to face the Stepford Twins.

That was my secret nickname for Ellen Cutter, CEO and president of Nestrom Media, and Liz Alexander, *Jill*'s brand new publisher, who had arrived shortly after the Nestrom Media purchase. If Martha Stewart, Kappa Kappa Gamma, and Park Avenue had a ménage à trois, Ellen Cutter would be the resulting love child. She had that affluent, blond, bland, studied ivory girl quality, a society carbon copy that made her a bit of a wallflower in the hipper Manhattan media circles. But she was smart, in a benign, conniving way. She had a way of making herself look real good, and taking credit where credit was not due – at least that was what the word that had drifted over from *Charisma*, her last tour of duty, was. Ever since her supposed efforts quadrupled *Charisma*'s ad dollars, she was the industry's reigning despot with a smile.

When Ellen first came on, I was impressed by her efforts to get to know me and actually secretly imagined that she seemed a bit starstruck. There were several lunches, a few postwork glasses of wine, and a couple of events where we gravitated toward each other. Underneath her WASPy exterior, she even showed a bit of an edge, like when she admitted going to a bondage club in my neighborhood. Was I crazy to think that we could get along? It seemed so now.

Liz Alexander had been Ellen's number two at *Charisma*. She was also her number two before that at *Joy!* And the duo even started out together, years ago, at some small food quarterly that no longer exists. She had reddish brown hair, straight as a pin, like Ellen's, and piercing green, Siamese cat eyes, with a stare that was always mistrusting, and sometimes downright frightening. Liz also had a conniving quality, but as the weeks went on, I found it wasn't nearly as benign as

Ellen's. I knew from about day two that I had to watch my back around Liz Alexander.

Liz had a certain holier-than-thou, putting-you-in-your-place attitude and she immediately started playing power games with me. For example, she'd never pick up the phone when I'd call. She would have her assistant answer, then grill me about what the call concerned before she'd take it. And if Liz ever called me, it was never directly. Her assistant would ask me to 'hold for Liz Alexander,' and Liz would never get on the phone until she was certain I was on the line. But after about the third time her assistant asked me to 'hold for Liz,' I cut her off and told her that I didn't have time to hold for anyone, and if Liz really needed to speak to me she could call me directly herself. And whenever we met, there was a little power play about who was coming to whom; Liz *always* wanted me to come up to her office. But after a while I'd occasionally insist that she come down to me, especially if the meeting involved other members of my staff, despite her audible sighs of protest. It was stupid, and catty, I know. But catty people needed to be given a taste of their own kitty litter.

Dreading my latest interaction with her, and Ellen, I hurried out the glass door, nearly tripping on the box of copy paper along the way. An elevator door was just sliding shut, so I jumped at it, sticking my hand over the sensor. 'Thanks,' I said sheepishly to the crowd inside as the doors slid open. When I went to push the button for the thirty-third floor, I realized I had gotten on an elevator going down.

Shit.

When I reached the bottom, I gave another sheepish smile

as I let everyone out and got back in. I frantically pushed the 'door close' button so I could have an express ride. For once, luck was on my side.

When I finally arrived on the thirty-third floor, I took a deep breath, stepped out of the elevator, and gave the receptionist my most confident grin. 'On my way to see Ellen,' I said, as if it wasn't a big deal at all. My stomach's incessant churning, however, betrayed the truth.

Now it was time for my 'Miss America' walk. I felt on parade as I glided past yet another sea of cubicles, but these cubicles were painstakingly neat with gleaming, polished wood trim. My heels sunk into the plush, thick new carpeting, so I had to concentrate extra hard on walking without tripping. I held my head high, taking in the décor – original, signed masterpieces and sleekly framed covers of best-selling issues. I noticed that not a one of them was *Jill*.

Continuing my pageant stride, I nodded at Michelle, Ellen's assistant, as I flitted past. 'She's expecting you,' she said dryly.

I gave a quick, assertive knock on the door and opened it before receiving a response. 'Hey,' I said, as nonchalantly as possible, when I entered Ellen's spacious lair.

Ellen was sitting at her desk, with Liz looming over her. They looked up in unison from the paper they were studying, as if they were some kind of pearl-wearing, two-headed monster.

'Please take a seat, dear. We may be here a while,' Ellen said, nodding toward the Eames chair placed on the other side of her desk. Ellen was my peer – thirty-eight years old at the most. So her sudden, condescending way of calling me 'dear' made my skin crawl. Liz's green-eyed glower on top of that made me want to jump right out of it.

Ellen adjusted the crimson hair band that kept her unmoving bob in place and perfectly matched her red sweater set. I noticed Liz had recently gotten her hair cut into the same severe lines, a style that said, 'I'm not only frigid, I'm a control freak, too!' Though today she opted for an unflattering, diarrhea-colored cashmere turtleneck, Liz was also fond of sweater sets. Two bitches in a pod, I thought.

'*Jill* is in serious trouble,' Ellen started gravely, yet calmly. 'Ad sales have been dropping.'

'Plummeting is more like it,' Liz added snidely. 'Existing accounts are complaining about the recent content. And forget about getting new accounts.'

This was getting to be like *Groundhog Day*. We'd had this discussion before. I made my usual retort. 'But circulation is up. Newsstand is up –'

Before I could even finish, Liz interrupted: 'We're talking about ad numbers, Jill.'

Fine, I thought. Let's talk about ad numbers. I was the only one who was selling ads, it seemed. When I showed up on ad calls, I didn't leave without closing the deal. Liz knew it. And so did Paul . . .

Where was Paul anyway? In the good old days, Paul Thomas, Nestrom's creative director, would have been my ally, sticking up for me in situations like this. Now, the Twins didn't even invite him to meetings. Still, I thought of what he might say. 'Are we approaching the right advertisers?' I asked. 'And have these complaining accounts ever bothered to look at a copy of *Jill*? Do they understand what they are buying into? It's not for everyone. It's not *supposed* to be for everyone.'

'It's not only the advertisers, Jill,' Ellen continued, giving me a cold stare. 'Nymph Airways is upset about that stewardess story. They don't advertise in *Jill* but their CEO is extremely well connected.'

Liz jumped in. 'And Watley Brown is infuriated that you printed her photo shoot rider. Her publicist called Ellen last night and threatened to cancel all of her clients' upcoming interviews and shoots for not only *Jill* but *Fashionista*, too.'

'Liz, you know as well as I do that publicists are full of shit,' I scoffed, knowing that the only reason they brought it up was that someone was pulled from their biggest title because of lowly *Jill*. 'The minute she has a C-lister she needs to promote, she'll be back. Besides, that's what Watley gets for her ridiculous demands. I mean, two dozen lavender-scented candles? Peruvian peaches, pitted while facing east, cut into precisely half-inch squares, and marinated in honey? A six-pack of purified oxygen in ten ounce cans complete with attachable face mask? That woman is insane! And the readers should know it.'

'That's really beside the point,' Ellen continued evenly. 'And we can't change what's been done. But I've been looking over the next issue's cover.'

She pulled the layout from a folder and stood it up on her desk. She read from it in a halting, disapproving monotone.

'How to sleep with someone famous.' Long pause, accompanied by a tense glare from Liz.

'His penis is not a toy.' Pause after nearly choking on the word *penis*. 'Or is it?' she finished. Pause. Glare.

Ellen continued, 'Another reason *not* to quit smoking.' Another, even longer pause. Another, even longer glare.

'We need to tone these down, Jill,' Ellen said.

'*Way* down,' Liz echoed.

I knew how to play the magazine business game. It was all about ad sales; I knew that. But it was also about keeping expectations in check. And it was also about targeting the right advertisers for your publication. *Jill* was a niche publication, and when conceptualized, its circulation was never meant to be more than half a million. Eight years later, we even topped that, closing in on 800,000. And the advertisers, for the most part, understood that *Jill* wasn't at all like the other glossies out there. *Jill* was unabashedly unapologetic about making young women feel good about themselves instead of pointing out their flaws. *Jill* had models of all sizes and color in its pages, not just the stick-figure heroin addicts the other publications favored. *Jill* favored subversive celebrities. And our core advertisers knew it.

'Come on, those are all obviously tongue-in-cheek. And what about our readers?' I asked. 'Toning down the cover-lines will alienate them.'

'Readers don't buy ad space,' Liz said smugly. I wanted to strangle her by her string of pearls. She had no idea how to – or to whom to – sell the magazine. Not to mention that before she arrived the publisher, in essence, deferred to me. An editor at my level – with her own name on the magazine – should have the power to admonish the publisher. Liz apparently thought it was the other way around.

'I'm not saying you have to tone down the content,' Ellen said, softening a bit. Sometimes I thought she actually did get what the magazine was originally about. I thought about our onetime camaraderie. How did she get to the point of calling me 'dear?' 'But we do have to tone down the coverlines,' she went on.

'We . . . can't . . . put . . . the . . . word . . . *penis* . . . on . . . our . . . covers,' Liz said in a staccato so tense I thought she was being anally tortured.

It was a losing battle; I knew it. 'Okay,' I conceded, 'I'll tone them down.' I'd use 'wanker' instead of penis, then. I'd find ways to keep them *Jill* quality. I started to get up.

'That's not all,' Ellen said, and I shrunk back down in the chair, waiting for the other shoe to drop. 'We need to get you a managing editor in place right away.'

'I agree,' I said, relieved, thinking the worst was over. 'I've got a pile of great resumes on my desk.'

'There's someone in particular whom I would like you to see,' Ellen said. 'I've already set up an appointment for you to meet her. Three P.M. Tomorrow.'

'Fine,' I said, looking at my watch. 'If that's all, I really need to –'

'That's not all,' Liz said, her eyes demanding that I keep my ass firmly planted in the Eames.

Ellen gave me a half smile. I was squirming inside, but there was no way I would let it show. Something bigger was afoot, though I couldn't imagine what it could be.

'The magazine needs to look more mainstream,' Ellen said, as she again fiddled with her hair band.

Mainstream. The word made me want to unleash a primal scream. *Jill* was the antithesis of mainstream. My magazine had full-on fatty recipes instead of diets; makeunders instead of makeovers; disarmingly revealing celebrity profiles instead of fawning puff pieces; and writers who were a bright band of personalities, not just bylines.

'I'm not saying the magazine has to *be* mainstream,' Ellen went on, as my blood boiled. 'It just has to *look* a little more mainstream.'

'It needs a total redesign!' Liz blurted.

That was it. 'What?!' I exclaimed, so bewildered that my jaw nearly fell into my lap. 'That's just not necessary!'

'It's not open for negotiation, Jill,' Liz barked nastily. 'It's an absolute must. And it needs to be done in six weeks.'

'Six weeks?!' I was approaching primal scream pitch, so much so I thought I'd shatter Ellen's sparkly glass windows. This time I stood. I clasped my hands together so they could not see them shaking. As much as I hated confrontation, I had worked way too hard to be talked to this way. 'Why six weeks? There's no way!'

'There's *always* a way,' Ellen purred, keeping her cool. 'I've seen it done, even more drastically, in less time.'

'I need it to sell for January,' Liz snapped. '*That's* why it needs to be done in six weeks.'

Ellen went on, 'So let's get ourselves a new managing editor. And let's get the redesign under way. Asap.'

I was speechless. I didn't know how to respond. I just stood there staring at her in shock, still convinced there was *no way*.

'The woman I want you to see is from a small publication, *New Jersey Lighthouses*. But she's *vastly* talented,' Ellen went on, tidying her desk and not giving me another glance.

Liz continued to glower, adding, 'You'll see; new blood will be good for *Jill*.'

A lump started in my throat. A lump of rage that I knew would eventually manifest into tears. *New Jersey Lighthouses*? Were they on crack? Even worse – a redesign? In six weeks?!

'No, I don't think so,' I said, shaking my head. 'I think *Jill* is fine the way it is. I don't understand why you're trying to turn it into exactly what it's not supposed to be. *Jill* isn't *Charisma*!'

'It certainly isn't. And like Liz mentioned,' Ellen said, 'it's not up for discussion, Jill.'

A small laugh escaped my throat. I didn't really mean it to, and I certainly didn't feel amused, but it was all so absurd. They had to listen to me. Didn't they? I was the magazine's creator and founder; it was based entirely on my vision. *I* was *Jill*. They weren't. And there was nothing they could do about that.

Ellen finally met my eyes. Calmly, quietly, she folded her hands together on her desk. It seemed she was reading my mind. 'I understand that *Jill* is your baby, dear,' she said, trying to soothe me, 'but the magazine's personality doesn't have to be so tied to yours.'

There it was. The other Manolo Blahnik had dropped. And it was a particularly pointy, spiky-heeled one. And I couldn't believe what I was feeling. I was hurt. That was a direct insult to *me*. They didn't like my magazine because they didn't like me. Not only did I want to cry; I wanted to quit right on the spot. But I quickly thought of the repercussions . . .

Josh hadn't been working all that much lately. We had a hefty mortgage. And we were spending an obscene amount of money on fertility treatments. There couldn't be a worse time for me to walk out. But I would be damned if I'd let them control my magazine.

'Six weeks,' I choked out in concession. 'I'd better get started then. Is that all?'

'That's all, Jill,' Ellen said, cheerily, while twisting her pearls. 'I knew you'd understand, dear.'

As I left her office, I was shuddering inside, holding back the tears that were welling and threatening to spill all over my loaner blouse. I was amazed at how much the Stepford Twins were able to shake me. And I hated myself for it. But I wouldn't cry just then. I couldn't. There was no way I'd give them that satisfaction.

I left the Thirty-third floor as quickly as I could but I was still in shock when the elevator hit eight. I couldn't even spend time preparing for 'the walk.' I just did it.

It was amazing how the 'red-carpet walk' turned into a 'perp walk' in just thirty minutes' time. Which meant that Casey must have warned everyone to back off. As I passed the sea of cubicles, my staff members turned down their faces, like ostriches ready to bury their heads in the sand, instead of wearing the usual pounce-ready expressions. How much did they know? I was humiliated. But more than anything, I was pissed off.

Redesign. I had to do it. And there had to be a way to compromise. Approaching Casey, I called out, 'Cancel every single meeting I have for the next few weeks,' before I sought refuge in my precious, albeit dumpy, four walls. I was never so thankful to have a door. I slammed it shut.

Casey tentatively tapped on it immediately after I closed it. 'Every single meeting, Jill?' she asked gently, opening the door a crack and sticking her head in. 'Are you sure? Even the ad calls?'

'Especially the ad calls,' I snapped, holding strong. While I did a redesign, Liz would have to sell ads for once.

Casey's head disappeared as she quietly reclosed the door. I wanted to let the tears come right then, but I fought them. Because I knew when they came, they wouldn't stop.

I spun around in my chair and studied the framed cover of *Cheeky* magazine, *Jill's* predecessor. It was my very first cover, as an editor-in-chief. Then I stared at the framed *Time* cover, with my beaming face looming over the words JILL WHITE, MEDIA WUNDERKIND. I sighed wistfully. Boy, was I young, then. I barely even knew what I was doing. Back then, I was actually encouraged to be flippant and irreverent.

How times had changed.

Shaking off the memories, I finally got myself together and buzzed Casey.

'Hey,' she answered, concerned.

'Hey,' I said. 'Whenever you're ready, come on in and we'll discuss the day.'

She hung up and within a second my door was opening. She had a hopeful smile on her face. 'We're getting barbecue for lunch if you want in,' she said, knowing hush puppies might cheer me up.

I thought on it. 'Maybe,' I said, 'but I'm not all that hungry.'

Her voice became suddenly singsong as she glanced down. 'Oh, Ruggles is here to cheer you up,' she said. 'How'd you get in he –?!'

She suddenly screamed, releasing a shriek that would

make a dog's ears bleed, before jumping onto my coffee table.

'What?!' I cried. 'What?!'

Casey was frozen, her face a mask of horror. 'Rat!' she spat out finally. 'Rat!!'

I climbed on my chair and looked down.

Yes, there was a Ruggles-sized rat, in all its fat, furry, twitchy-nosed, red-eyed, fang-toothed, and bald-tailed glory. There had been several sightings of said rat by several staff members ever since we'd moved. But neither I nor Casey had ever encountered it. Until now.

And here he was, poking around my office like he owned it.

I suddenly felt like I was going to vomit.

Jumping down from my perch, I rushed past a still-quivering Casey and raced down the hall, out the glass doors, across the vestibule, to the ladies room. I burst into a stall and heaved my morning Diet Coke in a splashing rush into the porcelain.

After another heave, I took a few deep breaths. I perked up a little. Nausea . . . now that was a good sign. A *great* sign. I felt instantly a whole lot better. Suddenly, the Stepford Twins didn't seem all that important.

I let out another deep breath and pulled down my skirt. *While I'm here, I might as well pee*, I thought.

But the next thing I knew tears were flowing down the Anna Sui blouse in a veritable monsoon.

I had gotten my period.

2

Local Girl Awarded Full Scholarship
to Connecticut Prep School
— Athens Daily Banner, August 1979

Yet another unsuccessful fertility treatment. And yet another not-so-veiled threat from the Stepford Twins. It was shaping up to be a great day.

To take my mind off the failed fertility treatment, I focused on my interaction with Ellen and Liz, which plunged me into a real depression. I thought of that Talking Heads song 'Once in a Lifetime' with David Byrne's bewildered voice questioning: 'How did I get here?' Thinking on it sent me back to the darkest period of my life.

I was fourteen, fresh out of a commune in rural Georgia.

Yes, a commune. Not the David Koresh, religious cult kind. It was a hippie, antiestablishment, grow-our-own food, conserve-energy, homeschool-our-kids kind. And it provided a somewhat happy, if unorthodox childhood, for me and my younger brother, Alex.

My parents were from the Northeast. They met when they were both on the tenure track at Yale – Mom as an art instructor, Dad as a philosophy professor. At the encouragement of one of their mentors, they left the rigidness of academia behind for communal life on a farm right outside Athens.

Whenever I think of my mom in those days, I picture her in low-slung hip-huggers with her hands caked in mud. She had long, straight blond hair; a perpetual tan; and deep, thoughtful dimples that came out whenever she concentrated really hard, like when she was working clay.

Pottery was her first love. I honestly think she enjoyed tossing pots more than spending time with Dad, me, Alex, and all of us combined. She would spend hours in the pottery shed, and sometimes I thought if we didn't go in to get her she wouldn't sleep, eat, or do anything else. When we would distract her from the spinning wheel, she'd seem like she was emerging from a coma, blinking and staring at us, like she had no idea who we were. The funny thing was, very few of those pots would actually make it to the kiln. Many of them sat unfinished, air-dried, and crumbly, lining the shelves and waiting for what, I never knew. I don't think Mom knew, either.

Dad was covered in hair. He had a head of brown spirals that reached down to his shoulders; a chestnut coat of fur on his chest; and a bristly russet beard and moustache, which made his piercing blue eyes, stand out even more. He had an offbeat sense of humor, a strong mischievous streak, and a quick and articulate tongue. He loved to get in tête-á-têtes with anyone who would listen. When the others at the commune became weary of his rantings, Dad would pull on his tweed blazer with the elbow patches – his only blazer – and go over to Athens and engage local students in his favorite coffeehouse. Sometimes he'd be gone for a day. Sometimes he'd be gone for a few days. But he'd always come back from those jaunts elated and rejuvenated. Whenever we would happen to be in town with him, young girls would rush up to greet him. 'Hey, professor,' they'd call between giggles, even though he wasn't one – at least not anymore. Not that Dad was a liar. But his ego would allow him to pad the truth a bit, and I knew those young girls were tasty feed for that hungry ego. Mom knew it too, though she'd go throw some pots and forget.

Dad was a great teacher, though, and schooling on the commune was probably far superior to that of the average public school. Not only did we learn all of Shakespeare's plays by the time we were eleven, but we honed our math skills, debated politics, painted, drew, sculpted, built, and fished, which was my favorite thing to do.

Whether I'd go out in our self-made rower with Dad, Alex, or alone (despite her earthiness, Mom had prissy tendencies when it came to fish guts), I found fishing to be the best escape of all. It was quiet. It was challenging. Everything except the mossy lake seemed far away and unimportant. And it was the one time when I felt completely myself, comfortable in my skin. Plus, there was nothing like landing a bass or a trout bigger than Alex's, and basking in Dad's proud smile.

But communal life wasn't all idyll. Deep down, I knew both Mom and Dad believed that it could provide a better, simpler, more tolerant, more equal, less evil life than the outside world. But no matter how much they tried to shun reality, it would inevitably creep in.

Work on the commune could be tiring. And as tolerant and mellow as everyone tried to be, there were frequent squabbles. During those times, Dad would talk about moving into town. But most of the townspeople weren't welcoming to having people like us as neighbors. The university set were the only people in town, in fact, who wouldn't mutter 'dirty hippies' when we passed by. The problem was that housing near the university was expensive.

So we stayed put, probably for much longer, than we should have. To cool off from disputes with the others, or just to remedy their restlessness, my parents would simply take off, sometimes for days on end. They'd drive miles to see a Grateful Dead show or leave to join a protest. Many times we had no idea where they were going, but we always knew why they left. And although Alex and I felt comfortable with the others on the commune, we still couldn't help but feel left behind.

Through it all, my parents never let go of the esteem of academia, which is why they encouraged me to apply to Northeastern prep schools. 'You need to see the world in other ways, too,' I remember Mom saying, perhaps a little too urgently.

'You can always come back, if you want,' Dad pointed out. 'But you need to go beyond the bubble. A great education starts with seeing all views. And there's a lot to be said for a good education,' he'd add wistfully, making it clear where he'd rather be. I wondered if their sending me off was fulfillment of their lost dreams. It was almost as if they were too committed to the communal lifestyle, or too proud to admit that it might not be working as they had hoped. More likely, I think neither of them had the energy to leave for good.

In spite of everything, I was proud of my upbringing; I still get sentimental about it even today. Too many times in my life I have become homesick for its simplicity – which is ironic because soon after my acceptance into prep school, I resented everything about it.

My parents couldn't have been prouder when I received a full scholarship to Hillander, the exclusive Connecticut prep school that was the alma mater of dozens of presidents, captains of industry, and Pulitzer Prize-winning writers. Though I doubted I would eventually fall into any of those categories, I was optimistic about the opportunities that were sure to come along, Even more exciting was the fact that I had never been around so many people my age. I was eager, and ready, to make a lot of friends.

It didn't quite turn out that way.

On the day I left the commune, my parents loaded me, Alex, and my duffel bag into their junky old van and we drove all the way from Athens to Washington, D.C. My parents and Alex stayed there for an antinuclear protest. I went to Union Station and got on a northbound Amtrak.

When I arrived in Connecticut at the station nearest Hillander, I asked the ticket clerk for directions and I walked three miles to campus. Along the way, I admired the golds, oranges, and browns that stretched along the tree-lined sidewalks, and I liked the crispness of the autumn air and how the wind caused the leaves to swirl around my feet. I have no idea how long it took me to get to campus, but I do remember the awe I felt when I arrived.

The towering gray stone buildings with venerable ivy-covered walls were just like the academies I pictured from books like *A Separate Peace and Catcher in the Rye*. I noticed a group of clean-cut boys crossing the quad on a tour, and I wondered which one would become my Holden Caulfield.

Everything was so different from Georgia. It was colder, for starters. I noticed that the people moved in a quick, serious manner, not slow and ponderous, like at home. Though it was fall, there was still plenty of greenery on the grounds, but whereas Georgia was emerald, Connecticut was pine. The dissimilarities alone showed me that I certainly had a lot to learn. But that was okay, because I loved to learn. I was hungry to know the world beyond hippie communes.

My excitement quickly melted away, however, the minute I arrived at my dorm. I'll never forget the looks on the faces of my roommate and her parents when I stepped in the door.

'Hi! I'm Jill!' I said excitedly, as I tossed my duffel on the floor.

Their expressions displayed a combination of fear, horror, and having eaten bad shellfish.

'You must be Alissa,' I went on, despite the awkward silence.

'Yeah,' the girl answered numbly, as she and her mother simultaneously looked me up and down. Alissa was all angles and edges: straight, blunt-cut blond bob, with each hair perfectly aligned; sharp but pretty features – pointed nose, prominent chin, triangular cheekbones, big square white teeth. She was topped off by confident, narrow shoulders helming a tall, thin frame, and if it weren't for her giant, round boobs, we probably even would have worn the same size.

But I was flat as a board and much more reedy all around. Plus, it didn't look like we shared the same taste in clothing. Alissa wore a perfectly pressed plaid skirt and neat navy crewneck sweater. That, combined with her mother's Chanel suit, and her father's sweater-vest and bow tie ensemble, made my Goodwill turtleneck and carpenter pants look even more ratty.

'We're the Fords,' her father politely said, snapping out of his own fugue state. 'Of Boston.'

'Oh,' I said. 'My parents were in Boston last year. For a Dead show.'

I noticed Alissa stifle a giggle then, as her mom opened the door and peered into the hallway. Her expression was more perplexed than ever when she pulled her head back in. 'And where *are* your parents, Jill?' she asked.

'Oh, they're in D.C.,' I explained. 'They dropped me off at the train station there.'

Mr Ford blinked. Alissa looked at me like I was growing another head. And Mrs Ford's face again went the fear, horror, shellfish gamut.

'Alone?' Mr Ford asked. 'You came up here *alone* for your first day of prep school?'

I didn't see the big deal. I was used to doing things on my own. 'Sure,' I answered weakly. Then I turned my attention to unpacking, trying to focus on anything but their stares.

Alissa and her parents did the same, diving into six suitcases and several large boxes. There was a bag of hair products, accessories, and styling tools; another bag of nail polish, compacts, lipsticks, and creams. There was one big bag just full of shoes – clogs, boots, loafers, sandals, sneakers, flats, pumps, slippers, and even golf shoes.

And then there were the clothes. Dozens of sweaters in colors I never knew existed. Skirts – short, long, midi. A dozen firmly pressed khakis, all the same color. Hangers full of starched Oxford blouses. Cowelnecks. Turtlenecks. V-necks. Izods. Tenniswear.

'I don't know where we're going to put all of this in this tiny room,' Mrs Ford harrumphed at one point.

'You can put some in my closet,' I kindly offered, since I had taken up only five measly hangers.

By the end of the hour, all of the closets and drawers were filled, but discomfort still took up most of the space.

Alissa looked so spooked at the prospect of living with me that I thought she might repack right then and there and follow her parents out the door. Instead, she stepped outside to bid her parents a tearful farewell. As they closed the door behind them, I couldn't help but tiptoe over to hear what they were saying.

I quickly wished I hadn't.

'It'll be fine, honey, I'm sure,' I heard Mr Ford mumble.

'I'm just not sure how I feel about my daughter living with a charity case,' was Mrs Ford's haughty reply, before another horrified sob escaped from their daughter.

And so I was marked from day one. A 'charity case.'

For the next four years, I searched the campus up and down for anyone, girl or guy, to befriend. The guys wouldn't give me a second look. They were rich, cultured, clean-cut, athletic and wanted girlfriends who were more feminine versions of themselves. The girls were all Alissa Ford clones, many of them Hillander legacies with family lineages that rivaled the House of Windsor. They treated me like if they got too close they'd catch poverty or, worse, unpopularity. They were confident, preppy, catty, and intimidating. It was an entire school of Ellen Cutters and Liz Alexanders. Even the less thin, less rich, less popular girls wouldn't associate with me for fear of becoming even more unpopular.

They had a million nicknames for me. 'Blue light special' referred to my Kmart wardrobe; they called me 'Daisy Mae,' because of my southern twang; and when I dumbly, naively shared details of my upbringing, they started to call me 'that Amish girl.'

I tried my best to change and fit in. There wasn't all that much I could do about my wardrobe, but my hair took up a good amount of time. I went into town one day and got a cheap cut from the local barber school. I wanted graceful 'wings' like the other girls in school. 'Layer it like this,' I told the student, insecure with her scissors, while showing her a picture of Jaclyn Smith. I ended up looking more like Patti Smith. Then a week later, I tried to fix it with a perm that could only look good on a poodle.

I bought cheap make-up at Woolworth's: pale pink lipstick, shocking coral rouge, fire engine red nail polish, midnight black mascara, and eye shadow – robin's egg blue, of course. Somehow, it never looked right, either, as much as I tried to copy the Hillander style.

My other attempts at fitting in were just as disastrous. I tried out for the tennis team, but even a fuzzy yellow ball could humiliate me. The rest of the school, it seemed, had been playing since in utero. Instead, I got really into music. On my lonely jaunts into town, I'd pick up a few cool used or remaindered albums at a dingy old record shop where I liked to kill time with the old hippie who ran it.

And I had a job at the library, which not only was great for extra cash, but it was where I'd always run into my secret crush: Walter Pennington III, a tall, handsome, and extraordinarily down-to-earth member of a high-profile political family. Walt had thick brown hair; a square jaw; and hallow, thoughtful eyes. But I fell for him because he had a layer of depth that no one else at Hillander seemed to have.

Walt was constantly checking out books, but not the usual guy books like *Lord of the Rings*, or anything by Robert Heinlein or Ernest Hemingway. He preferred reading the modern dramas of Eugene O'Neill, Tennessee Williams, and Edward Albee. But his absolute hero was Sam Shepard.

'They say he's going to win a Pulitzer this year,'I said shyly one day when he checked out a copy of *Angel City and Other Plays*. Suddenly, Walter Pennington III, who never before noticed my existence, was talking to me.

Nearly every day he hung around the checkout desk and we discussed plays like 'Buried Child,' and 'Cowboy Mouth.' 'He's just so quintessentially American,' Walter said fiercely. 'There's something at the core of his work that speaks to the tragic American psyche.'

Soon he was recommending other plays and playwrights for me to read. And when he'd return, he'd be genuinely interested in my opinion. I often fantasized about hopping on the train with him to New York to see an off-Broadway production, then talking about it over espressos in a Village coffeehouse afterward. It was a nice fantasy. And sometimes in reality I thought he might actually be interested in me. There was just one problem with Walter Pennington III.

He was dating my roommate.

I was no competition for blond Alissa and her big boobs; so actually dating Walt would be impossible. But I enjoyed our friendship, glad for Walt's company when he'd seek me out in the library. And sometimes, if he came by the room and Alissa wasn't there, he'd look through my record albums and we'd talk about things like what we thought The Ramones's 'Chinese Rock' was all about, or how we thought Marc Bolan from T-Rex was cool. He loved to see which albums I came back with from the town record shop every week; he even borrowed a bunch.

We grew closer, and we'd confide in each other about our dreams. Walt told me that he wanted to be a playwright instead of following the political path his famously widowed mother had planned out for him. 'My mom will be crushed, but I just don't have any interest in politics,' he complained. 'I just don't know how to tell her that I don't want to major in political science in college.'

It was too good to be true, however. Our friendship came to a crashing halt, thanks to Alissa.

One day in the library, Walt was leaning over the counter reading me a scene from a comedy he was writing. We were sharing a laugh over a clever line when suddenly – thump! Someone tossed a tome onto the counter before me. 'Aren't you supposed to be working? Check this out,' a voice demanded. The voice belonged to Alissa. She turned to Walt.

'And what are *you* doing here? I've been looking all over for you.'

'I was just . . .' his voice trailed off, for he didn't know what to say.

'Well, I need to finish my Shakespeare paper before tonight, or the whole weekend will be ruined,' she snapped. 'And I'd appreciate your help. There's no way I'm ruining Spring Fling weekend for boring Shakespeare.'

Spring Fling kicked off with a Friday night dance, then a local beach party on Saturday. It was a big annual deal, a sort of pre-prom, and everyone went with a date. I started to get angry, thinking how unfair it was that Alissa would be frolicking in the sand with Walt as I sat in the dorm. I decided to busy myself with returns to put it out of my mind.

'I mean, Jill probably has her paper done, right?' she said just as I turned away. 'Right, Jill?'

'Uh, yeah,' I answered. I had finished it a week ago.

'So she doesn't have any worries this weekend,' Alissa said. 'Who are you going to Spring Fling with, anyway?' she asked snidely, knowing full well that no one had invited me.

My silence gave her the answer she sought, and a smug expression replaced the sneer. 'Oh, so sorry,' she said, in mock pity. 'Maybe next year.' Then she laughed.

'Alissa, that's not cool,' Walt said meekly before she dragged him out the door.

The next day, Walt abruptly returned all the albums he had borrowed. He never approached me at the library again. And Alissa didn't speak to me for weeks.

So I should have been suspicious when one night she said to me, 'You know tonight is dorm ritual, right?'

I didn't know what she was talking about. 'No,' I said innocently. For a straight-A student, I was so stupid. 'What is it?'

'It's a bonding thing that's a tradition here,' she said. 'The girls do a silly ritual and vow allegiance to the woman named for the dorm so she won't haunt us during finals.' She added that Lisa, the sophomore who was the R.A. in the dorm and her good friend, was in charge. 'All I know is they will knock on our door to get us tonight. And we're to drop everything and go along.'

'Okay,' I agreed, knowing that not participating would surely earn me grief.

Then at 10 P.M., just as Alissa and I were turning in, the knock came. We followed the other girls down the hall and into the common room, which was pitch dark, except for the glow of a few candles. Lisa instructed us to sit, spaced out at least an arm's length in a large circle.

When we were all settled, she began, 'This is what you all must do to prove your loyalty to the Agnes Vance dorm at Hillander.'

I held back a yawn, hoping that this stupid ritual would be over soon.

She went on. 'I am going to blow out all the candles. Then you must strip down to your underwear. When I say, "begin," the first girl must take this crown' – she held up a golden cardboard hat from Burger King – 'and put it on her head. Then she must stand on one leg, put her hands in a praying position, and say, "I, state your name, am honored to be a princess in the court of Agnes Vance." Then she must count until five, very slowly, and pass the crown on to the next girl.'

It sounded so idiotic, but harmless, at least.

Or so I thought.

Lisa went around the room and blew out the candles, and the room grew eerily dark. Whispers arose, but she silenced us with a command. 'Strip!' she shouted. There was some rustling around the room, and some embarrassed giggles, but silence fell when the first girl began her pledge.

It went on, solemnly, and before I knew it, it was my turn. Alissa, who was next to me, handed me the crown in the dark. I stood up. I balanced on one leg. I placed the crown on my head and put my hands in the praying position. I was doing it all by the letter.

'I, Jill White,' I said, 'am honored to be a princess in the court of Agnes Vance.' Then I counted, following the slow pace of the other girls. 'One . . . Two . . . Three . . . Four . . .'

Before I could even say 'five,' the lights flicked on. And there I was, standing in the middle of the room, in my bra and undies, wearing a Burger King crown, balancing on one leg and praying. A peal of laughter arose from the rest of the girls, who were all clothed. 'I knew she'd be wearing grannies!' I heard someone say.

Then there was the flash of a Polaroid camera. The resulting photo was posted in the cafeteria the next day.

So Alissa had gotten her revenge. And any hope I had of being one of the girls had been dashed once again. I thought things couldn't possibly get worse.

Then my parents visited. Unannounced.

They were on their way to Rhode Island for – what else? – a Dead show, so they decided to stop in and say hi.

I was in my room, reading, when I heard some giggles outside my door. The next thing I knew there was a knock on the door. I opened it to find my parents standing there, in all their bedraggled, tie-dyed glory.

A year before, I viewed them as my heroes. On that day, they were my bane. I once had thought my father looked like an enchanted woodsman. But seeing him then, his scraggly hair stretching past his shoulders, his unkempt beard sprouting gray, I thought he looked homeless. And Mom appeared pale, tired, and in an untouchable zone of numbness like never before.

Needless to say, I wasn't all that welcoming. 'Why didn't you call?' I kept asking, over and over. They could have given me a chance to prepare myself. Maybe I could have arranged to meet them off campus. *Way* off campus.

Dad plopped on Alissa's bed, putting his bare, dirty feet near her pillow. 'Did you put on a little weight, sweetie?' he asked.

I had. Fifteen pounds to be exact. So nice of him to notice.

Then Mom snapped out of her coma and spoke. 'What's happened to your hair?' she asked vaguely. She stepped closer and inspected my face. 'Are you wearing make-up?'

That's when Alissa walked in. When she spied my guests, she was at first stunned – I had never had a guest, ever – then in fear for her life. At least Dad had the good sense to sit up and put his unwashed feet on the floor.

'Aren't you going to introduce us?' Dad asked, nodding toward Alissa.

I reluctantly, and hastily, made the introductions, as I pulled on my jacket, dying to get out of there.

'Hey, Alissa,' Dad said coolly, just before we were going to leave, 'do you know where we might score some good weed?'

Her eyes were full of judgment as she gave a snotty laugh and snapped, '*What*?' Suddenly, she was above smoking the occasional joint.

'C'mon,' I begged. 'I'm starving.' And I finally dragged them out of the discomfort zone known as my room.

I wanted to take my parents into town, but Dad insisted on staying on campus. 'How often do we get to come here?' he said.

So much to my misery, we ended up at the small café in the student union.

When we sat, Dad was preoccupied with appraising the students, reading the bulletin board, and getting up to chat with any professor who would walk through. Mom kept eyeing me questioningly.

'Did you get a perm?' she asked. Her earlier tone of disbelief had morphed into simple annoyance.

I nodded.

I knew what she was thinking. I didn't even ask her if she liked it.

'Just don't forget who you are, honey, okay?' she said, trying to be understanding, but still sounding very, very annoyed.

How could I ever forget who I was? My classmates were constantly pointing it out.

Like right that very second. A jock from my class, Judd Watson, walked in with his entourage. As he passed my table, he cracked, 'Freak alert!' to the hilarity of his cronies.

Mom grabbed my hand and softened. I was glad. I didn't

need her judging me too. 'Are you making friends, honey?' she gently asked.

I just shrugged. Her comfort made me want to wipe off my make-up, let my hair go back straight, put on my overalls, hop in their van, and leave Hillander behind for good.

'Jill doesn't need to be friends with these stiffs,' Dad said. 'She's smarter than them all put together. They're probably all Republicans anyway.' Dad's familiar, proud smile took over his face. 'Plus, we didn't send her here to make friends. Your grades with a Hillander education – there will be no stopping you in this world, honey. You'll leave every one of them in the dust.'

Then I knew – suffering through Hillander's hellishness would be easier than living with my parents' disappointment back in Georgia. So I stuck it out. When it came time to choose roommates for the next year, I boldly put in for a single, which sophomores rarely got. But miraculously, mine came through, most likely because every girl in the school doubled up with someone, anyone, so as not to get stuck with me.

So I spent the next three years in the solitary confinement of a single room, every night, every weekend, and every holiday. Yes, even holidays. My parents considered sending me a bus ticket for holidays an outrageous expense. So since they wouldn't go out of their way to bring me home, I never bothered to save up to buy a ticket myself. And no girl would be caught dead being seen with me, never mind inviting me to her home during breaks. So while most families were carving up a turkey carcass during Thanksgiving, I was sitting in my dorm room. Alone. I would while away many of those hours studying, eating and sometimes I even cut myself.

The cutting started my first year – probably because it was my most traumatizing year, and probably because I wouldn't ever let Alissa see me cry. My pain and rage had to come out somehow, I guess. The first time I did it was when I came into my room one day to find her reading my journal, ridiculing it out loud to one of her friends. In it, I had written fictional fantasies of how I wanted my life to turn out, what I'd like my 'dream guy' to be like, and my opinions on everything. I even made lists, like this one:

Things I want to accomplish in life

1. *Skydive*
2. *Be a good mom*
3. *Start a charity*
4. *Start a magazine*
5. *Travel to all seven continents*
6. *Fall in love*
7. *Find a friend*
8. *Become more likable*

I'm proud to say that to date I've accomplished #4, #6, #7, and #1, not very long ago for a feature story in *Jill*. The list is etched in my mind still, as are the emotions I felt when I heard Alissa's mockery and peals of laughter. It brought back the agony of every social rejection I had withstood at Hillander in one moment.

Alissa was so focused on making fun of my journal that she hadn't even seen me standing in the doorway. Before she could spot me, I crept back out of the room, so furious and upset that I locked myself in a bathroom stall. I remember sitting there numbly just waiting for the tears. But they wouldn't come.

Then I noticed a shard of metal sticking out from the broken toilet paper dispenser. I wiggled the metal back and forth, back and forth, until it snapped off. I ran my fingers over its edge, cutting my forefinger slightly, and watched intensely as the blood trickled down my hand. Strangely, it felt good. It felt cathartic. It was a relief.

Pathetic, I know. But it was the only way at the time that I would become distracted from the pain of being an outcast. As often as four nights a week, I'd hole up in the bathroom, now using a Swiss Army knife instead of the shard of metal, and cut – not enough to make the blood gush, though. No, I became an expert. I had practiced just the right touch. Just enough to make it hurt. Just enough to forget the real pain in my life.

I was bright enough to know that it was stupid. And I tried my best to taper off with other distractions, like music – and magazines.

When it was slow in the library, I'd pore over the glossies and mock them in my imagination. As I flipped through each page, examining each zitless face, each rail-thin frame, each blindingly white smile, I'd feel a well of disgust flood my soul. First, because I really resented not being anything like the models. But mostly, I was disgusted because I cared.

And I'd get angry looking at the flawless clothing. The perfectly applied make-up. The 'dream guys,' who were all Ken doll doppelgangers. I'd take the bogus quizzes, laugh at the puffy celeb profiles, and make note of the lameness of the advice from the 'expert' columnists.

Then one night, in a frenzy of boredom, I started to describe what I hated about these magazines, and what I'd be interested in reading about. One sample entry:

> *The latest Seventeen came in today. Why oh why do I subject myself to its inane, evil pages? Why do all these rags keep telling people how to be better? What if there were a magazine that just let girls feel okay about themselves? What if there were stories about useful things, like how to live with someone you loathe?*

Knowing now that Alissa was reading my journal, no matter where I hid it, I started to write to her directly, planting items that would infuriate her.

> *Girls can be so phony. I was in the bathroom today when I heard Alissa's best friend, Tracy Fisher, talking with Alexandra Hunt. Tracy was saying how she couldn't believe Walt would date someone like Alissa, that they were totally wrong for each other, and that Alissa was looking fat lately, too. I mean, even though it is true – she has put on a few pounds – that's nothing that a good friend should say, right? I think I'm better off not having any friends here . . .*

I smugly snickered inside when Alissa had a huge fight with Tracy a few days later, and they stopped talking altogether. And I felt a terrific sense of satisfaction noticing her eyeing her figure, and frantically weighing herself, from that day forward.

That's when I realized how dense Alissa was. She never figured out that I knew she read my journal, even when I out and out addressed her.

I remember writing this another time: Remember my name, Alissa Ford, because one day, when you're fading into a life of country club obscurity as nothing more than a proper prop for an uninterested husband, you'll read it somewhere and wonder how the girl you pegged as such a loser could somehow come out on top.

I wonder if she now remembers that passage as clearly as I do.

3

Jill White '83, Awarded Full Scholarship to Bennington

— Hillander Alumni News, September 1983

The one positive side effect of being an outcast was a 4.0 average, which guaranteed another all-tuition-paid trip to an institution of higher learning. But this time, I did some research, and this time, I made sure that my next campus culture would be as different as it could be from Hillander. Though my first instinct after graduating from Hillander was to beat it out of New England faster than you could say 'summa cum laude,' I fell in love with Bennington College in Vermont the minute I saw it.

Instead of the limestone and ivy that other New England colleges were known for, Bennington's farmlike environment, with its converted barns and rural surroundings, comforted me. It had a small student body (under 1,000), a no-athletics policy (no tenniswear to be seen!), no grades (no worrying about that 4.0), and a strong arts and humanities curriculum. But mostly, I loved Bennington because when I visited campus, I saw a lot of people like me. No cliques, no Alissa

Ford clones; just a bunch of individuals dying to express themselves through dance, art, writing, drama, their clothing and hairstyles – any way they could.

My essay and grades won me a full scholarship, so I decided to become a literature major. Once again I spent four years reading and writing, dabbling in fiction and expanding my literary literacy. But most of what I learned at Bennington had to do with friendship, something I was absolutely starved for when I arrived. I may have entered Bennington a loner, but I emerged with a tightknit circle of friends who vowed to stay that way for life.

This time, my roommate and I became best friends. Sarah Annastasatos was an art student from Long Island who loved to draw dreamy fantasy scenes of long-haired princesses riding on unicorns through enchanted forests. Despite her subjects, she was actually very talented, and it was amazing to watch her real skills and real self emerge over the years. By junior year, her cynical, honest, red-streaked self-portrait so impressed the head of the art department that he arranged for a showing of her work at a local gallery.

Sarah's bigger talent, however, was being a great friend.

Sarah looked a lot like her princesses; she had long, flowing, wavy, dark brown, waist-length hair; giant brown eyes, topped by expressive eyebrows that always gave away what she was thinking; and a lovely, oval-shaped face with a flawless olive complexion. I liked to think of Sarah as the rock tied to the end of my kite. When I'd be dizzy with distraction, she'd focus me. If I became too worried about minutiae, she'd calm me. When I drank too much and puked, she held back my hair. And she'd never mince words when I wanted a forthright opinion. It was almost as if Sarah were the parent I never had growing up.

But Sarah was more than a caretaker to me. She was fun. She made friends easily and constantly and was always excited to share them. She was the least judgmental person I'd ever met and, as a result, our large, ever-expanding but close-knit group comprised all types of people – musicians, potheads, gays, aspiring philosophers. She was the center, the one who brought us all together. Thanks to her, for the first time in my life, I felt normal, accepted – even average. And thanks to my newfound self-esteem, I no longer felt the need to cut myself.

It was a really happy time. We'd all spend nights hiking the trails on the fringes of the campus, smoking clove cigarettes and dreaming about our futures. Sarah had admittedly the lamest taste in music and she loved to dance. She and I would spend giddy late nights in our room making up interpretive pantomimes to her cheesy Rick Springfield cassettes, laughing until our sides hurt. We remained roommates for all four years.

My other best friend was my boyfriend. Yes, believe it or not, the pariah of Hillander was actually able to land one. Joe Dryer came from a family of local dairy farmers. He studied music and was an in-demand dj with the most popular radio show on campus. Sarah introduced us one night when we were having a floor party. She knew him because she had a part-time job in the record library at the station. I nearly died of embarrassment when she called him over and said, 'This is the Jill who calls in requests to your show all the time!'

'Really?' he asked, immediately interested. 'The same Jill who likes to play "stump the dj"?'

'That's me,' I said, trying to seem bored and not at all like I was glued to his show whenever it was on.

Joe had the best taste of all the djs, in my opinion. And he had a sexy voice. So I liked to call in and talk to him and make requests that I thought might throw him off guard. One time I thought Klaus Nomi – this bizarre German performer who wore a lot of white make-up and had a strange, operatic voice – would do it. But Joe knew him right away. 'I think we have a copy of "Simple Man" around here somewhere,' was his answer.

I laughed. 'You finally, truly impressed me with the Klaus Nomi thing,' I said, tossing him the bone that he deserved. He wasn't my physical type, really, though he was cute in an offbeat way: small and slender with short, spiky hair dyed Gothic black. And I loved his unique sense of style – vaguely preppy Oxford shirts a size too big with the shirttails always out; faded jeans; shiny black wingtip shoes. But strip him of his postpunk dj style, and he would look ordinary . . . like a dairy farmer. Though I wasn't physically attracted to him, I liked him immediately – selfishly, because he seemed like a nice guy, and more selfishly, because he seemed like he was very into me. It's hard to turn down someone who thinks you're the coolest chick since Chrissie Hynde, especially after four years of not a soul showing any interest in you. Besides, everybody else on campus started to hook up, so I thought it was due time for me, too. Soon, I started hanging out with him when he did his shows, and he introduced me to a whole world of music that I am still obsessed with: Joy Division. REM. The Smiths.

I even lost my virginity to Joe right in the radio station. It started when I playfully sat on his lap, launching a marathon make-out session. When he cued up a particularly long song – a remix of 'Everything's Gone Green,' by New Order – one thing led to another. Making out turned into foreplay, which turned into full-on sex acts. I was the aggressor, having decided it was high time I had sex. Joe seemed scared to death at first, but then he just relaxed and went along for the ride, despite his frantic glances at the studio door. He was concerned that the station manager would pop in, or that Sarah might want to scoop up some records. But we just went at it, right there in the dj chair. Sure, it was clumsy and a little bit painful, but it was also fun and so animated that while bouncing on top of Joe's lap I inadvertently knocked the needle across the record right as he came. After a jarring screech and some dead air, Joe threw on another platter, and then we laughed until we nearly cried. From that night on we were officially a couple.

Our sex life throughout most of our three-year relationship was pretty mediocre, however, as we were both amateurs. Still, we were inseparable for most of our time in college. I enjoyed being around him simply because he liked me for me, always making me feel beautiful with his easy acceptance and friendship.

One of my fondest memories of how sweet Joe was back then was when he took me skiing for the first time in my life. We laughed so much that day as I tumbled down the mountain. Though he was an expert, Joe didn't seem to care that he was missing out on the black diamond trails or that I was a complete klutz with frozen red cheeks and snot running out of my nose. But that was his true essence – he was kind.

I had nearly forgotten all about kindness after four years of Hillander.

But another thing I learned at Bennington, unfortunately, was how to break a heart.

Like I mentioned before, Joe's radio show made me more music crazy than ever. I was an especially devoted fan of Third Rail, a postpunk indie band from Chicago that was just starting to pick up steam on the college circuit. I adored the lead singer, Richard Ruiz, a sexy, wiry, androgynous man whose mess of curls set off amazing fantasies that I put to use many times during sex with Joe. So when Third Rail came to Bennington during our junior year, I flipped.

Joe, through the college radio station, had a gig as an escort/gofer for any visiting band. I, of course, demanded he take me with him to meet Third Rail.

The show was at the arts center. It was loud and wild and pumped me full of confident energy. But when Joe brought me backstage, I was actually surprised at how suddenly nervous I felt.

First, Joe introduced me to some roadies. Then I met Marc Miller, the lead guitarist, who offered us something to eat. He led us to a long buffet of cold cuts. My heart stopped a little bit when I saw a tall, thin man dressed in a faded black T-shirt and jeans toss back those curls as he regarded the spread. It was Richard Ruiz. *The* Richard Ruiz. I sidled up near him, pretending to check out the offerings myself, and waited for the right moment for Joe to introduce us.

Then I heard Richard grumble, 'Bummer. It's all animal kill.' His voice was deep and raspy, like a growl.

As a devoted vegetarian, I saw and took my opportunity.

'The Silo is open till two, and they have a pretty good veggie burger.'

He then turned toward me and shot me a slow, appreciative smile. 'Is that right? Because I'd probably even kill an animal for a veggie burger just about now . . .'

I laughed and then gave Joe, who was standing beside me, a subtle nudge. He snapped to. 'Well, she would know; she's a hard-core vegetarian,' he answered. I nudged him again and gave him a look. 'Uh, this is my girlfriend, Jill,' he said.

He *would* have to throw in the 'girlfriend' part. I stuck out my hand. 'Jill White. Good show by the way,' I said nonchalantly, trying my best to play it cool, using all my will to keep from gushing and looking like just another fan.

Richard smiled, grabbed my hand, and held it.

'Sooo,' I said, flustered, 'uh, I was going to run over and grab a veggie burger myself . . .'

'Bring back two, then,' Richard said, releasing my hand. 'One for me, one for you.'

I did just that, and me, Joe, and the rest of the guys hung out talking in Richard's dressing room until the wee hours of the morning. After my heart stopped doing that freezing-up thing, I was amazed at the confident conversation that came out of my mouth. I was talking to Richard Ruiz just like he was a regular person – like a peer. We had an especially great conversation about his lyrics, which often referenced obscure philosophers and poets. I was ecstatic that he seemed impressed by my depth of knowledge of them all.

The time flew, and at about 5 A.M., one of the roadies tapped on the door. 'Guys, we really gotta go now,' he urged.

'We should have hit the road hours ago. We've got a morning radio interview in Boston.'

So the night was coming to an end. I wanted to soak every last minute of Richard's presence, so Joe and I helped the guys gather their things and trailed along to their bus to say good-bye. Richard picked me up in a bear hug. 'Come with us,' he whispered in my ear.

When he put me down he stared intensely into my eyes. I turned to Joe, who was chatting with the drummer.

'I . . . I can't,' I said weakly.

'That's a real shame,' he said, sighing. Then he added wistfully, 'Idle youth. Enslaved to everything . . .'

It only took me a second to recall the rest . . .

'. . . by being sensitive I have wasted my life,' I finished for him. 'Rimbaud.'

'I knew you'd know that,' he said simply, offering me a smile before he turned to the calls of his bandmates.

'Let's go, man! We're going to be late!'

Richard gave me a disappointed wave before he climbed on the bus, and I felt like I was going to throw up once the engine hummed on. I felt like such a stupid groupie, but I was pretty certain that in the past five hours I had, for the first time in my life, fallen in love.

Joe came over in the meantime and grabbed my hand. 'Are you okay?' he asked gently.

The bus slowly backed up out of the lot while Richard's rugged voice echoed in my ears: 'Enslaved to everything . . .'

The bus pulled away, and I still, to this day, can't believe what I did next.

I looked at Joe; dropped his hand; quickly mumbled, 'I

have to go'; and chased after the bus, running down the street with all my might. When it hit the stop sign at the end of the block, I pounded on the door wildly. 'Wait! I'm coming with you!' I screamed. 'Open the door!'

The bus door flew open, and I ran up the steps and right into Richard, as the rest of the guys erupted in applause and whistles.

Laughing, he dragged me to the backseat and he planted his lips on mine. 'I've wanted to do that all night,' he said. So had I.

And that's when I first knew that I was capable of being as selfish and mean as anyone I'd ever hated . . . because I didn't even think to look back out that window at Joe. I just kept kissing Richard.

In one week, we hit Boston, Providence, Hartford, New Haven, and New York. In each new city, we had the same routine: sleep late, caressing each other in the mornings; rehearsal, when I would sit in the wings and watch brilliance in action; a healthy bite to eat; and then my favorite part – the downtime, when we'd steal away to a quiet spot, like a park or a coffee shop.

Those were my favorite times, when it would be just the two of us. Richard would share lyrics he was working on, and I'd read him snippets from a short story that I'd started on the road. And I felt so special when he'd confide in me, telling me things like how he was inwardly afraid of the band hitting it big.

'I just don't want to lose our raw edge,' he told me one day when we lingered in Boston Common.

'What makes you think you will?' I asked.

'The bigger we get, the more money we make, the more demands on our time . . . the more pressure to sell out,' he said.

'But that sounds like such a cliché,' I told him. 'You're above that.'

'Am I?' he said, concern covering his face. 'I'm only human. It's so easy to get sucked into the machine . . .'

He seemed so vulnerable. And I was so honored to be the girl he chose to bare his soul to. I dreamt of always being the girl who would ground him, no matter how famous he would become. 'Even if you do hit the big time and make a lot of money, think of what you can do with that. Think of the platform you could have. Think of the people you could reach. How you could spread your ideas. What effect you could have on people – on the world!'

I could tell by his smile that he liked what he was hearing. I was inspiring him; I just knew it. Thinking about my goal to start a charity from my 'Things I Want to Accomplish in Life' list, I went on: 'I mean, if you end up making a lot of money, there are a lot of causes you could donate it to.' I imagined us starting a charity together, the two of us saving the world in every little way we could.

'I just want people to hear my music,' he said. 'It's that simple. I want life to stay that uncomplicated. The tragic thing is, it never will.'

'That's why we have to live for today, then,' I said boldly, before kissing him.

'I agree,' he said. 'The future doesn't exist to me. The only thing that really does exist is the here and now.'

After that conversation, we went back to the bus and had the best here-and-now sex I could ever have imagined.

Sex with Richard at that time was incredibly eye-opening for me. It was intense, grown-up, sensual, and explosive, instead of the fumbling, quick and wanting variety that I experienced with Joe. With Richard, I finally understood what all the fuss was about in *Cosmo*. Richard taught me the reason every issue had a 'discover your G-spot' coverline, and he found A through F, too; it was like a veritable octave of pleasure each time we went at it. Which was at least twice a day.

My least favorite time during that week was showtime, crazily enough. The euphoric rush I felt during my first Third Rail concert became replaced by worry and insecurity. Before going onstage, Richard would warp into another zone, with rituals that I didn't understand and that he didn't care to share with me. There was a connection he shared with his bandmates – and only his bandmates. During those times, I'd feel like a true outsider, and I'd sit in the audience, feeling like just another fan. And when he'd be out there onstage, tossing his charm into the audience, I fretted whether he was catching another girl's eye – there were so many groupies screaming his name – and I wondered if he even thought of me at all. When he wasn't making eye contact with me while singing, I'd sulk. And I worried constantly about him meeting other girls. His bandmates, after all, went through dozens of girls in that week, tossing them aside like broken guitar strings.

At first, I'd feel superior to the groupie girls the other band members would hook up with. After all, it was different for Richard and me. What we had wasn't disposable. It was meaningful and real. It was love. But then it started to bother me that Richard didn't bat an eye about their behavior, like when Bobby Crash, the drummer, had two girls going – one preshow, one postshow. I couldn't stand the thought of Richard doing that to me. I couldn't even bear the idea that he had been with others before me.

Yes, very mature of me, I admit. But I was frantically in love. Every minute I searched for some clue that he felt the same way. I decided that when he did catch my eye during performances, validation was there.

I stayed away for an intense, whirlwind week of music, sex, and veggie burgers. And I would have stayed on, even, but the guys were then going west, and I didn't have any money for the airfare and no one offered to pay, despite several dropped hints.

'You need to go back to school,' Richard told me.

'I could go back anytime, anywhere,' I said, pleading inside that he'd beg me to stay.

'I don't want to be responsible for you screwing up your education,' he said. 'Go back to school. I'll call you when we come back east again.'

Parting was agony for me, while Richard seemed to take it in stride. I was having a hard time keeping my cool. I wanted to tell him that I loved him, right then and there at dumpy Port Authority, but knew that would be too banal. I knew he wouldn't communicate by those means either. Instead, he recited a line from another Rimbaud poem:

'Life is the farce which everyone has to perform,' he said to me before I left. He was right. I wanted to continue the fantasy. But life was inevitable.

The journey back to school was long, and as I came back

down to earth, guilt was my encroaching seatmate, though I tried to distract myself with thoughts of Richard's promise to call and what he might say. I wondered if he was missing me at that moment just as much as I was missing him, but I still couldn't help think of Joe. I hoped he'd understand, but even Joe's patience had its limits. The week was eye-opening in that it convinced me that we really didn't belong together.

Joe was the first person I went to see once I got back to campus, before I even stopped in my room. I tentatively knocked on his door. 'It's me,' I announced. 'Open up if you're still talking to me.'

After a spirit-crushing minute, the door did open. 'Barely,' Joe said shortly. He looked tired.

'I don't know what to say . . .' I started.

He sighed. 'That was a shitty thing to do to someone who is supposed to be your boyfriend,' he said.

'I know,' I agreed. But the thing was, he didn't feel like my boyfriend. I knew it even if he didn't. The feeling I had for Richard that week was what I thought having a boyfriend should feel like – constant, big rushes of emotion and intensity.

'So maybe we shouldn't be boyfriend and girlfriend anymore,' I went on quietly, as a few hallmates filed past. I looked past him into his room. 'Can we talk about this inside?'

Joe impatiently pulled open the door and sat on his bed. I awkwardly sat next to him.

'Admit it, Joe,' I ventured. 'I've been terrible at the girlfriend thing. And you deserve someone who's better at it.'

He shook his head. 'I don't know . . . I don't want you out of my life,' he said begrudgingly.

And I didn't want him out of my life, either. 'Of course

not!' I reassured him. 'But we don't have to cling to the notion of "boyfriend/girlfriend" just to be around each other. I think we'll make better friends than lovers, don't you?'

He shrugged. 'If that's what you want.'

I knew this was hard for him, but I was also convinced that this was the right thing to do. I looked at him pleadingly. I had been living on adrenaline for a week and my exhilaration was fast turning into exhaustion and I wanted this awkward conversation to be over. 'I think we'll be great friends without all that other pressure.'

'Okay,' he said, but I could tell he was let down. 'But I'll need some time before we start hanging out again.'

'I understand,' I said. 'As long as you don't hate me . . . I couldn't live with that.'

'I could never hate you,' he said. 'But I just need to be away from you for a while.'

I nodded. 'I'm just a big, dorky fan girl, I guess,' I said, downplaying the incident, but knowing inside that Richard was the true love I had waited my life to meet.

Joe laughed a little. 'Yeah,' he said, 'you are a groupie, aren't you?' He laughed again, this time with a bit of an angry edge. 'I guess I don't blame you, though,' he said, shrugging. 'I mean, that took balls. It must have been a pretty cool adventure. Not to mention the free concerts.'

'Yeah,' I said, glossing over his groupie comment. 'Though it was pretty tiring.' I went on to tell him a few details about the whirlwind week. I knew his anger would prevent him from understanding what had happened between Richard and me. And I certainly didn't want to hurt him any more than I already had.

After another apology from me and some tears, we parted as friends. I loved Joe, but I realized that I wasn't *in* love with him and, complete retrospective truth be told, if I hadn't been so flattered that he wanted to be my boyfriend, I never would have considered him anything but a friend. We hugged and I was so relieved that he didn't hate me.

Sarah, on the other hand, was a different story. When I floated back to my room, I was met by her hard, scolding stare.

'Nice of you to check in,' she snapped.

'Huh? Joe didn't tell you where I went?' I asked, completely oblivious.

She was sitting at her art table, her hands smudged with charcoal. She wiped them off impatiently as I flopped, exhausted, onto my bed. 'He told me. But you could have called,' she said.

'Sorry,' I said, midyawn, before closing my eyes for a much needed nap, which made her even angrier. I didn't think I could take any more confrontation in one day. I kept my eyes closed.

She came over to the bed and shook me until my eyes snapped open. 'You missed your World Lit presentation, you know,' she pressed.

'I know,' I said, probably a little too defensively. I didn't get her concern. Why would she care?

She grew annoyed with my apathy. 'Don't you ever think about consequences?!' she hollered. 'And how could you just leave Joe standing there like that?!'

I couldn't believe how mad she was, and I sat up. 'Look, I spoke to Joe and he's okay,' I assured her. 'But I don't get why *you're* so ticked off.'

Then Sarah's whole face fell, and she looked like she might cry. 'I was ticked off because I wasn't sure if you'd come back,' she whimpered. 'What would I do here without my best friend?'

I couldn't believe it. While I couldn't get over that someone like Richard Ruiz craved my presence, it was even more surprising to me that someone cared about my absence. I thought back to those times that my parents would just up and leave. I remembered wondering if they'd come back, wondering if they even thought of me and Alex when they were gone. I remembered the feeling of abandonment all too well. And I suddenly knew how Sarah felt.

'I'm sorry,' I said again, this time meaning it. Then I gave her a bone-crushing hug. 'Thank you for caring so much.'

Once again, I felt so fortunate for having such understanding friends. Almost losing them wasn't worth it, I realized, especially when Richard didn't call. Sarah stayed up many nights listening to me whine and cry about it. I was completely infatuated, and I was constantly thinking about where he was and what he might be doing and with whom. I was convinced that I never should have left him to go back to school, that it was my fault for not being available to him. Thoughts that he might have met someone new tortured me. I'd plague Sarah with those fears on too many nights. And when she wasn't talking me down from the ledge of heartbreak, she was convincing me that hitchhiking cross-country to find him wasn't a sane thing to do. Looking back now, I'm so glad that I didn't screw up my future – and my friendships – for a one-sided obsession. Sarah slapped a real epiphany into me, though, when I relapsed, moaning in a moment of temporary insanity about not wanting to be alone and that I should maybe even consider getting back with Joe.

'What?!' Sarah screamed. 'Now you've gone crazy. Listen to yourself. There's nothing wrong with being single when you're twenty-one years old, you idiot!'

I laughed my head off when she said that, because she was right, I was acting like a loser. It hit me. Yes, I was twenty-one, and I had a long love life ahead of me. I hoped.

While my time at Hillander stretched out like an endless ocean journey in an inflatable raft – with holes – the four years at Bennington felt like a cruise on a souped-up speedboat. I was amazed at graduation how quickly the time had passed. I was even more stunned at what had occurred over the span.

I had come into Bennington a scared, overweight, insecure prep-school outcast. I left healthy, happy, and secure in knowing exactly who Jill White was. As hard as it was for me to let go of my college years, I felt ready for the real world.

4

'87 Grad Named Editor-in-Chief of Cheeky Magazine

— Bennington Record, September 1988

They don't give full scholarships for real life so I had to land a job immediately after graduation. And I needed to act quickly as I really didn't have a 'home' to return to to figure out what was next. The commune had finally dissolved and my parents moved to Virginia, where Dad was teaching part-time at the 'University of' while Mom continued to toss pots and started to give private painting lessons. Their modest apartment was barely big enough for the two of them, never mind for me. Alex, meanwhile, started his second year on scholarship at Stanford, way across the country. So my friends were the only semblance I had of a 'family' at that time. The logical thing for me to do was to follow them to New York.

Sarah had landed a job at a behemoth ad agency as an assistant designer, and she was doing small illustration jobs on the side for jewelry catalogs. Joe was working at Merillion Records as an assistant, figuring that would be a great 'in' for him when he finally got together a band. I took on a job at *Dollar*, one of the leading financial magazines. I know I couldn't have found a more boring publication to work for, but publishing jobs were scarce, and I figured it was at least a foot in the door.

Sarah, Joe, and I moved in with our classmate Gerard Gautier – yes, the very same French Canadian who would find worldwide fame and fortune as a fashion designer. But back then we were a motley crew of nobodies: dark, elegant Sarah; less preppy, now pudgy Joe; flamboyant Gerard; and me – nose-ringed alt-girl, a combination of Molly Ringwald in *Pretty in Pink* and Ally Sheedy in *The Breakfast Club*.

We were our own commune of sorts, four of us jammed into a cramped one bedroom in a Jane Street walk-up. We sectioned off our private spaces with shower curtains (Gerard's idea). Joe and Sarah, who earned more than Gerard and I, paid a little more of the rent and had the luxury of sharing the bedroom. Gerard, who was doing graduate work at Parson's School of Design, slept in the living room. I slept in the hallway.

The West Village location couldn't be better. Everything else needed massive improvement. The living room was marked by water damage and a curious odor. The kitchen featured a stove that worked yet an oven that didn't. And our one bathroom was hastily built into the kitchen. Waiting to get in it each morning was an enervating ritual – especially for Joe, who had to follow after two girls and one gay man.

Not that I was ever in a hurry to get to work. I hated my job with a passion and had to unglue myself from my bed every morning to go. On workdays, the nose ring came out, and a conservative, monochromatic wardrobe snatched my body. Each day as I approached the towering midtown offices, I'd get a little sick in my stomach. The office was full of right-wing suits, mostly men, mostly assholes. My title, of 'editorial assistant' was an absolute joke, as my day consisted of answering phones, fetching coffee, listening to offensive jokes, and photocopying. The only way I learned anything about how a magazine ran was through osmosis. Still, it was something to put on the resume, and the only option I had for paying the rent.

Because we were all so broke, we had to find creative ways to amuse ourselves. So we tried to do whatever was free or extremely cheap. Sometimes we'd stop at crappy 'old man' bars for happy hour and gorge on the free steam-table snacks, though as a staunch vegetarian I was usually relegated to the pretzels and peanuts. Other times we'd sit around the apartment and talk about our futures: how Sarah wished to write and illustrate her own children's book, how Gerard aspired to conquer the fashion world, and how Joe wanted to win a Grammy – though he still had yet to put together a band. Me, I wasn't sure what I wanted besides out of *Dollar* magazine. I tried not to let myself think back to my journal and all the goals I had set for myself back at Hillander. It was too hard to reconcile the change-the-world attitude I had with what I was doing now.

The most fun we'd have was when Gerard got us into the clubs. He liked to dress in drag, and he became the quintessential club kid. Gerard's self-styled getups, inspired by everything from Julie Newmar's Catwoman to the FTD florist mascot, would always get him in the party photos of *Paper* magazine. As a result, he – and the rest of us – never had to pay the cover at hot clubs like Danceteria, The Palladium, and the Pyramid Club.

The only time I would really part with my hard-earned money was to go to concerts. Of course, when I saw that Third Rail was playing a few nights at the Peppermint Lounge, I didn't hesitate to grab tickets. Joe was my frequent concert companion, and despite his history with Third Rail, he came with me to that show. It was a quintessential good-sport gesture of the old Joe. And probably his last.

A small part of me still never quite got over the heartbreak of Richard Ruiz not calling after we spent a week on the road together. And instead of moving on, I ultimately went the denial route and chalked it up to his busy touring schedule. But knowing that he was in New York and that I might have a chance to bump into him again sent the old feelings rushing right back to me. I was reminded of our intense connection and was convinced that when he saw me at the concert the sparks would fly again.

That night, I pushed my way up to the stage during the first set, which wasn't easy. After what seemed like forever, I thought I caught Richard's eye. When he smiled at me, I thought, *Finally! He recognized me*. I was convinced we would resume our affair backstage after the show.

I dragged Joe, who had turned moody on me, to the stage door as soon as the show was over. Even though Joe and I were ancient history as boyfriend and girlfriend, I was sensitive enough to notice that he still had a sore spot when it came to Richard Ruiz. I couldn't really blame him. That night, however, I didn't really care. All I did care about was reconnecting with Richard.

I pounded on the stage door and announced my presence to the bouncer when he swung the door open in annoyance. At this point, other fans were gathering behind me. 'Please tell Richard that Jill White is here,' I urged, while others started to shout out their requests.

'One at a time!' the bouncer shouted. Since I was closest to him, he nodded toward me. 'What was your name again?'

'Jill White,' I told him.

He nodded, then pulled his hulking body behind the heavy door and closed it. I was all pins and needles as I waited for him to come back, while Joe was sighing impatiently. 'How long are we gonna stand here?' he asked testily.

The door flew open again, and the bouncer was clutching a clipboard this time. 'What was your name again?'

'Jill White!' I told him for the third time.

He glanced at the papers on his clipboard and shook his head. 'You're not on the list,' he said.

'But – but did you tell Richard? He wasn't expecting me earlier, but he'll know me,' I pleaded. 'Tell him it's Jill White from Bennington College.'

The bouncer seemed to have a good heart, and he gave in. 'Okay,' he said, resigned, probably wanting to get me in so he wouldn't have to listen to me any longer. 'One minute. I'll ask him.'

He disappeared behind the door again, and I turned to Joe. 'I'm sorry this is taking so long,' I said to him. He just shrugged.

A few minutes later, the door opened again. The bouncer was shaking his head. 'Sorry,' he said to me.

I was outraged. 'But – but – did you tell him it was Jill White? W-H-I –'

'I know how to spell White,' the bouncer snapped, losing his patience. 'And he's never heard of you. So go back to your college and give it a rest!'

I was crestfallen. I turned to Joe for consolation but was repelled by his smirk.

'Can we go now?' he asked.

'I'll bet that guy didn't even tell Richard my name,' I said. 'He probably said, "There's some chick waiting outside for you."'

'Yeah, I'm sure that's what happened,' Joe said. Was he being sarcastic? 'Now let's get out of here,' he demanded. As much as I needed someone to reassure me right then that it was all the bouncer's fault – or help me come up with some other logical rationalization – I saw that Joe was not going to step up. So I just followed him, saying a silent prayer that Sarah would be home when we got there. Unfortunately, she wasn't, but I knew deep inside just what she would say.

'Stop living in a fantasy world!' she'd yell, losing her patience with me. 'Forget about him and start dating someone who's not an asshole rock star and who will actually give you the time of day!' I could then picture her rolling her eyes, and adding, 'I don't know why you do this to yourself.'

Of course, the Sarah of my conscience that night would be right. It was time for me to move on. I decided then that I was officially on the prowl. And no one was more helpful to me in my mission than Gerard.

Gerard was extremely effeminate, a quality the girly girl in me just loved. We were about the same height, but he was much more slender, nearly a poster boy for heroin chic with his ashen complexion and willowy body. But though Gerard loved to experiment with party drugs – namely X – he was smart enough to never go near heroin but just look like he had. He had a great eye for color and he loved to dye his hair often, using it as a palette for whatever stylings he was fleshing out at the time. He was so good at it I let him color my hair, too, from streaky greenish blond to cherry red and everything in between. The best thing about Gerard, however, was that we had the exact same taste in men.

We'd go out to clubs and bars together and play 'gay or straight,' each picking out our favorites. Judging from appearances, one of us would approach the man in question and have a brief conversation, then signal the other on what we determined. For example, if I'd go talk to a guy and I thought he was straight, I would put my hand under my chin at some point in the conversation, letting Gerard know that not only was he straight, but that I was interested, and he should move on. If the guy was gay, I would cross my arms in front of my chest, signaling Gerard to work his way over so I could introduce him. If he was dull, weird, or just not right for either of us, I'd just end the conversation and go back to stand near Gerard. It was an efficient system that worked both ways, and thanks to Gerard's good taste I went on a few good dates, and even had sex a few times.

Other than scoping with Gerard and going to the occasional concert, my favorite form of entertainment was simply walking the city streets. I loved to wander south of the apartment and lose myself for hours while marveling at the diversity every few blocks would bring: old ladies sitting in their lawn chairs outside of Little Italy brownstones; the twisted streets of Chinatown, and its markets, full of exotic fish and gross hanging animal carcasses; the desolate, warehousey stretches of Soho; the brightly colored bodegas and junky discount stores of the Lower East Side, where I shopped for my used clothing wardrobe, and where salsa music blared out of tenement windows; and the Village, with its coffee-houses, gay bars, and bookshops.

Even though the apartment was way too small for four people, we were busy enough that it didn't feel crowded all the time. Gerard was at school all day and clubbing at night; Joe would go out to see bands with work friends; and Sarah met a guy at the Greek Orthodox church, so she'd often crash at his place – not comporting herself very orthodoxly – especially on weekends.

So I was especially surprised one Friday night when I came home from work and found Sarah sitting on the couch, her eyes ringed with tears.

'What's wrong?' I asked her when I tossed off my coat.

Her response was a hysterical mix of sobs and wails. I couldn't make out a single word.

I sat on the couch alongside her and squeezed her with a hug. 'What is it, honey?' Sarah was always so even, so whatever it was, I knew it had to be a big deal.

It took her a minute to catch her breath. When she finally spoke, I was shocked.

'I'm pregnant,' she blurted out.

'Shit,' was all I could think of saying, Then, 'Does Taso know?'

She shook her head. 'I don't know what to do,' she wailed.

I embraced her and calmed her. For once, I was the caretaker, and it felt kind of nice. 'Don't worry. We'll figure this out,' I said, though I had no idea what to do. Not only did I not know what to do, but I barely knew what to say. 'Let's take a walk,' I said, finally. 'We'll clear our heads. Plus, the guys will probably be home soon.'

'Okay,' she said and trailed after me out the door.

We walked for two hours, within which Sarah stopped crying and I asked upsetting but appropriate questions, like: 'Do you want to keep it?'

'Honestly,' she had said, with the tears threatening to well again, 'no. I can't be a mom, not now.'

'Then, we'll get it taken care of,' I had assured her. 'I think you're making the right decision.'

The following Monday, I called her gynecologist, got the name of a good clinic, and made her an appointment for the following week.

I took the day off from work. We went for coffee at the diner around the corner from the clinic. Once inside, we sat in the colorless, antiseptic waiting room for what seemed like eons. Sarah was silent the whole time. I chattered and tried to make her smile. It didn't work.

Finally, a nurse called her in. I gave Sarah's hand a final squeeze before she went. I was surprised that she emerged only thirty minutes later, and even more surprised that she was on her feet. She looked sad and tired, but relieved.

I hugged her. 'It's over,' I told her.

'Taso can never know,' she said softly, the tears starting again.

'He won't,' I promised.

No one ever knew except us two.

'You're a good friend, Jill,' she told me.

And after a few sad and crampy days, Sarah started to seem okay again. I was proud of how she – and I – had handled it all.

During those days of sadness, I pointed out all of the great things that were going on in Sarah's life to console her, like how Taso was a really great, caring boyfriend and how she was excelling at her job. But in the process of cheering her up, some glaring details of my own life came to the fore. I had no boyfriend and really hadn't had one since Joe. But even worse, the job at *Dollar* was corroding my soul. I had worked there over a year and it was time to stop whining about it and look for another job.

So each Sunday I picked up the *Village Voice* and the *New York Times*; headed over to my favorite coffeehouse, Caffe Reggio over near NYU; and scoured the want ads.

The market was brutal. Too many Sundays I'd leave Reggio with a stomach full of frothy milk, a brain wracked by caffeine jitters, and not a single hope. But then one day, it happened. My eyes fell on an ad in the *Voice*:

Wanted: Opinionated iconoclast with good writing skills and high energy level for editorial position at new magazine for teen girls. Some experience necessary. Anyone who has to look up 'iconoclast' while reading this ad need not apply.

The job sounded perfect. I knew what 'iconoclast' meant and I did have *some* experience, even if it was only in photocopying and tolerating assholes in suits. So I responded and within a week I had an appointment with Christine Clawson, a British transplant who was brought over to start a U.S. version of *Cheeky*, a magazine for teen girls.

Every day before the interview, I obsessed over preparing for it. Not by researching or rehearsing what I might say, however. I obsessed over what I was going to wear. Should I dress conservatively, so as to appear older and more experienced than I actually was? Or should I be stylishly fashion forward, like how I imagined the staff of *Vogue* to be clad? The tone of the ad made me think I should appear offbeat. Was there a way to dress iconoclastic?

I spent way too much time coming up with possible interview ensembles and harassing Gerard about what he thought of them. He hated every single outfit I had put together. 'Why don't *you* just dress me, then?!' I screamed at him the night before the interview.

'Why don't *you* just be yourself,' he answered, laughing. 'Instead of all of these caricatures: the editrix, the trust fund bitch, the prepster. Why don't you just dress as Jill White?'

He had a point. Plus, I had no other options left. 'Okay, okay,' I conceded. 'But just answer this question: nose ring in or out?' I never wore it to *Dollar*.

'What would Jill White do?' was his answer.

'Leave it in,' I answered.

The next day I showed up at the interview, nose ring in place, hair slightly teased but not quite as Sid Vicious as it could get, plaid skirt, Doc Martens, black ribbed turtleneck. As I sat in the midtown office waiting to meet Ms Clawson, it finally hit me that I spent so much time on my outfit that I hadn't prepared for the actual interview at all.

In the minutes before she called me into her office, I panicked. How many words per minute could I type anyway? Did I know all the appropriate copyediting symbols? What were my qualifications for the position? What was the position even for?

By the time the tall, English-accented woman stuck her head out of her office and called me in, I was a complete wreck. But her welcoming smile and well-worn jeans instantly put me at ease. 'I'm Chris,' she said, giving me an enthusiastic handshake. She ushered me into her office. 'Have a seat,' she said, indicating a comfy, yard-sale chair. I liked her already.

When I crossed my legs, she pointed out my Doc Martens. 'Nice,' she said. 'Did you know those were invented as a result of a skiing accident?'

'No,' I answered truthfully. 'I thought The Who invented them in "Quadrophenia."'

'One of England's best,' she said, sitting behind her modest desk. 'Tell me, do you consider yourself a "Mod" or a "Rocker," then?'

So far, this interview was a breeze. 'Definitely a Mod.'

She beamed. 'Me, too.'

I felt like we were instant friends, so I relaxed and just answered her questions candidly.

'What drew you to the magazine industry? Pay is terrible and hours can be hellish,' was her next question.

I thought for a minute about that one before I answered. 'In terms of pay, I never had any money, so I'm happy as long as I'm earning something. I like the feeling of accomplishment deadlines give, and there's something I like about the coming together of words and photos,' I said confidently and truthfully. 'But I guess what really attracted me is a dream I've always had of starting my own magazine. Something completely different from what is out there now.'

I could tell that last statement piqued her interest. 'Okay,' she said, raising an eyebrow. 'So let's say you're starting a new magazine for teenaged girls. In what ways would you make it different from the ones already out there?'

That was an easy question. I thought back to my journal, which grew into a slam book against Alissa's atrocious pile of glossies. 'I would start by putting models who look more like real girls on the cover,' I said. 'You know, less make-up, not as blond, certainly not as white, and no anorexics allowed.'

'I like it so far,' she said encouragingly. 'But what would the content be like?'

Another slam dunk. 'It could be a bit of a resource for real life, with stories like how to ask your parents about sex . . . or how to help your best friend when she thinks she's pregnant.'

'Who's writing these stories?' she went on.

I answered rapid fire. 'Young people with personality. And no experts! I think I hate the experts most of all!'

This elicited an out-and-out belly laugh from Chris. 'They're always so dry and condescending,' she agreed.

'Besides,' I continued, 'teenaged girls don't really listen to anyone except their peers. So I think it's important for the magazine to have a certain tone. The tone of a best friend.'

Every thought I'd ever had about magazines came out of my mouth, and the more I spoke, the more passionate I got, and all the ideas – big and small – I had had over the years on this subject suddenly and miraculously gelled into a single cohesive vision of a hip, irreverent, smart publication that spoke honestly to all the girls out there who, like me at sixteen, only felt completely inadequate after reading what was currently available on the newsstand. She hung on to my every word; then there was a pause as Chris regarded me thoughtfully. I was amazed that she was actually interested in my opinion. My boss at *Dollar* never asked for my opinions – not that I had a lot of meaningful insight into Wall Street to offer him anyway. 'I think we're on the same page, Jill,' she then said, as she pulled my resume out from a pile on her desk and scanned it. 'What was the last position you held?'

'Editorial assistant,' I reluctantly answered, wishing I had slightly more experience.

She nodded thoughtfully. 'I'd like you to come back to meet with a few others,' she said.

I was more than happy to. I had a good feeling about *Cheeky*. And when I did return a few days later, Christine Clawson offered me the job.

On that day, the best day of my life, I woke up a bored editorial assistant from *Dollar*. I came home the editor-in-chief of *Cheeky*.

5

Jill White, Media Wunderkind

—*Time*, September 1990

Dear Cheeky:

I was sick with mono and home from school and bored to death when your first issue came out. My mom brought it to me along with a bunch of other magazines. The other magazines were dumb and boring. But I read Cheeky cover to cover. It's the first time I read anything all the way through. I swear, I never even finish the books I'm supposed to read for school. Anyways, I just wanted to say thanks for giving me something to look forward to every month.

Sincerely,

Clarissa, 13, Skokie, IL

That was the first of *Cheeky*'s many fan letters. It still is proudly framed and displayed in my office.

The magazine enjoyed a huge, breakout success, surprising the industry and shocking me the most. How did we do it? By whim, by instinct, and by breaking every rule.

Very few staffers had any glossy experience, which ensured that our style was fresh. And we featured a distinct look, thanks to a renegade creative director who came right out of an underground music 'zine. Paul Thomas was an optimistic, energetic, extremely tall, straight-acting gay graphic designer who also liked to sculpt. When he invited me down to his Lower East Side studio to see his work – which consisted of doll parts and sex toys protruding from misshapen lumps of clay – I wondered what my mom would think of such an unusual use of her preferred medium. I became certain that she would like it.

My parents still lived in Virginia, albeit separately. There wasn't a whole lot of animosity between them; they simply grew apart. Mom was in a phase of self-exploration, finally blossoming into her own woman. We kept in touch much more frequently now, partially because she wanted to share her self-discovery, and partially because I think she was extremely lonely. Strangely, even though we were miles apart, I felt closer to her than ever before. Dad hadn't changed one bit. He still taught at the university, and he still basked in the praise – and God knows what else – of impressionable young students.

My brother remained in California, pursuing a master's. He had little patience for my parents, and though he'd occasionally call me, I hadn't seen him in a couple of years. Alex, even more so than me, completely isolated himself from his past.

No one at *Cheeky* knew about my roots; at the time I preferred it that way. As far as I was concerned, Jill White was really born the day I was anointed editor-in-chief. Because *Cheeky* wasn't just my job; *Cheeky* became my life.

I loved every part of it. Whereas I practically needed a crowbar, a crane, and three hulking wrestlers to pry me out of bed in the mornings when I worked at *Dollar*, I couldn't get up early enough to race to *Cheeky*'s ramshackle Hell's Kitchen offices.

There was a quick, easy camaraderie among the staff. Each month in my editor's note, which was called 'Jill's Journal,' I would highlight a different staffer. I'd point out how Maria, the features editor, was once a championship fencer in high school and now liked to spend her free time walking and playing with shelter dogs. Or how Scott, the music editor, had been in the original lineup of the Beastie Boys. These tidbits made the bylines human and even the editors started to get their own fan mail.

We did follow some conventions, only to break them in the same breath. For example, we did have a beauty column, but it was written by a rotating group of writers, one of whom was a drag queen. We'd feature products, but give our honest opinions about them, like: 'This facial scrub gave me the worst rash!' or 'My boyfriend loooooved the way this lipstick tasted.' We'd run side-by-side stories like 'Why You Should Boycott Your Prom' and 'In Defense of the Prom.' And our celebrity interviews were fun, honest, and sometimes downright unflattering. A-listers and the overexposed were never featured.

Soon, the letters took on an intensely personal tone, mimicking that of the magazine itself:

Dear Cheeky:
I'm so glad you exposed Kelli Hyer-Burke for the bubble-headed phony that she is. Watching that girl on TV makes me sick, and hearing her preach about her (surely phony) virginity makes me choke on my own bile. Her obsession with shopping and status came through loud and clear in your profile. It's so cool that you showed her for who she really is.
Karen, 17, Rutherford, NJ
P.S. Jill – sorry, but you have to get your hair cut. The photo of you with all those split ends in Journal last month made me shake my head in shame for you. I'm just saying . . .

And some of the letters were downright heartbreaking, validating our mission even more:

Dear Cheeky:
I tried to kill myself a year ago after my stepfather started to rape me. When I survived, it was even harder to get through every day. I was considering trying again, but then I picked up a copy of the March issue. Reading your story 'Breaking the Silence' gave me the courage to talk to my mom about it. And guess what? She threw him out. We haven't seen him in four months and my mom and I are much closer now. I never would have had the courage to say anything without you guys. I now

realize that I have so much to live for and that I shouldn't have tried to throw it all away just because of some creep. You saved my life.
Monica, 14, Portland, OR

After we clinched the readers – two million of them, to be exact – advertisers clamored to get in. And since the members of the staff were a very young and mostly underpaid staff, *Cheeky* achieved the impossible in its infancy: it actually made money. That caused the industry to sit up and take notice.

Insiders were intrigued by our little subversive, freshmouthed mag that managed to be successful without pandering to its advertisers. We won an ASME award, the top honor in the magazine game. And an endless stream of parties; openings; talk shows; and for me, even the cover of *Time* followed. Soon, the whole town wanted to know more about this 'Media Wunderkind.'

While my life was changing so quickly, I was always happy to have the constant of the Jane Street 'commune' to help me keep it real. I don't know if I was always successful, and when the commune inevitably started to break apart, I felt I had lost my anchor.

I knew we couldn't spend the rest of our adult lives living like we were still in a college dorm, but I wanted to hold on to it for as long as possible. Of course, I wasn't the only one who was making it careerwise. Gerard's designs were getting a lot of attention, and his first show was an enormous hit. Suddenly, he had serious backers in the fashion world. The more in demand he became, the less time he had for the nightlife scene. He quickly outgrew his section of the living room, so he was the first to fly the coop for a sprawling live/work space. We made a point of hanging out during fashion week, but otherwise, I didn't see him nearly as often as I liked. I truly missed his outrageous getups, his sharp wit, and his silly sense of fun.

When we were three, it made sense for me to move into the bedroom with Sarah, who not only was enjoying success at the ad agency, but was experiencing the first real, adult relationship of any of us. She stayed at Taso's more often than not, so 'our' room turned out to be a nice, private space for me. So I upped my share of the rent, which I could now easily afford, taking a bit of the burden off Joe.

Joe, unfortunately, still hadn't found his niche. His finances were dwindling as he was still languishing as an assistant at a floundering record company. It seemed that someone had to die in order for him to move up the ladder. The music business in general was in a slump, so jobs elsewhere were scarce. I didn't blame him for becoming depressed about it. It *was* depressing.

Whenever I would come home, I'd find him sitting on the couch watching TV and reeking of pot. This routine didn't help him make any strides toward his other dream of putting a band together, so that crumbled too.

I tried my best to cheer Joe up, but it seemed that whatever I would do would backfire. One night, I brought him a pint of his favorite ice cream, chocolate chocolate chip from Häagen Das. But a phone call distracted me when I came in, and it melted all over the bag before I could even give it to him. Another time, we had plans to have dinner at a kitschy Mexican restaurant, but I had to cancel because we were closing on an issue and I had to work all night to make deadline. Then I decided that a date would bring him out of the doldrums, so I set him up with one of the staffers at the magazine. Another disaster, 'Next time, choose anyone except your fan club president,' he said when he got home. 'All she did was talk about you. She didn't ask one question about me.'

I thought a celebrity-studded music-biz bash at Jackie 60, a club in an abandoned freezer room in the desolate meatpacking district, would bring the old Joe back. Plus, it would be a good opportunity for him to cozy up to music types. Sarah and Taso were game that night, and as it happened to be at Gerard's favorite hangout, even he said he'd meet us there. I was excited; the four of us hadn't been out together in ages.

The club was only a few blocks from the apartment. I stumbled there in shiny, patent-leather thigh boots, teetering in the middle of the cobblestone streets because I couldn't bear to walk on the blood-stained, rotted meat-strewn sidewalks. It was one of those electric Saturday nights – when you could feel the excitement and possibility in the air. It was a night where things would happen. I felt it in my bones.

When we approached the door, the dress code for the week was posted right on it:

Winning smiles, Tallulah Bankhead wigs with smeared red lipstick, flawless evening wear, tiaras and important jewelry, brown ribbons, tuxedos and tails, sequins, feathers and beads, sore loser faces, medals and O.B.E.s, glam drag, streaker, special effects make-up, classic fetish.

Joe opted for zipper-rubber fetish gear; Sarah did the fringy, feather-bead tiara thing; Taso, sweating through a vintage tuxedo, was clearly out of his league. We pulled open the heavy, steel door and walked down the stairs only to be stopped by the bitchy drag-dom at the bottom. 'Private party tonight,' she announced.

'We're on the list. Jill White, plus three,' I told her.

She then scrutinized my face and broke into a smile. 'Sorry, sweetie, I didn't recognize you! Come right in,' she said, all nicey-nicey now. Being recognized never got tiring in those days.

While everyone else flocked to the bar, the first thing I did – the first thing I always did – was scan the room. *Village Voice* columnist Michael Musto was working the crowd. All the famous drag queens like Lady Bunny, Joey Arias, and Flotilla DeBarge were vogueing. Debbie Harry was there, of course; despite her age, she was at every party. And a ton of other high-profile musicians peppered the room.

I immediately spotted the wild curls and square jaw of one particular musician far across the room. Richard Ruiz was slumped in a booth with a very young, very blond boy stroking his hair. I became determined to speak to him, and a few courage-enhancing gin and tonics made that happen.

When an empowering buzz kicked in, I strode over to the booth. 'Hello, old friend,' I slurred, trying to be casual, though anyone wearing a patent-leather jumpsuit was anything but.

'Hey,' Richard answered aloofly. It was a pat, generic 'hey,' the kind reserved for publicists whose names he'd forgotten, admiring fans, and the girlfriends of his bandmates.

'You don't recognize me, do you?' I said, shocking even myself with my boldness.

This caused the blond boy toy to squirm, excuse himself, and move off to get a drink.

Richard Ruiz studied my face for a minute, then spoke. 'Sure I do. You're that magazine editor,' he said, sticking out a hand. 'Cool to meet you. Your music coverage is great. Great to see someone featuring so much alt.'

I took his hand, a little embarrassed for being all 'don't you know who I am?' But not embarrassed enough to back down. 'The name's Jill. Jill White. But we have met before. A few years ago. I went on tour with you for a week.'

'Ah,' he said, recognition finally dawning on his face. 'That's right! Yale. The Rimbaud fan.'

'Bennington,' I shot back.

'Same difference,' he said, shrugging. 'How are you?'

'Fine,' I answered. The boy-toy came back with his drink, gave Richard another stroke, then skipped off to talk to a model.

'So . . . you're gay?' I asked, trying so hard to be cool and nonchalant that I was exactly the opposite. That had to explain why he didn't call . . . I felt a little relieved. I was just not his type, after all. There was nothing he, or I, could do about that. Right?

Wrong.

Richard scoffed. 'I refuse to label myself,' he said, making me feel like I was in elementary school. 'Gay, straight, bi – ridiculous tags. I'm attracted to the person, not a label.'

I nodded, thinking on it for a second. So maybe it didn't explain why he ditched me. It was still an interesting outlook.

'Sit,' he said, patting the spot that Blondie Boy Toy had vacated. He gave me such an inviting smile that I suddenly forgot that I had been mad at him for several years. I obliged.

'So, when is *Cheeky* going to do a story on Third Rail?' he leaned in and asked in his famous purr. 'I'm sure you're aware that we have a new album dropping in the spring.'

'Hmmm,' I answered skittishly. 'Well, you're a bit more mainstream than we usually like to cover . . . I mean, not to put a label on you or anything . . .'

He cut me off with his laugh. 'I guarantee that if you put us on the cover, it will be your best-selling issue.'

I hesitated, continuing my alcohol-fueled coyness. 'Well, I don't know. I guess I could use some filler for the May issue. I'd need an exclusive interview . . .'

'I could probably fit one in. Maybe. Perhaps,' he hedged, before he accommodatingly added, 'next week?'

'I could probably fit that in. Maybe. Perhaps,' I said, mimicking his words. 'I will have to look at my calendar, though.'

'Give me your card,' he said, as he subtly stroked my forearm. 'I'll call you.'

'Sure you will,' I said, highly doubting it, but producing the card anyway.

'Jill!' Gerard called to me from the bar just then, with a wave of a silk fan. I let out a guffaw upon eyeing his full-on geisha regalia. I toasted him, then noticed that my glass was empty.

'Friend of yours?' Richard asked.

'Ex-roommate,' I answered. 'And I gotta go. We'll be in touch,' I tossed off, before I slid out of the booth, leaving the chagrined rock star behind.

Feeling on top of the world, I held out my glass giddily when I joined Gerard at the bar. And why not? I had reconnected with the lust of my life while landing a big get for the magazine. 'Definitely another for me!' I said triumphantly. 'I hope you know I just blew off Richard Ruiz for you.'

'Good girl!' Gerard said, as he handed me my drink.

We laughed and clinked glasses as a third glass suddenly joined our toast.

'I'll drink to that, whatever it is,' a voice said. It belonged to Rory Bellmore, the former child actress. She was a beautiful African-American in her early twenties. Her skin was golden brown and her eyes emerald green.

'Hi,' I said, a little startled, and a lot starstruck. She was known as a nightlife fixture, despite going to rehab at a startlingly young age.

'Hey,' she answered, giving me a big, open smile and tossing her braids over one shoulder. 'I've been dying to meet you. I just wanted to tell you that I think *Cheeky* is awesome. I'm a subscriber.'

'And I'm a big admirer of your work,' I said. I was. I thought she made some brave choices over the years. She wasn't your typical Hollywood brat.

'When I was in rehab, I did a lot of writing. I liked it so much I thought I'd even start my own magazine,' she said. 'But then when I got out, an interesting role came along. And then another . . . Well, you get the picture,' she said shyly. 'But I still do write. Maybe you can take a look at my work sometime?'

I couldn't believe it. A celebrity was seeking approval from someone outside of her industry. From years of interviewing actors, I knew it was a very, very rare occurrence when one would show any interest in anything that didn't have anything to do with making his or her image better and career bigger. Rory's desire to have interests outside of her world made me like her instantly. 'Sure,' I agreed. 'I'd be happy to read your work.'

'Thanks,' she said, seeming truly grateful.

Conversation came easy between us, so Rory and I spent the rest of the night glued to each other: talking, laughing, bonding about our favorite bands (she was really into music, too, it turned out). The best part was, it caused Richard Ruiz to eye me until the party's end. The worst part was, it also caused Joe to glower at me until the party's end, for some reason.

By 3 A.M., I could barely stand due to exhaustion and a steady flow of gin. I looked around to see who might take me home. Joe had stopped glaring at me to chat up the bartender. Gerard was dancing. Sarah and Taso were making out on a bench along the wall. And out of the corner of my eye, I noticed that Richard was planting a wet one on Blondie Boy Toy. 'I should be going,' I finally told Rory. 'It was really great to meet you.'

'Maybe we should go out sometime,' Rory responded. She said it in such a way that it occurred to me that she might be flirting with me. I had heard she was bi . . .

Right then and there I decided that I liked her – a lot. I liked her so much that I was inspired to kiss her. Why shouldn't I? I thought again about what Richard said, about being attracted to the person, not the sex or the 'label,' and the next thing I knew my lips were tentatively touching Rory's. She aggressively kissed me back, and our tongues entwined for about thirty seconds. I relished the attention of onlookers around me, especially Richard's.

'I don't live far from here,' Rory said when our lip-lock broke apart. 'Do you want to . . . ?'

'Yeah,' I answered gamely, drunkenly, figuring why not? Label or no label, if bisexuality was good enough for Richard Ruiz, it was good enough for me. Plus, I had been working so much that I'd take any action I could get. 'Let me just say good night to my roommates.'

I teetered over to Sarah and Taso, who looked like they were getting ready to go themselves. 'We'll walk you home, then hop in a cab uptown,' Sarah said.

'I'm not going home,' I said. 'I'm going to Rory Bellmore's . . .'

Sarah rolled her eyes. 'Yeah, so what's up with that? I just saw you guys mauling each other.'

'I don't know,' I said naughtily. 'I think I like her. She invited me back to her house. Isn't she gorgeous?'

'Jill,' Sarah said, with an impatient laugh, 'you may be drunk. But you're not gay.'

'How do you know?' I answered. 'Maybe I'm bi,' I added, maybe a little too unconvincingly.

'Because,' Sarah said, sighing, 'you're one of the most guy-crazy people I know. You shouldn't lead her on . . .'

'I'm not. It feels right,' I said. 'Besides, it's about the person, not their sex. I think I'm extremely attracted to Rory Bellmore, the person.'

'Well, you're a big girl,' Sarah said, her patience

completely out. 'I give up. We're going. Have a good . . . whatever.'

When they left, I sidled up to Joe, who seemed startled when I interrupted his conversation with Michael Musto. 'I'm leaving,' I said.

'Okay,' he answered, with a hint of sulking in his tone. ''Night,' he mumbled, looking away. I didn't know what his problem was, but I would soon find out.

Nothing happened with Rory due to my passing out the minute we got to her sprawling, chicly outfitted loft. And I was glad, because the next morning I wasn't so sure if I did want to sleep with a girl after all. Still, I didn't completely write it off. The proposition came from Rory Bellmore, after all, one of the coolest celebs anyone could sleep with, male or female. Rory mentioned that she had to go off to L.A. for a few months, so I was off the hook for making another date with her. Not that I minded hanging out with her – she was great. I just didn't want her to get the wrong impression. Sarah's words from the previous night echoed in my head, working their way through my foggy brain and banging hangover headache. I didn't want to lead on Rory. She was way too nice for that.

But before I even had a chance to make the decision if I was gay, bi, or whatever, Michael Musto did it for me. Three days later, in Wednesday's *Voice*, this was the headline on his column:

WUNDERKIND WHITE GETS CHEEKY WITH BELLMORE

I read on, amused.

Media Wunderkind Jill White was more than cheek to

cheek with former wild child Rory Bellmore at Jackie 60 on Saturday night. Tongue to tongue is more like it. We knew Bellmore was a renowned switch-hitter, but we didn't know about White. Are they an item? 'We don't comment on Rory's personal life,' Bellmore's people said. Luckily, White's people don't have the same policy. I asked a close friend – and self-proclaimed former boyfriend – if she had Sapphic tendencies. 'Jill's just a starfucker,' the insider snapped. 'She's a celebrosexual.'

While I usually loved seeing my name in print, even if the words were not so flattering, Joe's comment was like a hard, stinging slap in the face. If it had come from someone else, I might have been able to laugh it off. But I couldn't believe it came from him. It was a cruel thing to say about a good friend.

'Celebrosexual . . .' Joe snickered when I threw the paper at him that night. 'I think that's pretty clever, don't you?'

'You're an asshole!' I shouted. 'Starfucker? How dare you! How could you say that about me?!'

'I didn't say anything that wasn't true,' he shot back bitterly.

'Grow up! And get over the Richard Ruiz thing already!' I hollered.

'You grow up! And stop being such a fucking groupie all the time!' he screamed.

A few slammed doors later, things would never be the same.

*

I called Sarah at work the next day and asked her to meet me for lunch. She hadn't been around to witness the fallingout between me and Joe. She eagerly accepted, telling me that she had some good news to share with me, anyway.

We went to the Sea Wok, this dinky midtown Chinese restaurant decorated with nothing but fish tanks. It had an obscenely cheap lunch special, and when we were recent graduates, it was the only place in the area we could afford. Even though the food wasn't that great and we could now afford better, it was a comforting, safe zone for both of us. We knew we'd never run into anyone from work there.

Sarah didn't flinch at the fact that I was twenty minutes late. She, and everyone else, had become used to my tardiness. I always felt guilty about it, but it seemed there was always something dragging me behind schedule.

'I'm sorry!' I called as I rushed in.

Sarah looked up from her menu. 'It's okay. My boss isn't in today. I can take a long one.'

'Cool,' I said.

'But I'm starving so let's order,' she said.

The waiter brought me an additional soy-stained menu, but I didn't need it. I always got the same thing: vegetable chow fun.

I waited in anticipation as Sarah made a decision, bursting to share with her what had gone down the previous night. When the waiter walked away to put in our order, I leaned in to Sarah and let it out: 'Did you read the *Voice* yesterday?'

Sarah shook her head. 'I had a crazy day.'

'There was an item in Michael Musto's column about me,' I said, rifling around in my bag to find the torn clipping.

'Congratulations,' she said deadpan. It wasn't the first time my name was bandied about in a gossip column. And she always scoffed at how I inwardly relished it.

I shook my head. 'Congratulations are definitely *not* in order this time. Read this!'

Sarah's face was emotionless as she scanned the piece. When she finished, she tossed it aside. 'What a dick. You can't be surprised, though,' she said.

That stunned me. 'What do you mean? I haven't done anything but try to help him out lately. And this is the thanks I get?!'

'That's exactly it,' Sarah said. 'Your trying to help him makes him hate you even more.'

I couldn't do anything right then but just stare at Sarah in horrified silence.

Sarah stared back at me like I was some kind of slow, mute child.

Finally, the outrage in me allowed me to form words. 'What do you mean *even more*?'

'C'mon, Jill, haven't you noticed?' Sarah answered, bewildered. 'Joe hates you. He has for a long time.'

Just then the waiter slapped our dishes down in front of us. Sarah didn't waste a minute digging into her moo goo gai pan.

I had lost my appetite, and I was fuming. 'What?! I mean, do I have to suffer for the rest of my life because I dumped him in college? Why did he even move in with me, then, if he hated me so much?'

'He didn't hate you back then, and it has nothing to do with college,' Sarah said, without missing a bite.

'Well, when exactly did he start to hate me?!' I demanded. I didn't know if I was more upset with Joe for hating me or with myself for not noticing.

'Jill,' Sarah said, finally giving her chopsticks a rest, 'ever since you started at *Cheeky*, he's been bitter. The more successful you become only accentuates what an utter failure he is,' she went on matter-of-factly. 'But it's not your fault. It's his problem. It's immature and bitter and wrong. But there's really nothing *you* can do about it. Joe chooses to be a loser. And he chooses to be bitter.'

Sarah went on to polish off the rest of her moo goo gai pan.

'How could I have not seen this?' I wondered out loud.

Sarah shrugged. 'You're busy.'

I looked at my noodles, sitting there cold and greasy, the brown sauce congealing on the edges of the plate. I couldn't touch a thing. 'Ugh,' I said in desperation. 'So now what do I do?'

'Well,' Sarah said, 'I really think the best thing for you to do is move out and move on. Why force this friendship? It hasn't been the same for you guys in a long time.'

I felt like she had just punched me in the stomach.

Sarah went on, 'It'll be the best thing for you, Jill. You don't want to be stuck in that apartment alone with him. That's not good for either of you.'

'But it's not like I'm really alone with him,' I said. 'I mean, even though you're not there every night, you're there –'

That's when she cut me off.

'That's the thing, Jill,' she said. 'Remember when I said I had some news?'

I had completely forgotten. 'Oh, yeah,' I said. 'Sorry. What is it?' I asked, slightly annoyed that she had changed the subject.

She held her left hand up, showing off a sparkling diamond ring. 'Taso and I are engaged!' she said happily.

'Oh my god!' I blurted, more in panic than elation.

'Oh my god!' I said again, trying to sound more supportive this time.

Oh. My. God, I screamed inside.

Then I awkwardly jumped up and hugged her. 'When?!' I asked. 'When did this happen?'

'Two nights ago. Over dinner at Milos.'

'Oh my god!' I said once again, because it was the only thing I could think of saying before I uttered, 'I'm so happy for you!' And I was. I was really, truly happy for her.

'Thanks,' Sarah said, smiling. She beamed. She seemed really happy.

'Let me see that ring!' I said, grabbing her hand, suddenly remembering the right, girly thing to do. 'It's beautiful!' I cooed.

'It was his grandmother's,' she said tenderly.

'So,' I said, putting two and two together, 'you're moving out. You're moving uptown.'

'Yes and no,' Sarah said. 'I'm moving out. But we'll be leaving the city. The market is so good for buyers right now that we want to nab a fixer-upper in the burbs as soon as possible. And I'm going to live in it and work on it. When Taso's lease runs out, he'll move in, too.'

Then, I started to cry. I cried because I was happy for Sarah. I also cried because I was going to miss her. And I cried because the only friend I had left on Jane Street hated my guts.

Sarah handed me a napkin to wipe my eyes. The sparkle of her ring caught my attention.

'Wait – have you been wearing that the whole lunch?' I asked, suddenly feeling so stupid.

Sarah nodded and laughed. 'Really, Jill, you do need to get your head out of your ass sometimes.'

It was such a Sarah thing to say, and it took away any hope of me pulling myself together. 'I'm going to miss you,' I said between more tears.

Who was going to watch my back? Who was going to set me straight? With Sarah leaving, I felt like I would lose all sense of reason. 'What am I going to do without you?' I sniffled.

Sarah smiled. 'You'll be just fine, Jill.'

I doubted it.

When I got home that night – purposefully late so I wouldn't have to deal with Joe – I walked straight into my room and wept the night away. I knew I had to start looking for an apartment right away. And that didn't really bother me so much. The Jane Street pad was a dump and I could afford better now.

I spent a few more taciturn weeks with Joe – with Sarah as a buffer, as she was spending more time in the apartment at my request. Finally, we had a tense 'house meeting' with Joe one night explaining that we would turn the lease over to him, though we knew there was no way he could afford the place on his own. So Joe started to look for a new place, too.

I came home elated one day, screaming to Sarah how I had found my dream loft and that I was actually going to buy it. I heard a jealous snort emerge from Joe but ignored it, as Sarah congratulated me. 'I can't believe we're both going to be home owners!' she said.

As the lease was expiring before my closing, I accepted Gerard's gracious invitation to move into his loft during the overlap. But I decided not to even wait; I paid the rest of my rent and began packing right away. On my official last day on Jane Street, Gerard was also nice enough to help me pack and move.

I remember going through every emotion possible on that day – from excitement to be living alone for the first time in my adult life to sadness that I was letting go of a precious part of my youth. And I wasn't the only one. Though he feigned indifference throughout most of the packing, Joe finally lost it.

I was taping up my last box and labeling it 'CDs', when Joe suddenly started to rifle frantically through his own stack of CDs. 'My "London Calling" is missing and you're not leaving this house with it!' he said suddenly.

'I did not take your "London Calling" CD,' I snapped back at him, the first words I had said to him in weeks. And I hadn't taken it. I didn't own that many CDs, and I knew for sure that the Clash hadn't made it into that box.

'Open that box!' he demanded. 'Let me see that it's not in there!'

'So typical of you,' I sneered, not budging, 'not to trust anyone.'

Joe came over to tear open the box himself. 'You've never done anything to earn my trust!' he shot back.

'Cut it out!' I screamed. 'I spent hours putting these boxes together and you're not going to start tearing them open!'

Gerard, who had been making 'keep' and 'trash' piles of clothing in my bedroom, came running out. 'Stop it, right now!' he screamed. His tone was stern, but also a little heart-broken, like a kid witnessing his parents fighting.

'Who do you think you are?' Joe then snapped at Gerard. 'You're worse than she is, thinking you're better than everybody!'

Then there was a thick, brief silence, as the room flooded with tension.

Gerard very quietly snarled. 'How dare you? I've never been anything but a friend to you, Joe.'

Joe turned away and started flipping through more of his CDs.

'Don't turn your back on me!' Gerard hollered.

'Why not? You've turned your back on me! Both of you! Everything just comes so easy to you guys, doesn't it?!'

Gerard softened a little and shook his head. 'We're not the ones who think you're not good enough to succeed. You think that of yourself. We always believed in you, Joe, but you gave up on yourself.'

'You guys may have never out and out said it, but I know that you always thought you were better than me,' Joe said, looking like he was going to break down in tears.

I still was speechless and I didn't know what to say. So I went over and offered Joe a hug, which he nastily shook off. 'Get away from me!' he said.

That's when I lost it again. 'I'm trying to. If you'd just let me finish packing, we'll never have to see each other again!'

'Fine!' Joe screamed, before he stalked into the kitchen.

Gerard and I exchanged bleak glances, confirming that our friendships with Joe were a lost cause.

We finished packing as soon as we could, then hauled the boxes into my rented van. I looked up at the apartment window, one last time, and started to walk toward the front stoop to at least say good-bye. But Gerard held me back.

'Don't,' he said to me, as he put a hand on my shoulder. 'He's just not worth it.'

I was crushed, realizing my friendship with Joe was truly over. Somehow I thought that some time would pass and he'd buck up and get over everything and we could just move on. But it sunk in that that just would not happen. It was bad enough that my real family had completely self-destructed. But as the moving van pulled away from the curb, I realized the same thing was happening to my surrogate family, too. And there was nothing I could do about it.

Except let go.

6

Renegade Teen Mag Cheeky Folds

— Folio, May 1997

I call the following years my 'Era of Detachment,' because it was almost as if I were leading someone else's life – like I was some kind of Jill White clone instead of the real deal.

My sense of home completely changed when I moved, for one thing. My dream loft on Charles Street was vast, sunny, and brand-spanking new. Yet it was empty, because I didn't have any money left to furnish it, except for a bed and a few bric-a-brac chairs. It didn't matter so much to me, though, because I was hardly ever there.

And this Jill White clone found herself in a relationship, at last, though I use the term loosely. Instead of lusting after Richard Ruiz in my mind, I became his actual on-again, off-again girlfriend. The most surprising thing was that when we were 'on-again,' I often found myself longing to meet someone else.

I was shocked when he called me, months after he had promised he would. He apologized, blaming his hectic schedule. I acted as if I hadn't even remembered that he said he would call, though I had thought about it several times a week.

He said he still wanted to give me that interview; I feigned a vague interest. By the end of the conversation, we had set up a time, a date, and a place.

When I arrived at his St. Marks' Place studio a week later, Richard was brimming with charm, hoping, no doubt, to get me into fawning mode. It almost worked; still, I was determined that this was going to be no different from any other *Cheeky* interview.

We sat together in his bay window and sipped spice tea. Once we were nice and comfortable, I switched on my tape recorder and fired away.

JW: Is it a habit of yours to pick up college girls, bring them on tour with you, sleep with them, promise to call, and then forget they ever existed?

RR: (After a bemused pause). No, that's not all true. I like to pick up college boys, too.

JW: How do you justify breaking so many young hearts?

RR: It's only rock and roll. You seem to have gotten over it.

JW: Not really.

RR: Can I make it up to you, then?

JW: Yes.

RR: How?

JW: You can invite me backstage to your show next week and pretend that I'm the only person in the room.

RR: Fine. Can we have sex again, too?

JW: It depends on how attentive you are backstage next week.

RR: Deal.

I did go backstage. Richard was more than attentive. And we did sleep together, that night and for years after. I even appeared in one of Third Rail's music videos, which I secretly thought was pretty cool. But Richard's lifestyle and frequent touring – not to mention his bisexuality – didn't make him the most available boyfriend. Even when he was physically present, he often didn't seem to be all there.

That especially held true in bed. I had imagined, for many years, that sex with Richard back in college had been unbelievable. But now I thought that back then I must have been turned on more by his famous face than his abilities.

The reality was that sex with Richard fluctuated between the bizarre and the routine. On occasion, during sex, he'd be struck with 'inspiration.' He'd start mumbling lyrics, then race out of bed – midact – to write them down. He was also annoyingly trendy when it came to sex. There was the tantric phase, the vibrating-accessories-of-the week stage, and the anal-thon. Most of the time I felt like some kind of blow-up doll he used for experimentation. The one constant, though, was that sex was always about him; it was never about us. That couldn't become more clear than on the night of 'the threesome,' the facilitator of our final split. On that night, Richard brought back a handsome young actor, thinking adding an extra person to our evening would be fun. I guess it was fun – for him. I, on the other hand, was more of an outcast than a participant. And I realized I didn't have that feeling only because there was someone else in the bed. When the actor left in the morning, obviously dazed and confused as to what had occurred the night before, I sat Richard down for a little conversation.

'What are we doing?' I asked, bewildered.

'Today, you mean?' Richard answered, as he crawled back in bed. 'I was kind of hoping nothing. I'm beat.'

'No, I mean in general. What are we doing? Together?'

He sat up and looked at me, slight offense in his eyes. 'Um, having fun – or so I thought.'

'Do you love me?' I asked, knowing full well that it was a preposterous question. I realized then that I wanted to hear an affirmative answer to that question. But not from Richard.

He looked startled. 'Uh, well, I do, but –'

'Don't worry,' I said, as I, too, crawled back in bed. 'Me neither.' I lit up a cigarette – not a habit, but something that helped me think once in a while. Being a rock star's girlfriend meant you could do things like this – smoke in bed – without the guilt. 'Richard, I think we're just spinning our wheels together, don't you?'

'I'm not sure what you mean,' he said, lighting a cigarette himself.

'I mean, we're not making any progress,' I said.

He shrugged. 'Sorry, Jill, but you don't seem to be the get-married, have-kids, get-a-house-with-a-white-picket-fence type of girl.'

'I'm not,' I said. 'It's just that . . .'

He put his cigarette in the ashtray on his night table, took mine from me, put it in the ashtray alongside his, and gave me a fierce hug. 'What we have works for me,' he said sincerely. I believed him. The problem was, it wasn't working for *me*. I wanted more. I wanted a relationship with a future. I was tired of living for the day. I wanted someone to say that he loved me, without an instant's hesitation.

'Look, Richard,' I said, 'I want you in my life.' Which was true. He was one of the smartest, most complex, and interesting people I knew. 'I like being around you. But I think we both deserve to stop kidding ourselves and move on. We're just plain better at being friends.'

I was surprised at the faint hurt in his eyes, and even more so by my conviction. He was the one who usually tried to break things off.

'Okay, then,' he said, finally, retrieving our cigarettes and taking a deep drag. 'Friends we are.'

'This time, no relapses,' I said.

'Fine,' he relented.

It was an incredibly freeing moment. I felt like, finally, even if it now became nonexistent, I was the one in control of my sex life. Still, there was a lot I'd miss about being a rock star's girlfriend. I met the most creative, amazing people through Richard and was able to develop real friendships with them. While I encountered a lot of musicians through the magazine, they always had a PR-placed veneer on them during interviews, no matter how cool and casual and 'not about press' they seemed to be. Plus there was a part of them that always tensed up when they were aware that someone media related was in the room. As Richard's girlfriend, they seemed to suddenly forget about all of that with me and I became more of a peer. I really got to know the real people behind many creative musical geniuses, like Kurt Cobain, Bono, and Mick Jagger. So I'll admit it: I loved the access to the music world being Richard's girlfriend gave me.

I also found that when you're a rock star's girlfriend people expect the least of you. So when you show any spark of intelligence, they are wowed. While most women would be pissed off by such underestimation, I loved seeing the looks on Richard's friends' faces when I'd draw them into conversation and we would actually connect. I also loved seeing the self-satisfaction on smug 'I picked a good one' look. And for me, well, it certainly didn't hurt my image as a hip magazine editor to have a boyfriend of Richard's status.

So these were just a couple of reasons why I put up with such an unsatisfying relationship. But I also did it because of insecurity: Richard's and mine.

I blame fame for enhancing Richard's eccentricities. Very few people understood Richard, and there were very few people he could be himself in front of. Third Rail had really become huge, and as his popularity rose, he came to trust fewer and fewer people. He never had a chance to develop friendships – other than with his bandmates – over the years, because he worked so hard and was on the road so much. So even though he barely remembered me from my time on the road with him when I was just a college girl, it was a comfort to him to be with someone who knew him before he hit it big. I think he clung to me because he didn't trust anyone else enough to get close to.

And I clung to Richard, because I was too lazy to go out there and get myself a new boyfriend. I was also afraid, I guess, of not finding the right guy. But I realized that I would never be able to find the right guy unless I got out there and tried and cut off my romantic relationship with Richard for good.

It turned out to be the right decision. Richard and I did stay friends; we never lost that underlying connection we felt and we grew even closer as a result. But during that time, I also grew apart from my best friend, which only added to that not-quite-myself feeling.

More than the Hudson River started to come between me and Sarah, unfortunately. For me, it started at her wedding. She hadn't asked me to be a bridesmaid because it was small and she only had her sister, which relieved me at the time. I was way too busy to be involved. But not being a part of one of the biggest events in her life isolated me even more from her, I now know in retrospect. I remember watching her walk down the aisle and wondering, when did Sarah become such an adult? I still felt like a college girl at heart. And I felt some resentment that she was growing up and moving on. I was too immature to realize that just because her personal life was progressing normally – and just because mine happened to be so stunted – it didn't mean that our relationship couldn't progress, too. But on that day I selfishly wondered if Taso gaining a wife, meant I had lost my best friend forever.

It should have been a happy day, the day of Sarah's wedding. But for me it was very sad. Gerard was my date, as Richard was completely out of the picture, and he'd never do something as conventional as go to a wedding with me anyway.

About a year after their wedding, Sarah and Taso had a baby girl and she became as wrapped up in her family as I was in my work. We tried to keep in good touch, but time slipped by so quickly. Despite her new responsibilities, Sarah made a good effort to stay in touch, but I was mostly to blame for our lack of contact. That fact really sunk in one time when I called her for her birthday – a week late. And though she did her best to hide it, I could tell that Sarah was pissed.

'Happy birthday!' I said all cheery on that occasion. 'I know it's belated, but I've had the craziest week – you wouldn't believe it.'

'When *aren't* you having a crazy week?' Sarah asked.

I agreed with her. 'I don't know why I do this to myself,' I confessed.

'Then why do you?' Sarah said. Then she hollered 'Hey, stop that!' Not to me, however, to Rosie, her daughter. I was used to, and annoyed by, those frequent outbursts. And she was used to, and annoyed by, me putting her on hold, which I did that very second to answer a question from Scott the music editor.

'Sorry,' I said when I came back.

'If you put me on hold one more time I swear I'm going to hang up,' Sarah said, exasperated.

Then I suggested the inevitable, though I dreaded it deep inside. 'Hey, let's get together,' I said. 'This phone thing just doesn't work for us. Get a sitter and I'll take you out for your birthday. We'll catch up, then – no distractions.'

'That sounds nice,' Sarah answered. 'I really could use a break.'

It wasn't until six weeks later that I had an actual opening in my schedule, so we made a lunch date for then. Then I had to cancel – twice – because of deadlines.

'Forget it,' Sarah had said when I cancelled the second time. 'Call me one day when you quit your job.'

I felt awful and begged her to allow me to make another date. When we finally did meet, my guilt made me spring for lunch in the Pool Room at the Four Seasons.

The food was certainly good but the rest of the lunch was a disaster. I think Sarah felt out of place there. She seemed annoyed at the media types who came over to say hi, and intimidated by the special treatment and attention we were getting from the maitre d'. She picked at her food and listened with half interest as I prattled on about who I'd met and who I'd interviewed. And I caught myself spacing out whenever she'd give me updates about Taso, the baby, and things like her kitchen redesign. I would toss out generic phrases like 'sounds wonderful' or 'I don't know where you get the energy,' so she would think I was listening and interested. But I knew she knew me well enough to know that I wasn't really.

That particular get-together made me wonder if we were beyond repair. Neither of us was to blame for the fact that we just didn't have that much in common anymore. Still, it saddened me and I wanted things to be like they once were between us. I just wasn't sure what that would take.

So playing the part of Jill White's best friend during that era was Paul Thomas, my creative director, which was convenient since my life really became all about work. I couldn't help but enjoy his company – we had perfect yin-yang synergy. I adored his avant-garde sensibility and he respected my editorial vision. And while his faith always bolstered my self-esteem, I helped keep him humble.

Deep down inside, Paul was very impressed by money and status. He liked to chide me for my prep school past, for example, even insinuating that I dated my classmate Walter Pennington III. As preposterous as that notion was, I secretly relished his suspicions and never confirmed nor denied them, under the guise that it would be too déclassé to tell.

I'm not sure why, but I never mixed Paul with my other friends and vice versa, so the relationship felt a little bit exclusive in that way. He was my buddy for documentaries – something we both had a passion for – and we'd end up catching one together on most Sundays. Paul always bought hoards of movie snacks and shared them with me: Sno-Caps, Milk Duds, Gummi Bears. By the end of the films I always felt I needed a few hours of dental work.

Despite my habit of not introducing Paul to my other friends, my worlds inevitably collided one day. We were waiting to go inside the Film Forum on Houston Street one Sunday afternoon when I saw a familiar, lithe figure sashay down the street right toward me. 'Jill White!' the figure shrieked. Though the afternoon sun was blinding me from that angle, I knew from the voice just who it was.

'Gerard, honey!' I called back. He ran to me and embraced me, picking me up and twirling me around. I hadn't seen him in ages because we had both been so swamped with work. He smothered me in kisses.

'Aren't you going to introduce me to your friend?' Gerard asked when he finally put me down.

'Oh,' I said, realizing Paul was standing there, gawking. 'Gerard Gautier, Paul Thomas.'

The men gave each other a firm handshake and we chatted

for a while. Gerard mentioned that he was on his way to a fitting in the neighborhood so he had to run. 'But I'll call you, my sweet, so we can get together soon. G&Ts on me!' he said, before he trotted off, waving.

'How do you know Gerard Gautier so well?' Paul asked, his eyes wide. I could tell he was impressed.

'He's an old friend from college, and then we were roommates for a few years, right here in the Village,' I confessed.

'Wow,' Paul said. 'High school with Walter Pennington III, college with Gerard Gautier. You certainly have lived a charmed life, Jill White.'

'Ha!' I laughed, waving the comment off. If he only knew the truth about my 'charmed' past. But I couldn't argue that I was living a damn good life at the moment.

It wasn't surprising to me, though, that Paul knew who Gerard Gautier was, because Paul had the best taste in clothes. He cut such a fine figure that being on his arm made any woman look good. So he became my preferred nightlife escort, too. I loved how he was always game for everything from the ASME awards to the Daytime Emmys – which leads me to the biggest out-of-body experience of that entire period: my turn as the host of the daytime talk show *Cheeky Speaks*.

After making the rounds from Larry King to Jay Leno as a designated 'teen expert,' I became so well known in the circuit that I was offered a show of my own. And even though I was strangely comfortable as a guest on someone else's couch, I was terrified to helm my own chats. But the publisher insisted that the exposure would help *Cheeky*, so I was pressured to accept anyway.

So I started to spend less and less time at the magazine's offices, and more and more time doing things like taking diction lessons to get rid of an air-unfriendly Southern accent that still peppered my speech. Or getting my hair bleached because 'brown doesn't read well on TV.' Such camera consciousness caused me to drop an unhealthy amount of weight. But as self-conscious as TV made me about my appearance, nothing terrified me more than being unprepared in front of a live audience.

When I wasn't being prodded, poked, and painted over, I was sequestered in the library researching a topic to death. I left the magazine in the hands of my trusted editors and tried to ignore their exasperation when I'd finally call them back, usually after they'd already had to make decisions without my input in order to get the issue to the printer on time. And my lack of participation showed when I'd see the first bound copies, and I'd try to ignore that, too. I was only one person, after all, and doing two full-time jobs perfectly was proving completely impossible.

Despite my pains, however, the show's ratings were weak. In a last-ditch effort to boost them, the producers pushed more salacious topics like 'I'm in love with a white supremacist' or 'I'm confronting my cheating boyfriend on national TV.' I didn't want to become the female Jerry Springer, so each day I prayed for an out.

The one good thing the show brought me was an even higher profile, and it expanded my personal network beyond my imagination. I found myself getting so involved in topics that I would frequently continue the conversation with some guests after the show – over drinks, dinner, coffee. One of those extended conversations even blossomed into a friendship. Serena Sax, the beautiful star of the sitcom *Roommates*, appeared on *Cheeky Speaks* to plug a charity she founded for children living with HIV/AIDS. When she related stories about the uphill battles of kids she visited around the country, I wanted to hear more. A follow-up phone call led to many lunch dates, during which I learned that Serena was truly committed to the cause, not just empty-headedly sponsoring it to get her profile up, like so many celebrities were known to do. I was so impressed by her sincerity that I not only made a sizable donation to the charity; I convinced *Cheeky*'s money people to sponsor a major fund-raising event. Working on that so closely with Serena – even when we were on separate coasts – led to an easy friendship between us.

The pretalkshow Jill White would never, ever have fathomed being invited to a dinner party by Myra Chernoff, the famously devious editor of *Fashionista*. I was floored – and flattered – that the she-devil of the magazine world would even look at me, never mind eat with me. But truth be told, I was reluctant to accept the invitation. How was I supposed to act around such a masthead legend? Plus, I was worried that my fraternization with her might get out to PETA, who relentlessly tormented her for her fur-wearing habits. (I was a card-carrying member.) But turning down an invite from Myra Chernoff could also mean career suicide. So I went.

I waved across Myra's crowded town house to my dear famous friend Gerard, then sat elbow to elbow with Peter Jennings, the dashingly handsome newscaster, and Bryan Miller, the *New York Times*'s restaurant critic. I chatted with

Gianni Versace, right across the table, and made small talk with Susan Sarandon over a lentil salad starter. I managed to say a few words to Myra herself without making a fool out of myself. It was all going swimmingly well.

Until the main course arrived.

It was a large, bleedingly rare hunk of venison.

My mind raced with the possibilities and their consequences. Do I tell Myra that I'm a vegetarian? I glanced over at her, holding court at the head of the table, her green eyes glowing under her famously severe bangs. I didn't dare.

Should I feign illness? She wouldn't buy it; just a minute before I was laughing heartily at Gianni Versace's off-color joke.

I could just eat the side dishes; but then I'd not only insult Myra but look like a complete idiot in front of the *Times* food critic.

Finally, I sucked in my breath, closed my eyes, and choked a few pieces down. The gamy flavor was revolting. There was no way I'd be able to eat the whole thing.

I eyed Gerard helplessly, who gave me an amused wink as he cheerily ate his meat. He had inside info, knowing that I was a vegetarian. I usually enjoyed his devilish sense of humor, but right this moment, as he was so obviously reveling in my discomfort, I loathed it. 'Myra,' he said, 'I haven't had venison this delicious since Paris!' Then he asked pointedly, 'Don't you agree, Jill?' Clearly, he was getting a giant kick out of himself.

Asshole, I thought, as I gagged down another piece.

Myra then took quick inventory of everyone's plates before her gaze lingered on my half-eaten venison. Why did my serving have to be the largest of the group? Myra's was the size of a matchbook. 'Jill? Don't you like the venison?' she asked sternly.

'Oh, yes,' I lied through my teeth. I noticed Gerard was making a poor attempt at holding back a laugh. 'It's one of my favorites. I'm just a very slow eater. I like to savor it.' And just in case Myra didn't believe me, I cut another piece and swallowed it, steeling myself from audibly gagging. Myra smiled in satisfaction before she changed the subject. Finally, all eyes were off me.

I shot Gerard a furtive evil eye and he smiled apologetically in return. Why did he even have to draw attention to me? And what was I going to do with the rest of it? If I ate it I might very well throw up right at the table.

A childhood trick was my only way out, it seemed. I cut the meat into pieces, put them into my mouth, faked chewing, then nonchalantly dabbed at my mouth while spitting them into my napkin. Then I brought the napkin down to my lap, stealthily pouring the remains of the meat into my very expensive, Gerard-designed loaner purse. After his actions at the dinner table, I had zero qualms about ruining the bag.

When Myra finally stood and directed the party to the enormous terrace for an after-dinner drink, I snuck off to the bathroom to empty the purse and flush the meat down the toilet only to find Sharon Stone slipping into it before me.

I searched an adjoining room but didn't find anything but closets. Myra had to have ten bathrooms in that spread – where were they when I needed them?! Down another hallway, I found nothing.

Myra then appeared. 'To the terrace, everyone!' she

demanded, shooing me outside. I had to wait a while to slip away, then. So I followed the crowd outside – while Chernoff's poodle followed me, jumping and nipping at my purse.

'Hello, little doggie!' I said, patting her on the head, and trying to keep her down.

But the dog was adamant, obviously smelling the venison inside. 'Down!' I pleaded. I'd be happy to slip her some later if she'd just leave me alone right then.

'Valentino must like you!' I then heard Myra coo approvingly.

I looked up into her glowing green eyes. 'Oh, I just adore poodles!' I answered, full of shit. I was never one for fancy, groomed-to-the-hilt dogs. And now this one wouldn't leave me alone.

She jumped up on me again, as Myra laughed it off. 'Valentino has always been a great judge of character,' she said.

So I let her paws go all over my Gerard Gautier dress. Then I made the mistake of bending down to pet her more, as a show for Myra. Thankfully, she was called away by Dominick Dunne, who had a question about her architect.

Just as she turned away, the dog's jaws clamped on my Gerard Gautier bag. She growled and shook it fiercely. I did my best to pull it free.

'My bag!' I heard Gerard say frantically. He came running over. It was about time he tried to help. 'Bad dog!' he scolded, hitting the dog on the nose, as I nervously looked over at Myra. I didn't want her to see us abusing her stupid, venison-obsessed mutt.

The best thing, I decided, was to drag the bag, and the dog, inside and try to rid the bag of the venison once and for all. 'Block Myra's view,' I whispered to Gerard, who dutifully stood right in her line of vision.

So I pulled the dog – her jaws still firmly clenched around the bag – and dragged her all the way to the kitchen. 'Good dog,' I said calmly as she started to snarl and growl, desperate to tear the bag into pieces. Inside the swinging kitchen door, I begged the cook, who was eating, for a decoy piece of meat. Seeing my dilemma, he cut me a hunk of leftover venison from his own plate and placed it on the floor.

Valentino pounced on it, finally surrendering the bag to me. 'Thank you!' I said, relieved, then raced out the swinging door and into the bathroom, where I emptied the smelly meat into the toilet and flushed it down.

Back outside on the terrace, I handed Gerard the shredded bag.

'Sorry,' I said.

He couldn't help but crack up. 'Don't worry, honey,' he said. 'The image of you and that dog in a tug-of-war is way more valuable than this thing,' he said, then gave me a peck on the cheek.

The next day was a complete misery. I was hungover, my venison-ravaged stomach ached like hell, and I felt horribly guilty for eating meat. The bright part of the day was that I got a call from my agent telling me that *Cheeky Speaks* had been cancelled, which was a giant relief. *Cheeky*, the magazine, however, would come over to haunt me in the form of Paul.

He brought me miso soup to settle my stomach, definitely

the act of a Good Samaritan. But I soon learned that his real motive was to have my undivided attention for once.

'You saved my stomach,' I said, as I gratefully slurped the soup.

'That's great,' he said, folding his long legs into lotus position at the foot of my bed. 'But I'm afraid I'm too late in telling you that you can't save *Cheeky*.'

The ache in my stomach was replaced by a sinking feeling. 'Talk to me,' I said, steeling myself for what he had to say. I knew it couldn't be good.

'Jill, the magazine is falling apart,' he started. 'We're down to fifteen ad pages next issue. And the advertisers who are left are threatening to jump ship if we don't tone down the content.'

'Fifteen!' I shouted, sitting bolt upright. 'That's not possible!'

'I warned you about this weeks ago,' he went on, as kindly as someone who had lost his patience could. 'And now the Moral Majority's campaign has really picked up steam . . .'

'Fuck the Moral Majority!' I said, nearly spilling miso soup all over my bed. 'They can't tell us how to run our magazine!'

'Maybe not,' Paul answered, 'but their letter-writing campaigns calling for a *Cheeky* boycott are sure scaring the crap out of the advertisers. And we won't have much of a magazine without those.'

I sighed. 'I had no idea it had gotten this bad. I'll be back in the office tomorrow,' I said. 'As soon as I stop throwing up. I'll fix everything – don't worry.' *Cheeky* was my baby, my passion. I knew its audience and its advertisers like the back of my hand.

Paul shook his head solemnly. 'I don't know if that's possible, Jill. Everything's changed. *We've* changed!'

I waved his comment off. 'Please. If we were able to make *Cheeky* a success with barely any experience, we can save it; don't you worry.'

But there was no putting Paul at ease. 'We're not the same people we were then Jill. Look at us. Look at you. Where are your Doc Martens? What's happened to your nose ring?'

'Please,' I said, rolling my eyes. 'That alt-girl uniform couldn't be more out. Every mall girl in Iowa has discovered "grunge."' Paul knew that I had coined the term *grunge* to describe the trend in fashion, and I thought he, of anyone, should remember that we had done it in *Cheeky's* fashion pages years ago. 'You know that.'

'You're taking me too literally,' Paul said. 'I'm just saying that things are different. Times are different. We've had a good run, but you can't go backward.'

Later that night what Paul was really saying sunk in. He was saying that *Cheeky* was losing its edge. He was also saying that *I* was losing my edge. And as I stared in the mirror that night, I realized that he might be right. As much as I loved *Cheeky*, maybe I had outgrown it. If someone walked past me quickly these days, he or she wouldn't give me a second glance, unless he or she was mistaking me for current 'it' girl Gwyneth Paltrow. Who was I if I wasn't the young, cool editor of *Cheeky*? That wedged a feeling of dread inside me. The dread spread when I returned to the office the next day, for the first time in weeks.

Things were indeed falling apart.

My scattered, neglected desk was covered in letters like this:

To the Staff of Cheeky Magazine:
I found an issue of your magazine in my fourteen-year-old daughter's backpack when she came home from school the other day. I flipped through it and was absolutely shocked at what I found. How dare you suggest that she and her peers are ready to have sex in stories like 'What You Need to Know about Safe Sex.' And how dare you promote unnatural sacrilegious lifestyles in other stories like 'I Love Having a Gay Brother.' In addition to making sure that this piece of trash never gets in my daughter's hands again, I will boycott your advertisers and any outlet that sells your rag. And I will look forward to the day that you all burn in hell for warping the minds of innocent American youth.
Sincerely,
Mrs Amanda Wilson
Salt Lake City, UT

I could line the cages of every kennel in the country with similar such letters. And while once we laughed at those damning tirades, it wasn't so funny anymore. Their boycotts were succeeding.

The camel's back broke when we lost two giant chainstore accounts. So we toned the content down a bit. But then the readers got pissed off, so we started to lose them, too. Paul resigned, taking a bigwig position at Friar Publications. And before we knew it, *Cheeky* was on the block, a headache that nobody wanted to deal with.

I hung in there, doing my best to salvage it, until it was sold with a mandate to morph into a completely different magazine. *Cheeky* as I had known it was truly dead, and I felt partially to blame. Maybe if I hadn't become so distracted it would have retained its freshness. Now the coolest thing about it was the fuchsia type on the spine.

There *was* no turning back. So I left.

Cheeky folded soon after my departure.

After too many years of workaholism, late-night parties, and social stagnation, my time had come for a break. It was time for the real Jill White to take over my life and start living it.

So even though a ton of tempting offers poured in immediately after my resignation, I took that break, confident that the magazine industry would be there when I was ready to come back.

I got lost in Europe for a while, and I was tempted to wile away the rest of my life in Roman cafes or in Spanish tapa bars. But after a few months, I felt a familiar tug, so I came back to New York, solid in what I wanted. One of those things was a real relationship. I couldn't believe where I found it.

It happened at Fashion Week, where I went to work the old connections and spread the word that I was back. There, I bumped into Serena Sax and her husband, Kevin Alouette.

'Jill! Thank God you're here. Come with us to the Donna Karan tent,' she implored. 'We'll need somebody to talk to.

It's going to be full of network bores.'

'What a tempting offer,' I joked. 'Why aren't we there already?'

Kevin excused himself to retrieve a friend of his whom he said was 'moping uncomfortably' in the corner. He returned with a slightly disheveled, sandy-haired puppy-dog type named Josh who looked like Bill Pullman's younger, blonder brother. He seemed to brighten when he saw that I was with the group.

After quick introductions, the four of us crossed Bryant Park, attempting to dodge stray press on the way. The entrance of the Donna Karan tent was mobbed, however, so we had no choice but to stop and wait to get in.

Flashbulbs popped away at Serena and Kevin as they posed graciously. Soon the questions started flying.

'Is it true that the next season of *Roommates* will be your last?'

'Will you and your costars be attending Jessica Armstrong's wedding next month?'

'When will you be having a baby?'

'Are you having trouble conceiving?'

Serena just smiled, seemingly oblivious to the reporters' rudeness. I, however, boiled at the questions' mounting nosiness.

One particular reporter was relentless. 'Is it true you had a miscarriage? Have you been seeing a fertility specialist?'

While Serena serenely continued to ignore the questions, I ripped into that reporter, who had been edging closer and was now about two inches from Serena's face.

'That's none of your fucking business!' I snapped.

'Of course it's my business,' he snapped back. 'My job is her business.'

'Then get a real job, you hack!' I shouted.

'At least I have a job,' he snidely shouted back. 'Suddenly *you're* above asking celebrities personal questions?'

Serena pulled me along, into the tent, before I could respond. It was true that many of our celebrity interviews were intense and revealing at *Cheeky*. But we certainly didn't badger people about personal issues, like how and when they were conceiving a child. Plus, I knew that Serena and Kevin were trying like hell to have a baby. To be questioned about it constantly by strangers must have killed them inside, no matter how good they were at hiding it.

'You're a good friend,' Serena whispered to me when we got in. 'But you'll never get the attack dogs to back down.'

'How the hell do you deal with it?' I asked incredulously.

'I just do,' she said. 'It's part of the job.'

'I don't know how they do it either,' Josh said, finally really speaking to me for the first time. 'I hate reporters. They really are the scum of the earth.'

'Well, the gossip ones are,' I answered.

'All of them stink,' he went on. 'I don't care if you're talking about *Time* or *Us Weekly*. They all have some kind of agenda. The magazine world is corrupt and full of shallow people.'

He was being sincere in defending his friends. And he obviously had no idea who he was talking to, so I gave him the benefit of the doubt. Plus, I thought he was kind of cute. 'I wish I could agree with you,' I answered kindly. 'But then I'd be admitting to shallowness.'

A look of dread crept on his face. 'Don't tell me,' he said.

I nodded. 'I'm Jill White,' I said. 'Of *Cheeky* magazine fame.'

'Sorry, Jill White,' he answered. 'I'm Josh Andrews, of Foot-in-Mouth fame.'

I laughed at his deprecation, while he gave me an embarrassed smile. I noticed it was a nice smile, if a little awkward.

'I don't know your magazine, so I won't judge it,' he said. 'And I'm sorry I insulted your profession.'

'You mean you've never heard of me?!' I said, in mock horror.

He shook his head sheepishly. 'I'm afraid I've never heard of you or your magazine.'

How refreshing, I thought.

'I'm actually taking a bit of a break from the business right now,' I said.

'Good for you, then,' Josh said. 'I'm in between projects myself.'

'What do you do?' I asked.

'I'm a playwright,' he answered. 'I wrote the masterpieces *Snow in April* and *Between the Lines*. They both had very successful off-off-off-off-off-Broadway runs,' he added sarcastically. 'I'm quite famous, you know. In the world of off-off-off-off-off-Broadway.'

'Well, I'm afraid I've never heard of you or your plays,' I sassed playfully back at him.

'Hey – do you want to split and go grab a bite?' he asked, suddenly emboldened, looking a lot less uncomfortable than he did earlier.

'I don't know,' I answered. 'I'm used to dating much more famous men. But I am hungry.'

'Great. Then let's get out of here,' he said.

That first date went on for months, it seemed, as we slept in; did crossword puzzles; ate takeout, rented movies; and acted completely, totally normal. There were no name-dropping conversations. No late-night parties. No press events. No weird sex. Because of Josh, the real Jill White finally started to come back to consciousness from a career-induced coma. It was nice. It was more than nice. It was love.

Eventually, we both got a little restless, realizing that we had to get back to work. Josh got to work on a new play. And a call from Paul Thomas, now creative director at Friar Publications, spurred me out of my brief retirement. He wanted to meet with me. 'Bring ideas,' he said.

I dug through old journals and files for inspiration. My best idea came from one favorite old letter:

Dear Jill:
I've been a Cheeky fan since I was sixteen. But I'm going on twenty-three now. I'm an adult and I have a good job, my own apartment and I'm even engaged to be married. But I still enjoy your magazine. I can't help but feel like my neighbors look at me like I'm some kind of emotionally stunted freak every month when Cheeky arrives in the mail. Have you ever considered starting a magazine for your older fans?
Sincerely,
Jennifer Czarnecki
Austin, TX

My readers had grown up. So maybe I was allowed to, too.

With a brand new mission, the old Jill White was back. She was a little more mature, and a little more the wiser. And soon, everybody would know it.

7

Jill White's New Magazine to Debut in Fall

— Wall Street Journal, January 1998

Jill was born after many hours of conception in Paul Thomas's office. She couldn't have had two prouder parents when the announcement was made. We received a bundle of congrats from well-wishers, including a bottle of champagne from Myra Chernoff, who I hadn't seen since the venison incident; a lovely floral arrangement from Richard Ruiz; a promise to pick whatever I wanted from dear Gerard's new spring line; a homemade, elaborately illustrated card from the gang at *The New Yorker*; and even a nice note from Lonnie Lessing, the notoriously nasty publisher of *Celebrity Gossip Weekly*. But the kudos I cherished the most came from none other than Walter Pennington III, who was helming a political magazine of his own. My heart fluttered when I read his slanted scrawl:

> *Even when we were teens you always showed a certain spark; I am very happy for you – Walt*

It's true that schoolgirl crushes die hard.

And Josh, of course, cheered me along the whole way. He had moved into the loft, and with his presence and fine taste in furniture, the space finally started to feel like a real home instead of just a big, empty box. Not to mention that our relationship grew deeper and more real by the day. He was most definitely 'the one,' I realized in a relatively short time.

One of the things I loved most about Josh was that he was a real romantic, and the antithesis to so many men I had come across in my dating life. He was a cuddler, for example, and not afraid to show affection. And he was always coming up with creative ways to express his love. Like on Valentine's Day, when he took out a completely cheesy ad in the *Village Voice* saying that he 'loved me 4 ever,' knowing what a sucker I was for anything blatantly kitschy or tacky. Another time, for my birthday and during a time that I needed some rest and some pampering, he surprised me with a reservation at a beautiful bed-and-breakfast in Massachusetts for the weekend. And there were so many other moments of thoughtfulness: daily phone calls at work, just to tell me that he loved me; flowers waiting for me at home, for nothing other than whim; silly trinkets, relating to inside jokes we shared.

Best of all, Josh was so understanding about the hours I had to commit to *Jill*. He knew she was an unruly, needy newborn that kept me up at nights and demanded my attention through the weekends, so he gave me ample slack. He also took the opportunity to throw himself into his own work, and while I pored over editorial content and hustled ad sales, he churned out play after play.

I wished at the time that Josh could share some slack-giving lessons with Sarah, whose congratulatory e-mail had an undertone of impatience.

Subject; congrats
Message: I read about your new magazine today in the Wall Street Journal. Congrats, Jill. I know this is what you always wanted. I can't help but wish, though, that I heard the good news from you in person. Would have loved to hear the excitement in your voice.
Love,
Sarah

I made a mental note to call her as soon as things lightened up.

Paul and the group at Friar were thrilled about the coverage the mere announcement of *Jill* received. They gave me free reign and full-on diva treatment, complete with big-shot salary, an expense account that included daily hair and make-up, and a vast entertainment budget. *Jill* was poised to become the publisher's lead title alongside its cornerstone, *Profile* magazine.

Putting together *Jill*'s staff was obviously my first, and most important, order of business. A few *Cheeky* alums came over: notably Scott, the music editor; Maria, from features; and Dana, a talented staff writer. I needed an art director with good big-league experience, and after studying portfolio after portfolio, I decided on the arty-pop stylings of Sven Janssen, whose resume included *Details* and *GQ*. Diana, a dynamo managing editor, came from a local weekly – I liked the idea of having someone who didn't flinch at short deadlines. It all fell into place fairly quickly. The only thing I lacked was a good assistant.

I thought about recruiting my assistant from *Cheeky*; deep down she never really impressed me but I craved to have someone comfortable with my quirks and habits. Word on the street, however, was that she had a drug problem, which I always suspected, and it had spiraled out of control.

I interviewed an exhausting amount of people, none of whom moved me. They were either dull, neurotic, too rigid, too spacey, or too dumb. I was just about to settle on having a never-ending series of temps, a la Murphy Brown, when one day, on line at CVS, I found her.

She was wearing vintage Levis, clunky motorcycle boots, and a tight black turtleneck with thin ribbing. She had smartly cut chestnut hair that fell in an efficient curve just down below her ears. A tiny baby was slung on to her chest in a Baby Björn carrier, a basket full of drugstore items hung cradled from her left elbow while her left hand clinched a thick file, and her right hand pressed a cell phone to her ear. A friend, or coworker, stood alongside her.

I had stopped in to grab some emergency Excedrin and ended up behind the pair at the register. As I waited, I watched as the chestnut-haired woman soothed the baby, proficiently made an appointment on the cell phone, chatted with her friend, and paid for everything with a confident coolness that I so wished was contagious.

'I can't believe you agreed to come in today,' the friend said to her. 'Morgandorfer is well aware you still have three weeks' maternity left. You need to draw the line with him.'

The chestnut-haired woman nicely hushed her friend as she cased the crowd to see who else might be standing there. That tipped me off that they must have been talking about Robert Morgandorfer, the music biz mogul whose offices were directly across the street. So Chestnut, unlike her friend, was discreet. I liked that.

'He doesn't trust the temp with confidential documents, and I told him I was coming into town anyway,' she answered quietly.

So she was dedicated, and loyal, too. I liked that more.

I decided right then and there that this was the type of woman I wanted – no, needed – as my assistant.

'I gotta run,' she said to her friend as the clerk bagged her items. 'I'll call you later,' she said. She gave the friend a quick peck on the cheek and took off.

As the friend paid off her purchases, I tapped her on the shoulder. 'Who was that?' I asked incredulously, as if I had spied a superhero.

The girl eyed me nervously at first, but then I think I saw a faint recognition cross her face. 'Her name is Casey Harris,' she said. 'And her boss totally takes advantage of her.'

I pulled out one of my cards from my purse. 'Give this to her, and tell her to call me. Tell her that I do know where to draw the line.'

The friend studied my card and smiled. 'Sure thing,' she said.

A week later, Casey called. She wanted to meet for coffee.

We did, and we instantly clicked. I took to her sharp sense of humor, and I respected the fact that she drove a hard bargain. She negotiated a four-day workweek for herself, as well as a comfortable salary that would prove to be well worth it. When Casey officially came on board a month later, my staffing was complete.

Her first assignment was to buy up every woman's magazine she could find. She did, piling them in the conference room after each trip. Each editor was assigned a few to study for our first real editorial meeting.

When the time for the meeting came, we all sat on the floor in a circle in the (yet unfurnished) conference room. I started by asking each editor to read a list of the lead stories in each.

'How to Keep Your Man,' Diana piped up.

A few murmurs followed. 'That's in practically all of them in one form or another,' a voice added.

'Okay, so *Jill's* answer to that would be "How to Lose a Loser," ' I said.

As Casey scribbled that down, laughter erupted throughout the room. But I was dead serious. 'See, we're going to give each story our own twist,' I explained. 'What's next?'

Maria raised her hand. 'There's all of these advice columns of women asking women what men are thinking. Why not just have a guy answer the questions?'

'Awesome,' I said. 'You're thinking on the right track. We could include a column called something like "What Is He Thinking?" and it will be written by a guy.'

The ideas came fast and furious after.

'Here's a workplace column, but the stories are so tired and predictable,' Dana pointed out.

I nodded thoughtfully. 'What kinds of columns are never in women's mags that you wish were?'

'Tech and gadgets,' Casey offered. 'I love that stuff but I can only find info in boring men's magazines.'

'Yes!' I said. 'We're going to have the world's first girl gadget department ever.'

'Sounds like we'll be rating vibrators,' Maria snickered.

'And there's absolutely nothing wrong with that,' I countered. 'I'm sure our readers would actually love that kind of content.' And since *Jill*, unlike *Cheeky*, was targeting twenty-somethings, the Moral Majority couldn't complain that I was corrupting America's youth.

'How about a "Hoax" column, where we set up practical jokes?' Casey suggested, her sense of humor emerging. 'We can pull them on celebrities, politicians, designers . . . you name it.'

'Love it!' I said. 'Add it to the list.'

'Here's a common coverline: "Lose Ten Pounds This Month"!' Scott then shouted. 'Weight loss stories are in every freakin' one of these rags.'

A chorus of murmurs agreed.

'Great. What's the twist, then?' I asked.

'Uh, "Gain Ten Pounds This Month"?' he answered.

All of the women in the room scoffed. Scott was trying, but we knew better. 'Nah. Even the most secure women don't want to read that,' I said. 'What else can we do?'

'What about stories that celebrate food, that say it's okay to eat, or something like that,' Rosario, my entertainment editor, interjected.

'I like it,' I answered, thinking it over. 'Include recipes –

the fattier the better. And I don't ever want to see the words *slimming, diet*, or *low-fat* or anything with *low* in it. A story on the best French butters, but never low-fat nondairy spreads. Got it?'

From the enthusiastic nods I saw all around the table, I was certain that they *did* get it.

The art department had a mandate: diversity. I wanted my pages to draw visual attention solely for the fact that each spread was different. I demanded models of all varieties – no Barbie clones or anorexics need apply. I also directed them to keep airbrushing to a minimum. I wanted the women, especially the celebrities, in our magazine to look as real as possible.

The editorial department was instructed to always pursue an angle of intrigue, and to write, when appropriate, with an edge of smart humor and irreverence. Everyone was reminded to acknowledge our reader as confident and independent minded.

All we had to do was pick the perfect cover girl to embody that for our first issue. I had decided that we would feature only women who had something going for them besides a perfect face.

I also decided that for the first issue it had to be an actor. I asked the editors to e-mail me the qualities that they thought that celebrity should have.

Here's what I received:

Offbeat but popular.
Smart.
Adventurous.

Controversial.
Open – willing to divulge good dirt.
Hollywood glamorous but not Hollywood per se.
Not too young, not too old.
Risqué.
Bon vivant.

One person kept coming to my mind as I read the list over and over: Rory Bellmore. I was convinced from the few times I ran into her over the years that she still had a crush on me, even though she had married a Japanese actor known for his karate action movies, so I thought she might be an easy get.

I was right. To my delight, Rory accepted. To my fear, she did so with the condition that she write her own cover story. I had remembered her telling me all those years ago about her writing, but I had never made the time to actually read her work. I wasn't sure I wanted *Jill* to be her 'practice publication,' especially since it was the first issue. But she was the absolute embodiment of the *Jill* girl, and I'd do anything to get her on that cover. I decided to let her give it a shot despite my trepidation, figuring that we could always editorially salvage what was there if we didn't like what we received. Shocking us all, however, Rory turned in an extremely intelligent, captivating account of her years in rehab. It was brilliant; it was honest; it was human. And it was destined to sell magazines.

After months of toiling, when I finally had a moment to breathe, I remembered that I owed Sarah a phone call. I had thought about calling her a few times, but my guilt always made me ashamed at my lack of communication with her, and Sarah was not one to let me off the hook that easily. So I buried my head back into work until I finally got up the strength to suck it up.

'It's been nonstop since we made the deal,' I told Sarah when I finally called her. 'Most pubs have at least a year to get off the ground. They want me to do it in half the time.'

'You get off on the pressure, though, Jill,' she said in support. 'You'd hate it if it were any other way.'

We went on to have the first real conversation that we had had in a long time, and I truly missed her right then. Sometimes I wished we were back on Jane Street cozying up in the living room with a couple of beers and talking about the sillier side of life rather than its pressures.

'I miss you,' I blurted.

Sarah gave a flattered laugh. 'Well, I'll be delivering some sketches in the city next week,' she said. 'Wanna get together for a drink before I have to rush home?'

'Sounds great,' I said. I was looking forward to the diversion.

Sarah was right: I do get off on pressure. But while I enjoyed it, rearing *Jill* through her initial stages had its hazards to my health. My brain, for one thing, wouldn't function correctly for anything that wasn't related to the magazine. I was sort of desensitized to anything un-*Jill*.

While that's not a valid excuse, it does explain how I just couldn't seem to do anything right when it came to my friendship with Sarah.

The day that Sarah and I were to meet was just like any other day in the months since *Jill*'s birth – a nonstop series of meetings, phone calls, reading, drumming up business and hype. I was just about to hit the wall of exhaustion when Serena Sax happened to breeze into my office that very afternoon. She and I had become very friendly since I began living with her husband's best friend.

'Lunch?' she asked as she peeked in.

'Hey! What are you doing here?' I said, as I jumped up from behind my cluttered desk to offer her a hug.

Serena put down her Bergdorf shopping bags and returned the embrace. 'I was on the fourteenth floor for a *Profile* photo shoot, so I thought I'd kidnap you for the afternoon.' She looked me up and down. 'Looks like you could use a break.'

I totally could use a break. But I couldn't help but feel guilty for wanting to take one. There was so much work to do. 'I don't know . . .' I said.

'Casey!' Serena called out. 'Is her afternoon clear?'

'She has a very cancelable phone call at three,' Casey called back. 'But other than that . . .'

'Great! I'm not taking no for an answer, then,' Serena insisted.

Casey went along with the conspiracy of slacking off. 'She's reaching levels of OCD that would even freak Rain Man out. Get her out of here and bring her back a new woman,' she said.

'All right,' I agreed, as I grabbed my purse.

'No looking back,' Serena said, as she pulled me out the door.

And I didn't. If I had looked back, though, I might have seen my cell phone, buried under a pile of papers.

And I might have noticed a note to myself:

Don't forget! Drinks with Sarah, 5:30.

Serena treated me to a long, spectacular lunch at L'Espinasse, right in her hotel, the St. Regis. Immediately after, we got massages in her suite. Then after showering off, we headed down to the King Cole bar for some champagne. It was nice to live the life of leisure and luxury – if only for a few hours.

As we sat in the bar, we clinked glasses when the pianist ripped into the Cole Porter classic 'Friendship.' I thought of what a good friend Serena had been that day.

I also suddenly thought about Sarah.

'Shit!' I screamed, loudly enough to earn a glare from the pianist. I looked at my watch. Seven-thirty. 'I was supposed to meet Sarah for bellinis at Cipriani hours ago.'

Serena regarded her watch. 'I imagine she realizes she has been stood up by now,' she said.

I panicked. Throwing some money on the table, I apologized to Serena, thanked her, and bolted out the door. I ran up Fifth Avenue like a maniac, even though I knew that Sarah had way too much self-esteem to still be waiting there.

I burst through the door and frantically described Sarah to the tuxedoed maitre d'.

He shook his head. 'I'm afraid you missed her by about an hour.'

Dejected, I slunk out the door and hailed a cab. The shame of my screwup plagued me the entire ride home.

I skulked into the loft to find Josh as my glowering

conscience. 'Where have you been? Haven't you gotten my calls?' he demanded.

I shook my head and searched my bag. 'I must have left my cell at the office.'

'Sarah called,' he went on. 'You were supposed to meet her. When she said you didn't show, I started to worry.'

'I know,' I said. 'I'm an idiot. I just plain spaced. She'll probably never speak to me again.'

'But where were you?' Josh pressed.

'At the St. Regis with Serena Sax,' I told him.

Josh shook his head. 'You know I love Serena, honey. But don't forget who your old friends are.'

He was more than right. So I picked up the phone and called Sarah. When I got her machine, I babbled an embarrassed apology.

A few sad hours later, I reluctantly logged on to my e-mail before I went to bed.

As I had dreaded, a message from Sarah waited:

Dear Jill:
I was glad to receive your message tonight because at least I now know that you are okay and nothing happened to you. Because despite your utter lack of respect for me, I care about you. Or at least I did. You've done nothing but show that our friendship is low priority to you in return. You're too busy, or too uninterested, to keep up your end. So, I'm done, Jill. I wish you well, but I can't allow myself to be treated like this by my 'friend.'
Sarah

She was absolutely right. I felt like shit. I felt worse than shit. I felt like shit that had been shat upon. I went to bed heartbroken, and defenseless, and spent the night crying in Josh's arms.

The next morning, I wrote her a long, sappy, handwritten letter about how important our friendship is to me.

She didn't respond.

I sent her flowers a few weeks later.

Still no response.

I had pretty much given up by the time fall rolled around. In a last-ditch effort, I sent Sarah and Taso an invite to the *Jill* launch party along with a handwritten note:

Sarah –

I never would have been able to do this without your support and friendship. I would be happy, and so touched, if you came.

Love, Jill

I didn't expect to hear back, but I still carried around an ounce of hope that she'd someday forgive me.

Though many in the industry would say that it was premature, in a little over eight months, the whole *Jill* team had reinvented the standard women's glossy. Decked out in the latest Gerard Gautier, I felt on top of the world on the night of *Jill*'s launch party. All of my nearest and dearest came to the enormous celebration at Balthazar restaurant. It was the hottest party of the season.

I flew in Alex, my brother, who was now a researcher at

Stanford. It wasn't until I laid eyes on him – and his very Dadlike beard – that I realized I hadn't seen him in ages. It was great to catch up with him, and his life in California sounded like it perfectly suited him. I also brought in Mom, from Virginia, who also happened to be on the masthead as *Jill*'s book editor. She needed cash, she loved to read, and in a fit of inspiration I assigned her to do a review. She did such a good job that I decided, why not keep her on the payroll? But the assignment meant more than money to Mom. Hearing her shriek with excitement after seeing her first byline made me feel so good inside. It reinforced the vague notion that even if I was a shitty friend I could be a pretty good daughter.

That held true even with Dad, whom I tried my best to keep in touch with. He had a habit of disappearing, then resurfacing – especially when he needed to borrow money. Last I heard from him he had moved to Maine with his new girlfriend. I tried to salvage what was left of our relationship, but unfortunately I couldn't even find him to invite him to the party. Even though I was pissed at him for being so absent, I wanted him to be there, too.

The paparazzi showed, of course, and their flashes went wild at the preponderance of A-listers who crowded the room, especially the couples like Uma and Ethan, Ellen and Anne, Serena and Kevin.

But my eyes were drawn to one particular couple who came through the door: Sarah and Taso.

Upon spotting them, I rushed over and nearly smothered Sarah in my embrace. 'You came!' I said, as she laughed. When we broke apart, I broke down in tears. Having her there meant so much to me.

'So I guess you're done being mad?' I said, as I wiped the embarrassing stream from my face.

Sarah gave me a forgiving smile. 'I just want my best friend back,' she said.

'You've got her!' I answered.

Gerard then came over and grabbed me from behind. 'The gang's all here,' he said. 'Let's take a photo.'

'Josh, would you?' I asked.

Gerard took me and Sarah in a stranglehold hug, as Josh snapped away.

'It feels like forever since we've all been together,' I said, when we broke apart.

'And look how far you guys have come,' Josh said. He was right: Gerard had become one of the fashion world's top designers, Sarah had a near perfect marriage and family, and I finally had my own magazine.

'A toast!' Gerard then said, swiping a few glasses of champagne from a passing server, and handing them off. 'To old friends and new adventures!'

'Yes, to my oldest and truest friends!' Sarah said.

As the three of us eagerly clinked glasses, for a minute I thought of Joe. I wondered where he was right now and was saddened that he wasn't a part of the celebration today. But when I thought back on how bitter he had become, I realized he probably wouldn't be as supportive as the friends who were standing right before me. He'd probably look at the whole event as a personal affront.

But still, I wanted to send positive karma out there to him, even if I never did see him again. I wanted Joe to one day be as happy and fulfilled as the rest of us. 'And to

Joe, wherever you are,' I said, holding up my glass.

'I'll drink to that,' Sarah said. 'Have either of you heard anything from him?'

Gerard and I both shook our heads.

'Shame,' she said. 'He used to be such a great guy.'

'*Used to* are the key words there,' Gerard said.

The party was a hit, foreshadowing the success of the magazine. *Mediaweek* named me editor of the year shortly after *Jill's* debut, and six months later *New York* magazine named me one of the '40 People to Watch Under 40.'

With the pressure of starting up the magazine finally off, Josh and I made time to spend some weekends in the burbs with Sarah, Taso, and their kids. She had two, now – having added an adorable little boy, Nicholas, to the family. I could kick myself for the years I declined invitations to their cozy suburban home, in fear of bucolic boredom. It was quite the opposite – I found the tranquility of their yellow-shingled Cape Cod to be like a spa for my soul, and I especially adored Rosie, who was growing up to be quite the girly girl. I laughed my head off when I spotted her drawing unicorns and princesses, just like her mother once drew.

'Just like your early work,' I remarked to Sarah.

'Which means there's still hope for her, I guess,' Sarah said, laughing.

Over the years we tried to spend as many weekends there as we could, because it was the perfect antidote to the pressures of work and the city. Coincidentally, or maybe not so, my maternal instincts grew along with my fondness for Sarah's happy home. Something else grew, too.

After one Saturday visit, I woke up Sunday morning realizing something quite unplanned, yet quite extraordinary had happened to me. My period was often late but this time, on a whim, I took a pregnancy test.

A magazine wasn't the only thing I was capable of conceiving, it seemed.

8

Media Giant Nestrom to Acquire Friar Publications

— The Wall Street Journal, February 2001

It was right after the turn of the new year when I figured out that I was pregnant. I kept it to myself for a day, fretting briefly about how to tell Josh. Though I knew he was crazy about kids and he often talked about us having them, it was unplanned, after all, and I was slightly concerned about how he'd react. My fears, of course, were unfounded. It's crazy how an unplanned pregnancy can send you straight back to the mental state of a teenager.

Josh, however, was capable of regression, too, and he didn't even have a hormonal excuse. We had a giant snowstorm the morning I decided to tell him. And whenever there was snow, Josh became twelve years old. He bounded out of bed, then shook me awake when he saw that the streets were blanketed in white. 'Put on your snow boots and let's get out there,' he urged. 'Let's walk around.'

I understood his excitement. It was the first major snowfall of the season, it was a Monday, and these were the rare days that New York transformed into a small town, like some kind of peaceful white hamlet in New England. Instead of working, people took to the streets – literally – by walking down the middle of deserted thoroughfares. They let loose with playful snowball fights, sledded in the parks, cross-country skied on the highways, and jumped into giant drifts.

We bundled up and joined the fun, our mittens clasped together as we shuffled along through the powdery sidewalks. The air was crisp, the sky was white, and the smell of burning firewood from the Village brownstones wafted from their chimneys.

We passed through Washington Square Park and stopped by the mounds where clusters of kids slid down on plastic discs alongside cafeteria tray-surfing NYU students. We noticed one rosy-cheeked little girl, about three years old, who was ignored by the older kids as she patiently waited her turn to slide down. When she realized she had no power over whether her turn came or not, she wandered over to the side good-naturedly shrugging as if to say, 'The hell with you all.' She plopped down on the ground to build a snowman, taking a few breaks to suck the thumb of her mitten.

As we watched her, Josh and I laughed, touched by her confident nonchalance. 'She's so over them,' I said.

'Yeah, well, bossy kids are so last year,' Josh added, then grabbed my hand and gave me a peck on the cheek.

It was the perfect moment. *Now*, my inner voice was saying. *Do it now*.

'Do you think our child will be as cool?' I asked, toeing the waters.

Josh's face lit up. 'Without a doubt,' he answered. 'No question. With such a cool mom . . .'

I grabbed his hand and we moved on to watch the happy mutts frolicking in the dog run. 'I guess we'll find out soon enough,' I said coyly, before giving him a meaningful look.

Josh beamed, completely elated. 'So you want to start soon, then? I didn't want to press, you know, with all you have going on with the magazine . . . How soon are we talking?'

'Oh,' I said, calculating the time in my mind. 'I'd say as soon as August.'

'Great!' he said. He crouched down to pet a German shepherd. 'That'll be perfect. We'll start trying this summer, then.'

'The thing is,' I started, 'we don't even have to try. I was thinking that August would be a good time for our baby to arrive. You know, it is about eight months from now . . . and by my calculations, I'm probably four weeks along already. All this will be confirmed Friday though, when I have my first appointment with my ob-gyn.' I finally stopped talking and smiled at him expectantly.

Josh stood up, his eyes wide. 'You're serious?' he asked in amazement. 'Do you really mean . . . ?'

I nodded, and he scooped me up in his arms and twirled me around. 'I'm gonna be a dad!' he shouted. 'We're going to have a baby!'

'Mazel tov!' a passerby shouted back.

We laughed triumphantly, and I was relieved and thrilled at his reaction. As Josh kissed me right then, I felt closer to him than ever before.

When we broke apart, Josh pulled me toward the fountain, which was filled with snow instead of water.

'Stop here,' he said. 'And turn around and close your eyes. I'm the one with a surprise now.'

He spun me around so my back was to the fountain and made me put my mittened hands over my eyes. 'Count to twenty, slowly,' he said as he stepped away.

I couldn't imagine what he had up his sleeve. But I did what he asked.

By the time I had reached twenty, he had come up behind me and placed his hands on my shoulders. 'Open your eyes,' he said.

I did, and he slowly spun me around. There in the snow he had written these words:

MARRY ME JILL

I gawked at it, frozen. Strangely, it hadn't really occurred to me that we should get married just because of the pregnancy. But Josh was more traditional than I was, so of course I could see how it crossed his mind.

'Well? Hurry up and answer before it melts!' he said. 'Or do I have to say it?'

I was at a complete loss for words.

Josh then bent down on one knee and took one of my mittened hands and held it to his heart. 'Jill, will you marry me?'

'That's so sweet, but you don't have to do this,' I said, still stunned.

'I know that,' Josh said, still kneeling, the knees of his jeans soaking through. 'I want to marry you, kid or no kid.'

Right then, it occurred to me that not only did I want to have his child, but I wanted to marry Josh, too. 'Okay,' I said. 'Now get up before your jeans get drenched.'

We kissed again, then headed to Caffe Reggio for a celebratory hot chocolate. As we sipped the cocoa we made plans for our future. We decided to do a quickie city hall ceremony in a few weeks with only our closest friends in attendance.

Sarah was my matron of honor; Kevin Alouette was Josh's best man. Serena was there, too, with their newborn daughter, Alexis. After years of fertility treatments, and a very delicate pregnancy, she and Kevin were finally proud parents.

It was a lovely, quick and casual ceremony. I wore an ivory Ferretti dress and I carried a small bouquet of white roses. Josh shucked his usual informal attire for the one suit he owned. We exchanged rings, mine an heirloom from Josh's family, his a brand-new platinum and gold band. Afterward, as we bade thanks and good-bye to our friends, Josh and I made our way to Bouley for a romantic, celebratory lunch.

As we walked, little flurries of snow started to fall and rest on the bare branches, decorating them only briefly before a chilling breeze came and blew the flakes off. We quickened our pace to get out of the cold. Even though it was the dead of winter, my heart felt like it was spring. The future seemed to have so much potential, and each day I grew more and more eager to become a mom. I often caught myself daydreaming about what kind of mom I'd be. I wanted to have some of the same elements of my own mom, like her earthiness, I thought. Yet I hoped to be more independent, less disconnected, a confidant and an inspiration to my child. Above all, I just wanted to be good at being a mom. How I'd go about it was anybody's guess.

Josh grew increasingly excited, too. He was handy, so he

had taken on the project of preparing a mininursery in a corner of the loft. He was already preparing to be a great stay-at-home dad, too, spending days cooking and the evenings pampering me in every way possible. He was proving to be a great husband and I was certain he'd make an even better dad.

Coincidentally, shortly after Josh and I married, another union was in the works. The world's biggest publishing conglomerate, Nestrom Media, had been wooing Friar Publications for months, and now the sale was going to become a reality. Nestrom was the home of *Fashionista, Erudite, World Traveler, Feminist, Algonquin, Epicurean*, and many other high-circ, high-quality, cash cow magazines, and the envy of everyone in the business.

I had announced my marriage at the office, but I kept the pregnancy to myself. Only Sarah and Taso, Serena and Kevin, my parents and Alex knew. I wanted it to stay under wraps at work until the merger was complete, if possible.

The gossip columns did speculate about the possibility of my being pregnant, however, due to the news of my hasty marriage. But I was able to torpedo further scrutiny by saying that I needed to go to city hall to research a story anyhow (not a false statement), and I thought it might be nice to tie the knot while there. The columnists bought it, and thankfully juicier gossip about higher-profile people diverted their interest.

When news of the merger finally came through, Paul and I were summoned to meet with T.J. Oldham, the billionaire chairman of the company. Our appointments were separate, however, so I fretted about meeting him alone. People that rich and powerful made me nervous. To make matters worse, my appointment preceded Paul's, so I couldn't even get some inside info to prepare beforehand.

As had become my nervous habit whenever I had something majorly important to prepare for, I focused on what to wear. I put in an emergency phone call to Gerard. Understanding the urgency of the situation, he came over and rifled through my closets before recommending a newish eggplant-colored Roberto Cavalli pantsuit with satin accents. It was elegant, dressy, yet offbeat. Gerard assured me that that suit with a blow-dry was a power combination.

All I knew about T.J. Oldham before I arrived was that he was very rich, and very eccentric. I didn't even know what he looked like. So when I walked into his Fifth Avenue penthouse, I was caught off guard by the man who greeted me in the foyer. He was short, balding, and rodent-like, with a long face and big thick glasses that exaggerated the size of his eyes. He looked to be about in his midseventies and he wore a moth-eaten dark blue sweater over a white shirt with an outdated collar. Add the black pants, and he had the look of some kind of mustied-over rabbi or vague-minded college professor. Obviously, this man didn't spend hours fretting about what to wear, like I had.

I hesitated before greeting him. Could this be the billionaire magazine tycoon? Or was it just some sort of elderly, poorly dressed assistant of his?

My answer came with his introduction. 'Miss White?' the man asked meekly.

'Yes,' I answered, smiling awkwardly, and expectantly.

'I'm T.J.,' he said.

'Oh, Mr Oldham, it is such a pleasure to meet you,' I said, sticking out my hand for a shake.

'No,' he said, waving my hand off. 'I'm sorry, I don't do that. It's a germ thing I have, plagued me all my life,' he explained, as he ushered me down the hallway. 'Don't take it personally.'

'Oh, I'm sorry,' I said, not sure how to respond to that.

'Don't be sorry,' he said, as he led me into a massive great room. 'And please call me T.J. Mr Oldham was my father. And I wasn't very fond of him.'

I nodded, and once we were settled in the great room, I was rendered speechless by not only the enormity, but the brightness of the space. It was decorated entirely in white and chrome, with snow-colored carpeting, pearly couches, sheer cream curtains, an alabaster coffee table, and shiny metal lights throwing white-hot illumination throughout the room. T.J., in his black and blue ensemble, resembled a squat cockroach in this blinding penthouse heaven.

'Jill!' A voice startled me then, snapping me out of my milky reverie. I noticed then a woman sitting on one of the cushy cotton-colored couches. She wore a hound's-tooth jacket; black pants; and a black headband; keeping her golden bob in place. She rose to greet me, taking my hand into both of hers for a gracious shake. 'I'm Ellen Cutter,' she said. Her pallor was nearly as colorless as the room, especially in comparison to the pink shade of lipstick she sported that day. But she was, if you dissected her features, pretty, with a delicate Barbie nose, round eyes set far apart, a Chicklet-perfect smile, a gentle chin. All together, though, it was a somewhat bland combination. She was blond, but by no means a bombshell.

Ellen Cutter was the CEO who would be overseeing *Jill*. Our previous CEO, Donald Crawford, would 'not be making the transition,' as Paul had explained to me. Translation: he was being kicked out. I knew that transition time was prime time for cleaning house. So, all the better for me to keep my pregnancy secret. Not that I felt I had anything to worry about. *Jill* was one of Friar's hottest publications, after all.

'Sit here,' Ellen said, patting the cushion next to her on the couch. I obliged. T.J. sat across from us in a marshmallow chair.

I noticed T.J.'s oddly broad shoulders, then, and determined that even though he was quite short in stature, he had the ability to make others see him as seven feet tall, especially when seated behind a desk.

He motioned to a basket sitting on the coffee table filled with a largely colorless display of untoasted bagels, cream cheese, and sturgeon. 'Please, help yourselves,' T.J. said, as a maid came into the room to ask us what we'd like to drink.

I passed on the food but asked for some orange juice.

T.J. shook his head, slowly, his goggly eyes wavering behind those enormous glasses. 'How about something clear, perhaps?' he countered.

'Oh, okay,' I said, again taken off guard. I questioned whether I even wanted to work for such a freak. I figured I'd at least wait around for his redeeming qualities to emerge. 'A sparkling water then?' I asked.

'Very good,' he said, as if I had ordered a fine vintage wine. Ellen asked for the same and the maid went off.

T.J. then presented me with a thick accordion folder. 'These are clippings,' he announced while handing it over.

I took the file, opened it, and peeked inside. They were clippings, all right. Clippings upon clippings about me. My mother couldn't have kept a better collection of my ephemera.

As I started to look through them, T.J. began regurgitating some facts. 'Hillander Prep. Bennington College. Editor-in-chief of *Cheeky* at twenty-four. Seven hundred thousand circulation for *Jill*. Impressive stuff,' he said.

'Thank you,' I said, again not sure if that was the right response. This was getting weird. It was like having a stalker. A stalker who was about to pay me $1,000,000 a year for the privilege.

'And you're recently married – congratulations,' he went on. 'And may possibly be pregnant. Are you?' he asked, his owl eyes fixed on me.

I hated lying, but I had to. 'Certainly, you don't believe everything you read,' I hedged, laughing.

He laughed along. 'I know that from firsthand experience,' he said, leaning in to grab some sturgeon with his bare hands. 'You should see my clippings!' he boasted. 'I'm having them archived electronically. Otherwise, they would fill warehouses and warehouses!'

The way he spoke struck me as odd. Not for what he was saying – it was the way he said it. He was disarmingly soft-spoken, and even though his words could be looked upon as arrogant, he came off as a bit insecure, almost like he was looking for my approval.

I gave it to him. '*The Wall Street Journal* called the Friar purchase "brilliant" on your part,' I said. 'I'd say that was accurate.'

His owl eyes lit up, seemingly getting even larger. 'I now have a dream portfolio of magazines,' he said, like a proud little boy. 'I'm a collector, you see. A collector of magazines. And I'm very, very proud of my collection. Especially now, with the acquisition of Friar.'

'As you should be,' Ellen said, playing the perfect side-kick.

'The tabloids all say that I bought Friar because I wanted *Profile*,' he said, leaning in intensely. 'That's not entirely true. I'm a great admirer of yours and I think *Jill* rounds out our women's niche perfectly.'

'And it was particularly genius because now there isn't a market left untapped for Nestrom,' Ellen added, as if she were T.J.'s wooden dummy.

The maid finally arrived with our drinks, and I clung onto my sparkling water, scared to put it down and ruin any of T.J.'s hospital-clean surfaces.

'We're going to take *Jill* to the next level,' he said. 'I'm going to make sure that *Jill* is on every supermarket checkout stand in the country.'

That pleased me as Friar alone definitely did not have Nestrom's distribution muscle. What did not please me was that just as he made his declaration T.J. took off his shoes and his socks and began to rub his feet nervously. I tried not to appear shocked, though it was damn hard, especially when I noticed his freakishly long, yellowed toenails. Ellen seemed to be taking it all in stride, but she must have been used to his strange behavior by now. Now, I couldn't be more grateful that we hadn't shaken hands when we'd met.

What a strange, strange man, I thought. He was a living,

breathing oxymoron – an openly foot-rubbing germaphobe who ate with his hands; a color-loathing eccentric who lived in an antiseptic penthouse, yet whose appearance could be described as slovenly at best; a billionaire who was famously, guardedly private, yet who obviously got great, big kicks from his press.

And just as I decided that he was one of the most revolting people I'd ever met, he rattled off a litany of what I was now entitled to as a Nestrom editor-in-chief. It was a list that would make Queen Nor blush.

'Private car service, to and from work and social events, every day. I don't ever want to see my editors arrive anywhere in a Yellow Cab. Professional hair and make-up every day, arriving at your home in the mornings to ready you, and on call for all public events. You're a Nestrom editor now. We pay for your lunches. You'll have a generous clothing allowance and a travel and entertainment budget you'll be very happy with. I can offer you a no-interest loan if you want to upgrade your housing. We have an arrangement with Starbucks for free coffee . . .' He went on and on doling out perks like some kind of Christmas elf. I took it all in like the little girl in 'The *Nutcracker*.'

When the meeting finally concluded, and T.J. saw Ellen and me off into his private elevator, I was stunned to realize it had lasted only an hour. I felt like I had been in there for an entire workday.

I turned to Ellen as soon as the doors slid closed. She shed her professional exterior by bursting into laughter.

'Wow,' was all I could manage to say.

'There are no words,' she said, clearly picking up my

unarticulated thoughts. 'But he really is a prince to work for.'

'Good to know,' I said. 'I really didn't know what to expect, and I did a good amount of research. Though he gets a good amount of press, somehow they never divulge anything personal about the man.'

'Oh, well, he pays handsomely for exactly that to happen,' she said. At my questioning look she added, 'Let's just say that T.J. is known to . . . subsidize certain gossip columns.'

'Oh,' I said, in surprise, perhaps naively. I was starting to realize in the big leagues things always seemed to happen for a reason.

'Well, welcome to the team!' she then said, giving me an awkward hug. 'I have a feeling we're going to be good friends!' she added. Though she was a little too 'rah, rah' for me, I played along. I had to.

'It's been great to meet you,' I said.

She shot me a conspiratorial smile. 'Oh, but we have met before.'

'We have?' I asked. I searched my memory. Though I knew her by name and reputation, I was pretty certain we had never met. I was pretty good at remembering such things, especially when it was someone in her position.

'Yes,' she went on. 'We met at Paddles a few years ago . . .'

'Paddles?' I questioned. I honestly had no idea what she was talking about.

'That S&M club in meatpacking?' she said, dropping her voice to a whisper, even though we were the only two in the elevator.

I still had no idea what she was talking about, but I played along, so as not to embarrass her. 'Oh, right!' I said.

'I was so bummed when they shut down,' she said wistfully.

'Yeah,' I agreed. 'Nowhere else compares.' Although I had a reputation for being a terrible liar, this one rolled off my tongue expertly.

At her request, I then followed Ellen to Nestrom Tower in Rockefeller Center to scope out our new space. When we arrived, we had to wade through the cluster of PETA protestors near the entrance, barking on their bullhorns to cage and skin the fur-loving Myra Chernoff.

'They're here every day,' Ellen whispered to me. 'Once, they even got past security and made it up to her office! She was in fear for her life!'

'I'll bet,' I said, though I secretly sympathized with their cause.

Ellen and I chit chatted some more once we arrived in her office, and then her assistant, Michelle, escorted me on a tour of the entire building and its editorial offices.

Though I was certainly considered an industry vet at this point, I was still awed by Nestrom's prestige. The names on the masthead were legendary, but everyone – from the editorial staff to the assistants, from the ad men and women to the security guards – seemed more glamorous than anyone else anywhere else in the business.

Erudite was the first group of offices we walked through. It was a buzzing, noisy corner, full of journalistic animation. Michelle introduced me to Brandon Crestwell, the WASPy but coarse editor-in-chief, who gave my hand a firm shake as he puffed on a cigarette. 'We'll do lunch sometime,' he promised before he picked up the phone and cursed out some unfortunate caller.

'Obviously he thinks the city's smoking ban doesn't apply to him,' Michelle said, in exasperation. 'Everyone is too intimidated to complain, though, and T.J. just turns the other cheek.'

Then we sailed through the *Fashionista* floor, a stark contrast from *Erudite*, with its severe silence. No one looked up as we passed; everyone seemed stoically intent on whatever it was they were doing.

I asked Michelle if I might say hello to Myra Chernoff.

She shook her head. 'I would not recommend it,' she said. 'She hates unplanned interactions.'

'Okay,' I said, shrugging it off. I sensed there was no love lost there.

I was particularly excited when we approached the offices of *Feminist* magazine, because Geraldine Siegel, its founder and editor-in-chief, was one of my college heroes. I loved her writing, her intellect, and her brave journalism. Many people say that she single-handedly started the women's movement.

When we peeked in Geraldine Siegel's office, she was standing on a doctor's scale. She held her finger up to indicate a minute while she fussed with the sliding weights. Then she sighed and hopped off.

'Jill White!' she said enthusiastically. I was thrilled that she knew my name.

'I'm so honored to meet you,' I said to her and went on to tell her how her collection of essays was my college bible.

After a few minutes of pleasantries, we let her get back to work.

'That woman is completely obsessed with her weight,' Michelle muttered as we entered the elevator lobby.

I was shocked. 'What? Are you sure she's just not doing that for a story she's researching? She really gets into character, like when she went undercover as a casino waitress,' I said.

'Unless she's been compiling this "research" for twenty years, then no,' Michelle said.

I couldn't have been more let down and disillusioned. Geraldine Siegel, the renowned women's libber, obsessed with her weight?

Maybe the aromas emanating from *Epicure*'s test kitchens constantly wafted into her office, I thought, as we moved on to the next floor, where I was blown away by the stews, salads, and colorful desserts being made there. Now that was impressive, as was Randi Reed, *Epicure*'s editor-in-chief, who was so pleasant and down to earth. We even made a dinner date on the spot.

I returned to Ellen's office dazzled by the ink, glamour, and gloss pouring from every corner of that legendary building and I was thrilled to become a part of it.

'So what do you think of the Nestrom mothership?' Ellen asked, as I stepped into her office to thank her and say goodbye.

'I'm truly excited,' I said. 'Moving day can't come soon enough.'

'Hey – let's grab a celebratory cocktail, then,' she said, taking a look at her watch.

I hesitated and tried to think of a quick excuse, not wanting her to guess that the pregnancy rumors about me were true. But nothing came, and I didn't want my reluctance to seem too obvious. I supposed that I could have a soft drink with her and say that I was on medication. Or I could just nurse a glass of wine.

'It's just about cocktail hour,' she urged.

'Okay,' I agreed, realizing that it probably wasn't a good idea to turn down an invitation from the CEO this early on in the game.

'Great!' Ellen sounded truly pleased. 'If you don't mind waiting a few minutes, I just have a few things to go over with Michelle first.'

'No problem,' I said, taking a seat in her office.

She called Michelle in; then, as I busied myself flipping through a recent issue of *Fashionista*, Ellen became all business, rattling off a dizzying list of demands to Michelle.

'Call my manicurist. Tell her that I don't like the way this color catches the light and I want a redo in my office before my first meeting tomorrow. Catalog all the call reports from this week. And back up all of the files on my PC.'

'I just backed them up yesterday,' Michelle replied.

'Then do it again!' Ellen snapped. 'A lot has transpired in a day. Sheesh.' I could tell that Ellen didn't like being questioned or contradicted, and I respected Michelle for not letting her feathers become ruffled at all.

Ellen dismissed Michelle right then, grabbed her things, nodded at me, and just as we were stepping out the door, she remembered one more thing. She called back to Michelle. 'Oh! That damn cat we got last week? It's not working out. Go to my townhouse before the kids get home and do something about it.'

'Like what?' Michelle asked, seeming genuinely horrified.

'Find it a new home, take it to the ASPCA, or let it loose in the streets, for all I care,' Ellen said impatiently. 'It peed on my sixty-thousand-dollar couch. It is no longer welcome in my home, I want it gone. *Today*.'

'What are you going to tell the kids?' Michelle asked, bewildered.

'*You* can tell them when they get home that it ran away,' Ellen said. Then with a wave of her hand, she dismissed Michelle again and turned to me. The witch I'd just witnessed vanished. A perkier Ellen immediately took her place. 'Let's go!' she said. 'I'm thinking Tao.'

'Sounds fine to me,' I answered, still distracted by what would happen to that poor cat . . . But I felt even worse for Michelle, who seemed so quick and capable and way too smart to be disposing of inconvenient cats and spoken to like she was some kind of indentured servant from the Middle Ages.

'My car is waiting,' Ellen said, indicating a black Benz sitting smack in front of the exit. I was happy to walk the six blocks over to Fifty-eighth Street. It was early March, and hints of spring were peeking out. But Ellen would have none of it.

'We're going to Tao!' Ellen barked at the driver as we slipped inside and settled into the cushy interior.

The driver turned around. 'I'm sorry? Come again, madam? Town?'

'No! Tao!' she hollered again, before emitting a loud sigh and a 'jeez!' for good measure.

'Do you have an address, madam?' the driver proceeded politely despite Ellen's rudeness.

Another loud sigh from Ellen. 'I don't know. It's on Fifty-seventh somewhere. *You're* the driver!'

I couldn't take it anymore – I felt embarrassed just being with someone so rude. I decided to bail the man out, even if it was to contradict my new boss. 'It's actually on Fifty-eighth, sir, between Park and Madison. Thanks so much.'

He gave me a grateful look and drove off.

'I'm going to be naughty!' Ellen then said, whipping out a park of cigarettes from her purse. She offered me one.

'No thank you,' I said, declining. Great – after a night out with Ellen my unborn child was bound to pick up emphysema and fetal alcohol syndrome in one fell swoop.

She lit up, filling the backseat with smoke. I felt nauseous. Thank God it was a short ride.

We arrived at Tao, sailed in the door, and took a seat in the lounge. It was still early and not as crowded and sceney as the place was known to get.

Ellen kept up with her 'naughty' routine by ordering a martini; I asked for a wimpy white wine spritzer, which she chided me for.

'I have a bit of an upset stomach, and I took some medication,' I said in my defense.

'Fair enough,' she said. 'But one of these nights you're going to have to have a real woman's drink with me.'

'I'll look forward to it,' I said, thinking that a drink would be welcome after nine months of pregnancy and hours of labor.

Then her cocktail arrived. But Ellen took one sip and she sent it back. 'Not cold enough,' she said, waving the waitress off.

When it came back, she sent it back again. 'Not dry enough.'

Was all of this a misguided effort to impress me? Or was this what she was usually like? She was being so rude to the server that I wouldn't be surprised if the next martini came with a phlegm floater. I was kind of disheartened. We were vastly different people, and it would have been easier if I could like Ellen Cutter. But it was hard as hell to warm up to the cat-killing, martini-swilling, assistant-berating prima donna sitting before me.

We chatted about nonsense for the next forty-five minutes, and then I politely looked at my watch and mentioned that I had a dinner date with my husband. 'We're newlyweds, after all,' I reminded her.

'I understand,' she said. She demanded the bill, paid it, and left a two-dollar tip.

I trailed behind her as she marched out of the lounge like she ran the joint. 'Oh, I have to go to the restroom,' I said just as we reached the door.

'Okay, I'll wait in the car then,' Ellen said.

'You don't have to wait for me,' I told her.

'Don't be foolish. I'll drop you home,' she said.

I turned back to the lounge, not really having to go to the bathroom. But I did feel the need to make up for Ellen's rude behavior. Searching the lounge, I tracked down our waitress and slipped her some additional cash. 'Sorry about that,' I said.

'Thanks!' she said, giving me an empathetic smile. I think she could tell I didn't exactly have a good time.

When I got outside, Ellen was just finishing a cigarette –

inside the car. I opened my window a crack, feeling woozy.

'Thanks for dropping me home,' I said. 'It really wasn't necessary. I would have been happy to take a cab.'

'Please,' Ellen said, slurring a little from her two strong martinis, 'I'm in no hurry to get home.'

Just then her cell phone rang, and she gazed at it and sighed before she finally flipped it open.

'Hello,' she said shortly.

I was grateful for the call. It meant a few minutes that I didn't have to make conversation.

'Well, sweetheart, I don't know why Snowball ran away. That's just the way cats are.'

She rolled her eyes at me, then added impatiently, 'I don't know if she'll come back. I wouldn't get your hopes up.'

Another pause. Another eye roll. 'If we get another cat, how do we know it won't run away too? Sweetie, just put Grace on the phone, please.'

Another pause.

'Grace!' Ellen shouted so loud that I instinctively flinched. 'How many times do I have to tell you never to put my kids directly on the phone with me! Jesus! Why can't you remember that?'

Silence as she shook her head.

'They're *always* crying. I don't want to hear that excuse anymore. Now make sure they're nice and quiet and over this cat thing by the time I get home.'

She slapped her phone shut. 'My latest nanny is just awful!' she said. 'But I don't know where on earth to find a decent one. I've used every "top" agency in this city and have yet to find anyone acceptable.'

'That's tough,' I said, wishing the driver would floor it.

I was so grateful when we finally arrived at Charles Street. I didn't spend a minute lingering before I stepped out of the car. 'Thanks for the drink!' I called just as I closed the door.

'Yes! It was fun!' Ellen called out the window. 'We'll have to do it again soon,' she said.

Not if I can help it, I silently answered as the black car pulled away into the night.

The following morning was full of glorious spring tidings, for the temperature grew even warmer. Josh and I woke up early, and excited, to go to our next ob-gyn appointment. I was at nine weeks, and we had expected to hear our baby's heartbeat for the first time.

I, myself, was feeling pretty healthy. I wasn't overly emotional like I had expected, and my nausea had passed about two weeks ago. I had gained very little weight, so things were status quo. So far, it seemed like I was having the easiest pregnancy I could have hoped for. If it hadn't been confirmed I was pregnant, I wouldn't even think I was.

Turns out there was a reason for that. When we went into the examination room, we were expecting to hear the vibrant thumping of our baby's heart.

Instead, there was nothing but silence and the crackling of the microphone. The doctor moved me into various positions and listened, but still, there was nothing.

I saw the concern covering her face and felt Josh's grip on my hand grow tighter.

'Let's do a sonogram,' the doctor said, obviously concerned.

I grew upset. 'Is there a problem? Why isn't there a heartbeat?' I felt panic rise in my chest. I had never expected this.

'The sonogram will give us answers,' the doctor answered. I knew she was trying not to be alarmist. But I also knew that things just weren't right.

They weren't. The sonogram didn't show a heartbeat either.

I was devastated by the news. Day after day, I obsessed over what I might have done wrong, what I could have done to induce miscarriage, though the doctor said there wasn't anything that could have prevented it.

Josh was braver, and constantly reassuring me. 'We'll try again soon, honey. Don't you worry – this one just wasn't meant to be,' he'd say over and over.

He did his best to comfort me but I still felt empty inside. After I had my D&C, it was a little easier to move on, especially with all of the changes happening at work. But even though the workday was enough to distract me for a while, when I came home, I became sad all over again.

I kept it together emotionally very well for a while. Almost too well. It concerned me, and I wondered when I'd finally let it all out.

Then a few weeks later, just when I thought I was ready to move on, something else happened that released all of the emotion I had locked up inside since the miscarriage.

I opened the apartment door that morning to retrieve the newspaper. A shocking front-page headline met me at my doorstep:

WALTER PENNINGTON III, AND WIFE, CARRIE BAINES, KILLED IN AUTO ACCIDENT

I was absolutely stunned to the point of immobility. I kept staring at the paper, afraid that if I touched it the news would be validated.

He was only thirty-six; she was thirty-four. He and his wife were so young, with so much potential, yet gone in a flash. They were struck by a jackknifing trailer truck as they drove up to the family cottage in Newport.

There was an actual photo of the wreckage – of twisted metal and covered stretchers.

As I stared at the picture, I lost it, embarking on a crying jag that lasted for hours. I wasn't close personal friends with Walt, but I couldn't help but feel a loss. Why was the world robbed of someone I knew was innately good? *He never got to be a playwright*, I thought, which made me even sadder. Even though he dabbled in political journalism, I knew he probably still held fast to his dream of becoming the new Sam Shepard one day.

It brought back all the sadness I felt from the miscarriage. I was so angry. Why was our child never even given an opportunity to live? Life was unfair. It was also fleeting. None of it made any sense.

I vowed right then to cherish every minute – good, bad, and ugly.

9

Liz Alexander Named Publisher of Gill

— *Folio*, September 2001

To paraphrase Spider-Man, with the big leagues comes big responsibility. And big changes.

I did get to know Ellen Cutter better right after the merger. I felt like I had no choice but to tolerate way too many lunches, dinners, and cocktail hours where she ordered wait-staff around like those people were put on this earth solely to please her every whim. On these occasions, I always felt compelled to overcompensate for her bad manners and would transform into Glinda to her Wicked Witch, full of profuse thanks and prone to overtipping. And while the countless waiters, waitresses, and bartenders seemed to appreciate my efforts, I had the feeling that Ellen disrespected me for my behavior. Which made it all the more curious to me why she was so eager to take our working relationship outside the office so often. We couldn't have less in common, and I felt really uncomfortable when she would start bad-mouthing other Nestrom staffers and try to get me to do the same.

Even more curiously, it seemed that whenever a hot new restaurant opened Ellen wanted to be among the first to dine there – with me. And, for some reason, she always wanted me to make the reservation. I wondered why she didn't prefer to go out with her husband; Lord knows I'd rather be anywhere with Josh. But one night I discovered the real reason why she wanted to hang out with me so much.

We were at Ellen's favorite – Tao – and as I navigated the noisy crowd to meet her, I noticed a photographer peering over the hostess's shoulder. 'Cutter?' I heard the hostess say.

'Yeah,' the photographer answered. 'She said she's dining with Jill White. I'm not going to disturb anyone, just take a few snaps and go. Good for the restaurant's profile, too, you know,' he said as I snuck behind him.

Then it made sense. When we were out dining at these hot new places, the paparazzi would often snap our photo together, and it would inevitably end up somewhere like *New York* magazine, or Keith Kelly of the *Post* would run it in his media column, mentioning us as 'publishing's new dynamic duo.'

How could I have been so blind? It suddenly started to fall into place. No wonder Ellen always asked me to make the reservations – my name was more recognizable than hers. She was clearly using me to get both a better table and her own name and face in print. I imagined such exposure put her in good favor with T.J.

Feeling used, I started to turn down Ellen's invites, citing too much work, or needing to spend time with Josh, especially when more and more often the dates would encroach on my personal time – like when she'd want to get pedicures on a Sunday, or when she'd horn in on a premiere I wanted to bring Josh to, or when, knowing my connections, she'd ask me to get her front row seats to a Third Rail show. I quickly grew tired of it, especially now that I knew Ellen's motives were suspect. Not coincidentally, the more I begged off, the more things began to change between Ellen and me.

During that brief honeymoon period, the entire staff of *Jill* moved into the Nestrom Media building in Rockefeller Center, settling in on the same floor as *Fashionista*. I flattered myself thinking of what an honor it was to be on the same floor as the legendary Myra Chernoff. Maybe she even requested to have us share her floor. I had visions of her waiting to greet me with a giant welcome basket – maybe with more of that expensive champagne she sent me upon the launch of *Jill* . . .

Scary how delusional I could get sometimes. I soon discovered that the space was usually a transient stop, like a holding depot or halfway house for newly acquired publications. I had heard rumors that it was because no one could stand to share a floor with Myra Chernoff, or vice versa. But I was wary of believing the hearsay. After all, the bigger you get, the bigger the gossip about you. She couldn't possibly be as evil as legend painted her. Could she?

There was no *Fashionista* welcome wagon waiting when we moved in, and I was even wary of just striding over and saying hello because of Michelle's warning that Myra didn't like 'unplanned interactions.' I spent a few days fretting about how to approach her, but then fate intervened and placed us on the same elevator.

I rushed into the building one morning, late for a meeting,

when I saw the elevator doors begin to slide closed. I ran over and waved my hand over the sensors so the doors would open again. Myra was standing inside, alone, wearing an ivory Prada suit complete with dead animal collar, and sporting her famous classic bob, now brown with impeccable blond highlights. I was aware of the legendary rumor that no one was supposed to ride the elevator with her highness. I was unsure if that unspoken rule included other editors-in-chief.

She looked at me, annoyed. I tried to break the tension. 'Hi! How are you? So, we're floor mates now.'

She returned my greeting with a tense nod.

'Hold the elevator!' I heard someone scream, and I instinctively pressed the 'door open' button to the sound effect of Myra's enormous sigh.

Rosario, our blue-haired entertainment editor, rushed in. 'Hey!' she said in cheerful greeting.

Myra moved to the corner, staring at Rosario's hair as if the color would run onto her ivory suit. For a minute I thought she might pull the emergency stop and climb out the ceiling hatch just to get away from us. When we finally reached our floor, she bolted out of the elevator like she was escaping a couple of poorly dressed axe murderers. Not quite the welcome I had expected.

The tone was set on that day, so we all pretty much kept to our side of the floor. The only person who spent time on both sides was Paul, who would occasionally find the time to pop into my office to catch up and who also found himself a boyfriend in Roger, *Fashionista*'s handsome, well-bred production manager. There was really no reason for any of us to go over to the *Fashionista* side of the floor anyway. It was so uninviting, with its decked-out staff, smug attitude, and echoing silence. Its people equally avoided our blaring radios, bouts of hilarity, and compendium of clutter.

Turns out there was one *Fashionista*, however, who yearned to cross over to our side of the tracks. Her name was Jocelyn Kramer. Casey came into my office one day clutching Jocelyn's resume.

'Relative of yours?' I accused as she handed it over to me. She knew I wasn't hiring. The usual drill was to copy it and file it away for when I did have an opening, and then push it on to HR.

'No,' Casey answered. 'But I would like you to give it a look.'

I did right then. 'Jocelyn Kramer, Editorial assistant – at *Fashionista*?' I read aloud. 'Even if I did have a position, wouldn't I be accused of poaching?'

Casey shrugged. 'Not if she came to you first.'

'Why am I interested in her?' I asked, knowing there had to be more to the story to garner such attention from Casey.

'Because you are a compassionate, compassionate woman,' she answered, in her famous half-serious, half-sarcastic tone.

'And why, pray tell, would any Fashionista be deserving of such sympathy? Better yet, why in the world would she even want to join the ranks of the great unwashed?'

'I met her in the ladies' room this morning,' Casey said, plopping down in my guest chair.

'Oh, so you go way back,' I joked, still not getting why this girl warranted such special attention. We ran into Fashionistas in the ladies' room all the time. Upon spotting us they usually lunged for the disinfectant in the primping basket by the sinks.

'She was bawling her eyes out,' Casey went on. 'She was crying so hard I thought that maybe someone close to her had died, or that she had gotten some bad news from the doctor.' She paused.

'But,' I pressed, looking at my watch. I had a lunch date and was hoping Casey would wrap this up soon.

'But when I asked her what was wrong, she told me that she was crying because Myra threatened to fire her if she didn't lose weight! She made the heinous mistake of eating a bagel at her desk when Myra walked by. In front of *everyone*, she told her she was way too heavy to be eating so many carbs, and that if she ever wanted to get anywhere at *Fashionista* she'd have to start rethinking her image.'

'Ew,' I said. How awful.

Casey went on, in outrage. 'It gets worse. When I saw her, she had just come from HR, where she was told that if she couldn't handle the environment she should think about leaving!'

'You're kidding!' I said, knowing full well she wasn't. Only a company like Nestrom could get away with such bad behavior without getting sued. Any aspiring magazine journalist who even threatened a lawsuit could kiss the chance to work at any of the magazines in the Nestrom empire goodbye forever. I definitely felt for the girl.

'I just thought that if there was any room in our budget . . .' Casey went on.

'That we might rescue her,' I finished. It was so like Casey to want to help her. We often joked that her home was the

Westchester branch of the ASPCA because of all of the shelter pets she adopted.

'Well, I'd just like to see if there's anything we can do to give her a chance at a real career in the business before the poor thing is euthanized,' she said. 'At least keep her in mind. I got the sense that's she's really a *Jill* girl at heart. And I think it would be great for her to know that not every boss has to be the Wicked Witch of the West.' Then Casey gave me one of her meaningful, doe-eyed looks. 'We need to break the cycle by breeding more Jill Whites and fewer Myra Chernoffs.'

Casey knew that flattery got her everywhere when it came to me. And I wasn't above recognizing that. 'Set her up for an informational interview,' I said. 'No promises, but I'll see what I can do.'

'You're the best!' Casey said. She left my office, smiling, as if she had done her good deed for the day.

I did my good deed when I hired Jocelyn two weeks later. I liked her: she was cheerful; friendly; good-hearted; and, most important, a really talented writer, and I didn't think she should have anything to do with *Fashionista*. I immediately felt comfortable with her, like she was my little sister.

So I made her an assistant editor; at the same time, I made a permanent enemy out of Myra Chernoff for 'stealing' not only one of her most promising writers, but an easy target for her venom.

Soon after Jocelyn crossed over, I had one of my now-regular elevator run-ins with Myra.

'Hi!' I cheerfully greeted her, as became my custom, if merely to see how she'd react to my pleasantries.

She wore an exquisite emerald cashmere sweater, which brought out the green of her eyes. I waited for the usual glance of distaste; this time, however, her icy glare came with a heaping side of odium, and tense silence, as she turned away. Sometimes she would let out a grunt of disapproving acknowledgment. This time, nothing. That made me nervous. And when I was nervous, I became dangerously chatty.

'Loved the piece on the ingénue actresses,' I said, earning another death glare. 'Great choices, all of them. Insightful interviews, too. The whole thing was so well written . . .'

'Really?' she then quietly snarled. 'Perhaps you'd like to poach that writer, too.' Snap.

'I – I –' I knew she had to be referring to the fact that Jocelyn 'transitioned' over to *Jill*. I wanted to explain to her that Jocelyn had approached me, and that I hadn't 'poached her' at all. But nothing would come out of my stunned mouth.

The elevator doors slid open. And Myra glided out, tossing me another hateful glower, for good measure.

It was definitely no fluke, then, when I received a call from Ellen as soon as I got back to my desk.

'When are you running the Lila Bass cover?' she asked, skipping the formality of even greeting me.

'As soon as possible,' I answered truthfully. 'I want to strike while the scandal is hot.' The scandal was that Lila Bass, a famous model whose rock star boyfriend got her hooked on drugs, was now back on the needle. After a halfhearted but highly publicized visit to a treatment center, she was angling for a comeback. We agreed to interview her only to have her ramble on and on about her 'bravery' while appearing to be completely stoned. Rosario's resulting profile was terrific, startling, and incisive. 'Not a Pretty Picture' was the coverline we couldn't wait to run . . .

'You have to wait,' Ellen answered, 'until well after her *Fashionista* cover runs.'

'*Fashionista* cover? I don't believe it,' I said, and I didn't. Myra famously shunned any model who exhibited such bad behavior. Plus, she publicly commented that 'any model who used drugs would never be featured in *Fashionista* again.' If there was one thing I knew about Myra Chernoff, it was that she was true to her word – especially if it was in print. So there was no way in hell she was running a Lila Bass cover. 'She has quite unforgettably said she'd never put her in the magazine again,' I reminded Ellen.

'Well, apparently she is reconsidering it. And we don't want her to appear on both covers at the same time,' was Ellen's defense.

All of this was obviously Myra's Jocelyn-inspired retaliation. 'Well, then, why doesn't Myra postpone her cover,' I said, just to be a brat, and just to see what kind of answer I would get.

Ellen laughed at what we both knew was a preposterous notion. 'Jill, you know as well as I do that Myra doesn't change anything for anybody.'

To think I once ate venison for the woman!

'But the two magazines are not even competitors,' I said. 'Can't they both run in the same month? Changing this now is going to screw up our whole schedule.'

'Jill,' Ellen went on with measured patience, 'Myra Chernoff is a legend, and she makes a lot of money for

Nestrom. So her needs take priority. That's the reality. And now this conversation is over.'

And I was completely not surprised when after I had reluctantly pushed my cover back a month Myra conveniently changed her mind.

In the early days of our working together, Ellen might have at least faked being on my side or pretended to intervene with Myra, though of course I knew that Myra would win out. I also received Myra's message, loud and clear: she wasn't to be fucked with. And I had little interest in continuing to fuck with her.

Besides, it would turn out that I would certainly have more important fish to fry right in my own pond.

A few days later, Ellen called me into her office to let me know that Lynn Stein, *Jill*'s publisher, was being let go.

'Why?!' I asked, shocked as I jumped out of one of Ellen's Eames guest chairs. I exchanged a glance with Paul, who sat in the other Eames. He shrugged and shook his head. Obviously he hadn't been consulted either. I was outraged. 'Lynn's work on *Jill* has been exemplary!' And I stood by that statement. Lynn was a powerhouse from day one of *Jill*'s inception. She was a big part of making *Jill* Friar's leading title, with her sales savvy causing it to surpass *Profile* in advertising dollars.

'It was a mutual decision,' Ellen said, adjusting her brown leather headband, which matched the copper color of the day's cardigan. 'We're in a different climate now from the days of *Jill*'s inception,' Ellen said, feeding me the corporate speak that so effortlessly tripped off her tongue. 'This is no longer Friar Publications, and her vision just never seemed to jibe with Nestrom's. In the end, she just wasn't Nestrom material.'

What the hell did *that* mean?

While I was confused by Ellen's motives, I had absolutely no doubt that Lynn would end up on her feet, joining some lucky publication somewhere else. But I felt a strong sense of loss. One of my initial concerns about the merger was Nestrom dismantling my original team. Of course, T.J. and Ellen had assured me they'd never want to 'fix something that wasn't broken.' What a couple of liars.

'The better news,' Ellen went on, fueling my fury even further, 'is that we have a replacement lined up already.'

I smelled a rat right then. A giant, sweaterset-wearing one.

It turned out that Ellen had conveniently already replaced Lynn with Liz Alexander, one of her old cronies from *Charisma*. This choice really disturbed me. Whereas Lynn had a true *Jill* sensibility, Liz came directly from a publication that was the complete opposite. It just didn't seem like a good fit.

I met Liz for the first time over lunch with Ellen at 44 in the Royalton Hotel. She was tall with long, shiny reddish brown hair and piercing green eyes framed by sinister, overplucked eyebrows. As she sat next to Ellen at lunch, I noticed how pale her complexion was, even in comparison to Ellen, who I thought was the whitest person I had ever seen. There was no mystery where she took her fashion cues from. She sported an Ellenesque aqua sweater set that day complete with matching headband. Right then and there it became clear to me why Lynn might have been fired. I suspected that Ellen's problem with Lynn had more to do with her image than her vision. Lynn might not have been stick thin and she had her own quirky ideas about fashion, but she was an excellent salesperson and clients loved her. But Ellen wanted an Ellen clone. And outspoken Lynn was by no means a 'yes' woman.

I stood and introduced myself as soon as Liz came to the table. 'I'm Jill White,' I said.

She offered me a dead-fish handshake and an equally enthusiastic hello. Ellen, on the other hand, received a decidedly warmer greeting – a kiss on both cheeks and a full embrace. 'Bunny!' she said. 'I'm so excited we'll be working together again!'

'Bunny?' I echoed, stifling a laugh.

'Nickname from the old days,' Ellen said demurely.

'Oh, but those were the days, weren't they?' Liz prodded. 'We'll never have those carefree days again. Two hot, smart women taking over this town! We were quite the pair!'

It went on to be one of the strangest lunches in Jill White/Ellen Cutter history. Ellen and Liz spent a lot of time catching up, chatting like the old friends they obviously were, while I sat there like excess baggage. I attempted to find common ground with Liz. It just didn't work. I talked about music, dance, theater, travel, movies, other publications – but I just couldn't penetrate her frosty exterior. I gave up and tuned out, suddenly feeling like I was back at Hillander sitting at a cafeteria table with Alissa and her popular friends trying desperately to fit into the conversation only to be ignored and dismissed.

Thanks for the memories, you guys! I thought.

When it came time to order I noticed that Liz must have

picked up restaurant etiquette tips from Ellen, too. Except she was even more annoying. 'Does this have garlic in it?' she asked about a scallop dish.

'Yes, ma'am,' the server said.

'Can I get it without the garlic?' she whined.

'I'll ask the chef,' the waiter patiently answered.

He went off to ask the chef, came back with an affirmative, that yes, the chef would leave the garlic out of the scallop dish. But she changed her mind in the few minutes that that had taken.

'I think I want the trout instead,' she said. 'But with no butter or salt. And I want it deboned. And grilled instead of pan fried. And I don't want green beans on the side. I want broccoli and cauliflower.' She snapped shut her menu and shoved it at the waiter.

As if dining out with just Ellen wasn't mortifying enough. Here was her finickier and even more impolite little sister. I dreaded even the thought of how many of these double whammies I would have to suffer through.

The waiter, of course, seemed uneasy with her demands. After all, her version of the dish was nothing like what was on the menu. 'I'll ask the chef if he can do all of that,' he said tentatively.

Liz smiled condescendingly. 'I don't see why he couldn't. I'm the customer. His *job* is to cook what I want to eat.'

'But it's a full house and . . .' The nervous waiter's comment faded with Liz's shriveling stare.

'Ma'am?' he asked, turning to me.

'I'll have the asparagus risotto,' I answered. The waiter paused, waiting for the other shoe to drop. 'That's all, no substitutions. However the chef likes to cook it,' I said, earning a dismissive glare from Liz. 'Thank you so much!' I added, definitely a little too Glinda-like for Liz's taste.

He turned to Ellen. 'I'll have the same thing she's having – the trout – prepared exactly the same way,' she said.

'Ellen and I always have had the same taste!' Liz said gleefully, leaning in to touch Ellen on the elbow. 'We're just like twins!'

That was another odd thing. During the whole lunch, they touched each other constantly, one pale hand on another pale hand, patting shoulders, commenting on and touching each other's hair. It was disturbing, but I amused myself imagining them as twins, just like Liz had said. But in my imagination they were like some kind of freaky twin vampires . . .

The two of them picked at their specially prepared, high-maintenance trout while I downed my risotto. They were either in intense conversation together the whole time, or on their cell phones, one of my biggest pet peeves in restaurants.

'What?!' was Liz's greeting to whoever was on the other line. Then she groaned. 'Can't you just get to the point? I'm busy!'

A pause as she rolled her eyes. I wanted to roll my eyes too. I hated being forced to listen to one-sided conversations.

'I don't know what I feel like for dinner – I haven't even had lunch yet,' Liz snapped. 'I'll call you later,' she added, in a hyperannoyed tone.

After she slammed her phone shut like a pouty child, she sighed. 'Men are just so aggravating!'

I surmised, then, that the person she was talking to like some kind of cretin was actually her husband.

'Tell me about it,' Ellen said, jumping on the man-hating bandwagon. 'I fantasize about sending my husband away on monthlong vacations all the time.' Then in her first effort to include me in the conversation, Ellen turned to me. 'Don't you agree, Jill? Women are always being referred to as balls and chains, but I think men are much worse in a marriage. In fact, marriage in general is so overrated.'

'They're just such time and attention suckers,' Liz added.

They both expectantly stared at me, awaiting my input. 'I actually like being with my husband . . .' I said tentatively but truthfully. 'I mean, if he were to be going on a monthlong vacation, I would want to be right there with him.'

Liz actually gasped at my sentiment.

After that luncheon, I reluctantly accompanied the duo to Ellen's office, where we finally had a brief business talk – such a relief from the inanities of the lunchtime conversation, yet I still couldn't wait to be done with their company. The meeting finally over after an eternal fifteen minutes, I decided to pop into the ladies' room on that floor. As I sat in the stall, I heard the clip-clop of heels come in. Two women were in midconversation. It was Ellen and Liz.

'You really talked her up but I just don't see what the big fuss about her is,' Liz was saying.

Then came Ellen's voice. 'Well, T.J. seems to think she's very talented. And her high social profile is good for the company's image.'

'Talent? What's so talented about shoving your personality down people's throats?' Liz then snapped. 'Who names a magazine after herself anyway? Only a narcissist, if you ask me.'

There was no doubt in my mind. They were talking about *me*. I didn't move a muscle, trying desperately not to be noticed as I overstayed my welcome, taking it all in.

'She can be kind of fun, sometimes,' Ellen said. 'We had been spending a lot of time together. Then all of a sudden, she wasn't interested in making plans with me outside of work.'

I was surprised by the sound of hurt in her voice.

'Well, now that we're working together again you have your kind of person to spend time with – in and out of the office,' Liz said. 'See, it just goes to show you, she can't be trusted. I totally get that vibe from her. She's flighty; she obviously only cozied up to you when it suited her interests . . .'

Her voice trailed off as they washed their hands and sauntered out the door.

I was stung. After hearing her tirade, I was amazed that Liz had even agreed to come over to work at *Jill* from *Charisma* and even more stunned that after ignoring me over one two-hour lunch she could have such a strong negative perception of me and the state of my psyche. Liz had it wrong, and completely turned around. But maybe I had gotten it a little wrong with Ellen, too.

Most important, hearing their conversation made it quite clear to me that I couldn't trust Liz Alexander.

Turns out Paul didn't trust her either, I found out later that day, as I lingered in his office and the two of us whined about the hasty hiring.

'As long as she and Ellen stay out of the creative side of things, we'll just have to trust that they know how to sell *any* magazine,' he assured me. Though just his saying that made me realize he was just as uneasy as I was about her.

'Why are you concerned at all then?' I asked.

Paul sighed. 'Because I – and you – just lost a great publisher and supporter in Lynn. And Liz is Ellen's former lackey from *Charisma*. Which means both Ellen and Liz go back years with T.J.,' he said. 'I can't compete with that relationship.'

I understood his concern, since *Charisma* was a Nestrom publication. And even though Paul and Ellen were supposed to be equals under T.J., the addition of Liz shifted the power more to Ellen's side.

You see, the chain of command at Nestrom operated like the military. T.J. was obviously its general. He had a battery of colonels, each responsible for several publications. Paul and Ellen were both colonels overseeing, among others, my magazine. Paul was *Jill*'s creative director colonel, responsible for the editorial content of the magazine and the way it looked. Ellen was *Jill*'s CEO colonel, in charge of all things business related. I was a major on the creative side, reporting to Paul. Liz was a major on the business side, reporting to Ellen. That is the normal order of things.

But soon after Liz's arrival, it was like Donald Rumsfeld had come in and messed up our chain of command. Liz started to act more like a colonel; Paul was seeming more and more like a major, and I felt like I was looked upon as some kind of lowly enlisted man.

Strangely, a teeth-whitening product made this shift – and Ellen's new attitude toward me – even more apparent.

We had tested several brands of whitener and compared the results for a story. There was one brand in particular that didn't work, and we said so. It was very typical *Jill* content, and typically, no one would bat an eye about it. And no one did – at first. A few hours before the story was scheduled to be shipped to the printer, though, I got a phone call from Liz.

'I want you to drop Sparkle from the teeth-whitening story,' she said. Her tone was clipped and demanding.

'Why?' I asked, flabbergasted. It wasn't like Sparkle was an advertiser. That's what usually ruffled the business side's feathers.

'Because I've been trying to get an appointment with their parent company, and if that runs, I'll never get one,' she answered.

'Who cares?' I said. 'Aren't their other products denture related? They're not right for *Jill* anyway.'

'They are obviously branching out into other products,' she hissed. 'Potential future advertisers.'

Not very good products, I wanted to say. But I knew that Liz couldn't care less if what we advertised worked or didn't as long as we got the money.

It was bad enough that I felt pressure to pander to current advertisers. Now I had to worry about potential *future* advertisers? Screw that. 'It would be journalistically irresponsible for me to take it out,' I said, holding ground.

'It would be even more financially irresponsible to keep it in,' she insisted, before hanging up.

The next thing I knew, I got an e-mail from Liz, which she'd cc'd to Ellen, Paul, T.J., several young children in Vietnam, the Pope, and Antarctic ice fishermen. Needless to say, that pissed me off. There was no need for her to involve the whole freaking world in our battles.

To: Jill White@nestrom.com
cc: Ellen Cutter@nestrom.com;
TJ Oldham@nestrom.com; Paul Thomas@nestrom.com
From: Liz Alexander@nestrom.com
Subject: Sparkle Teeth Whitener
Jill, per our previous discussion, Sparkle is a potential advertiser and I am trying to win that account. Keeping the negative content about it in the teeth-whitening story would guarantee a loss of that potential advertiser. I really feel strongly about this.
Liz

I decided to be the bigger person and compromise.

From: Jill White@nestrom.com
Re: Sparkle Teeth Whitener
Liz, we are shipping tonight and if we drop the content we will have to fill the extra space. Frankly, I really don't feel that we have to make such a drastic change for a potential advertiser, especially one whose products aren't really geared toward our audience. But if it is so important to you I could tone the text down.
Jill

It didn't matter. The next e-mail I got was from Ellen:

From: Ellen Cutter@nestrom.com
Re: Sparkle Teeth Whitener
Jill – take it out
E

But I wasn't going down quietly:

From: Jill White@nestrom.com
Re: Sparkle Teeth Whitener
Ellen – I will take it out, but note that this really puts my staff in a bind now. We will all have to work through the night to figure out a new layout before it ships. We can't always be making last-minute changes like this.
Jill

As a result, I shot myself in the foot:

From: Ellen Cutter@nestrom. com
Re: Sparkle Teeth Whitener
Jill – You are right. To avoid having to make these changes last minute, add Liz to the routing list of editorial copy in its initial stages.
E

That was definitely *not* the right answer. It just wasn't Liz's place to be so involved editorially.

I stormed up to Paul's office, scaring the hell out of him as I charged in unannounced. 'Wait until you hear this!' I said, not even noticing he was in the middle of a phone call.

'I have to call you back,' Paul mumbled. Then he quietly placed the receiver down. 'Whatever it is, is it important enough to warrant your nearly sending me into coronary arrest?'

'Sorry, but yes,' I said, pacing back and forth in front of his desk. I then proceeded to explain the Sparkle saga in detail.

'I can't let her have that much editorial control. She has no creative judgment or experience. Letting her have input this early in the process is just going to slow everybody down!'

'She's a total nightmare,' Paul agreed. 'I'll see what I can do . . .'

'Just try to talk some sense into Ellen for me,' I pleaded.

'You know I'd do anything for you, Jill,' he said, giving me one of his assuring smiles and making me feel a little better. 'Now, can I get back to work?'

I nodded and left his office feeling more secure. Paul had a lot of charm, and he was in a more powerful position than I. But I still couldn't help but wonder if he was strong enough to lasso in Liz Alexander.

My suspicions were correct, unfortunately. Despite Paul's best efforts, Ellen didn't budge. Liz was officially added to the routing list for copy.

But that wouldn't be the last time he'd go to bat for me. Unfortunately, the next time would.

Liz's new kick in scrounging for easy advertising dollars was to push the envelope for editorial ethics. Don't get me wrong – none of us were hard-core rule followers, but there were some gray areas where things got icky between the business side and the creative side.

The best example was when Liz wanted me to profile a certain Italian designer in exchange for some ad pages.

'I have a great idea for a feature,' she said to me, all sugar and pleasantries, on the phone one morning. 'Why don't you interview Graciela D'Alessandro?'

I laughed silently, wondering what she was up to, knowing that Liz, as usual, had to have a hidden agenda. 'Why?' I responded. 'She's in no way a designer in her own right and we've never considered covering her.'

Her voice changed as I questioned her, then her famous clipped tone set in. 'Because she is one of the most important and interesting designers today, that's why.'

'I wish I could agree,' I said. 'But as I see it, all she's done is inherit her husband's empire. And ever since her husband's death, the quality of the line has taken an obvious nosedive. What's the real reason?' I asked, growing more impatient. Why was she acting like Graciela's publicist?

Liz's tone turned venomous. 'The tragedy of her husband's death would make the interview all the more interesting to our readers.'

'Really?' I countered. 'She whores his name out like it was a teen runaway at a truck stop. And anyway, I didn't realize we had such a big Italian widow demographic.' I knew I was probably sassing her too much, but I couldn't stand it when people weren't straight with me.

'Look,' Liz said, clearly on the edge of losing it, 'you know how this game is played. She bought some ad pages. And I want more. Just a couple more pages can make the difference between a good quarter and a bad quarter. And we all know who the bad quarters reflect on most.'

Finally, the real reason she wanted a Graciela profile, complete with a delicious, threatening topping of blame. Half the time she would press the point that *Jill* the magazine and Jill the person were not the same entity. But when things weren't going her way, she liked to point out that it would reflect poorly on both the person and the magazine if I didn't listen to her.

I'll admit, sometimes I did listen to her, wanting to save my hide and, of course, I enjoyed seeing a nice, fat, successful issue of *Jill* – thick with ad pages – as much as anyone. But this time she was just plain wrong. I might have considered it if Graciela were interesting, hip and did something extraordinary other than inherit her husband's business. But that just wasn't the case. 'Graciela D'Alessandro is nothing more than a middle-aged, ill-tempered, pill-popping narcissist. If I profile her,' I warned Liz, 'I will show her as she really is.'

'No. You. Won't,' she shot back in a fuming staccato.

So she pulled out her favorite weapon of choice whenever we had a stalemate: an e-mailed cc'd to everyone in the world.

The next thing I knew, I got a response from Ellen:

To: Jill White@nestrom.com
From: Ellen Cutter@nestrom.com
Re: Graciela D'Alessandro
Jill – I think a minifeature on Graciela's new line would fit in the style section just fine.
E

As long as I didn't have to profile the crazy bitch herself, I'd live with it. This was the last straw, however, for Paul, who called a meeting with T.J. and Ellen to discuss his concerns about the direction of the magazine. He left me and Liz out of it, to prevent a cat fight, I suppose. And it was his last stab at yielding whatever little amount of control he had left. In the process he unknowingly painted a giant bull's-eye on his chest.

The following week, not so coincidentally, this mysterious and not very blind item surfaced on 'Page Six':

Which aptly named Nestrom creative director was recently sighted sporting his John Thomas to anyone who would look in the skeevy restroom of Two Potato on Christopher Street? We knew he was flashy but pegged him as too classy to be a flasher. Who knew? A disappointed onlooker noted that he soiled two good names in the process – his own and that of his company.

I immediately called him.

'It's not true!' he screamed. 'You know I wouldn't be caught dead on Christopher Street!'

'I know, honey, I know,' I said, trying my best to console him.

'Who could have done this?!' he stormed.

I had a pretty good idea who did it, but no proof.

'Roger is beside himself. How do I respond to this?'

'Don't,' I told him. 'It will eventually go away.'

The gossip did eventually go away. But so did Paul's power, and his reputation in the eyes of the press-obsessed T.J.

After the whole Paul incident I decided I needed to get away and reconnect with my staff, whom I felt I had been neglecting amid the political shitstorm. I thought it would be good for us to have a retreat, but not the team-building, touchy-feely kind. I called a meeting to ask what the staff memebers thought they'd like to do on a day trip.

The suggestions came fast and furious.

'Spa!'

'Paintball!'

'Bowling!'

'Yoga!'

'Skydiving!'

The last one caught my attention. I remembered how it had been #1 on my list of things I wanted to accomplish back in the days of my Hillander journals. But as I got older, it had become less and less appealing. And after September 11, it had been hard for me to even get into a plane, never mind consider jumping out of one.

That was exactly why I should do it, now, I thought. I felt a need to confront a demon, and that would be it.

I confessed my interest and my fear of skydiving. A few others on the staff also mentioned a fear of heights. I inspired them, however, to at least try to do it. It would certainly be easier to conquer these fears as a group than alone, I reasoned. Plus we could get a story out of it: 'Conquering Your Worst Fear in One Scary Step.' In the interest of good journalism, we all agreed to do it.

So one early morning the following week we were all on a bus on our way to Kutztown, Pennsylvania, to jump out of a plane. It was a clear, sunny, warm fall morning. We were told that the weather conditions would be perfect for our jump.

We were suited up, given a class and I was doing pretty well until we stepped into the teeny, tiny plane. As it rose, I felt my color drain. Exactly *why*, again, were we doing this?

I looked at Casey, panic in my eyes. She looked excited and ready to go, but she instantly picked up on my trepidation. 'You're going to be fine,' she said. 'We'll all be attached to the instructors. Let them do the work and the worrying and just relax and have fun.'

She gave me an encouraging pat on the back when my turn came. And I just closed my eyes and gritted my teeth and before I knew it the instructor and I were sailing out the door.

Falling through the air was completely exhilarating. I felt so free, and powerful, as the adrenaline rush kicked in when we dropped. Looking down, I was mesmerized by the vibrant colors that made up the patchwork fields below us. It was breathtaking.

When our chutes came out, our speed dropped, and we floated, and I felt so calm, as if nothing in the world could bother me. My fear seemed so far away then, like it belonged to a different person. Everything that was so big in my life – the magazine, the Stepford Twins, my miscarriage – seemed so small, too.

My coworkers who were already on the ground cheered as I touched down. I ran toward them and we laughed and hugged and shared the same joy with each remaining staffer who floated down.

After we all had made our jumps, we piled on a bus and went to a local tavern, triumphantly clinking together foamy mugs of beer.

I think that was the best beer I ever tasted.

I returned to the office after that with a new well of confidence, which even a surprisingly negative performance review couldn't shake.

I felt so frustrated as I sat in Ellen's office with a mute Paul by my side. 'We need you to become more active in selling the magazine,' Ellen said to me, using a tone that should be reserved only for scolding a misbehaving middle-schooler.

'I'm an *editor*,' I reminded her. 'My priority is to *create* the magazine each month, not sell it.'

'You are *Jill*. You are responsible for the brand,' Ellen countered. 'And like it or not, you are tied into it – and its sales.'

'But I have been helping with ad calls,' I said, stating my case. 'I've gone to at least a dozen since Liz has come on board.' I didn't mind helping out by introducing Liz to some of the major accounts, but the bottom line was that it was my job to create the magazine, and Liz's job to sell it.

Ellen stood up from behind her museum-worthy Frank Lloyd Wright desk. She lifted up a memo from her desk and handed it to me.

'According to Liz, you've only been on two ad calls with her,' she said, offending me with her accusatory tone. I read the memo. She wrote that I was 'uncooperative,' 'frequently unavailable,' and 'reluctant to sell the magazine.' What a bitch.

So Liz was playing the paper game, then. I made a mental note to have Casey document every ad call I did from that moment on. I held my temper as I calmly handed the memo back to Ellen. 'This simply isn't true. Of course I want to sell the magazine, and I have made myself as available as humanly possible for someone who is responsible for the editorial content.'

Ellen sat back down. I could tell that what I was saying

wasn't penetrating. 'Look,' she said, 'the bottom line is that T.J. has given us some lofty goals. We now have a mandate to bring in new advertisers. Liz can use all the help she can get. For now, you must make it your priority. Let your staff handle the editorial side. They are perfectly capable of it.'

'Maybe she's bit off more than she can chew, then, as publisher of *Jill*,' I said. 'I mean, maybe we just didn't hire the right replacement for Lynn.'

Ellen stared me down. I could already tell that I had said the wrong thing. 'Liz Alexander isn't the problem,' she said. 'She's one of the best publishers in the industry and I suggest you start taking her advice.' She turned to Paul then. 'I'm sure Paul will be a great help to you on your end while you and Liz work as a team to reach our new goals.'

I glanced at Paul, who gave me a defeated 'you have no choice' look. He verbalized. 'I'll be happy to pitch in and help pick up the editorial slack.'

'Great!' Ellen said, sealing the deal and seeming thrilled to have proven exactly who was in charge. 'So I'd like you to meet with Liz, make an aggressive ad call schedule, and send me the final itinerary, if you will.'

I rolled over and agreed, knowing that, indeed, I didn't have any choice.

I made an appointment with Liz for the next morning. I didn't even fight with her this time about where we were meeting, for fear of seeming 'uncooperative.' So as much as I hated it, I made the journey up to her office.

I hated going to Liz's office for several reasons. The first, and most childish, was that it was bigger than mine, and she loved to show that off. But what really agitated me about her office was that she rearranged it every few weeks, so I was always completely disoriented upon entry. Maybe if she spent less time rearranging her overpriced furniture and original Ertes, she could sell the magazine. But that's just one woman's 'uncooperative' opinion.

We got right down to business. I bit the bullet and scheduled twelve calls with her over the next five weeks. From early morning calls clear across the country to local calls that would include dinner and drinks late into the night, I knew I had to do the best I could on all to get Ellen off my back and get back to the work that I loved to do.

Our first call was in New York, thankfully, with a new cosmetics company whose products were 'guaranteed organic and environment friendly.' Liz wanted to take the reins on this one, so I let her. But I was horrified by what I saw.

First, she looked all wrong. Liz wore a yellow tweed Chanel suit with buttons as big as fried eggs, while the ad execs were clad in Stella McCartney. Mistake number one. How did she, all wrapped in Chanel, ever expect to connect with these people? Then she droned on in a darkened room over a Power-Point presentation that was rife with embarrassing misspellings. Her dry, dull pitch caused more than a few eyelids to flutter. It was a disaster.

For the next call, we flew to Seattle. I nicely asked Liz if she wouldn't mind if I did the pitch, since it was for KewlTunez, a music downloading site, and since I had a big interest in music and all. I tried my best not to seem like I was wresting the task from her. But surprisingly, she readily agreed, seeming even somewhat relieved.

Because of the nature of the client, I dressed in jeans, an ancient Third Rail T-shirt, and a Marc Jacobs jacket that the designer had sent me for Christmas. In a red Chanel suit this time, Liz stood out like a sore thumb even more. The woman had a serious learning disability.

No PowerPoint for me. I simply pulled out a letter.

'Dear Jill,' I read aloud, casually sitting on the edge of the conference room table. 'Thanks for recommending the Stalkers CD. After reading your review I ran out and bought it and now I'm hooked. As I'm overworked, I don't have time to keep up with the new bands, so I always turn to you guys to let me know what's good. Your suggestions are always spot on. I don't feel so out of touch anymore, thanks to you! Carole, twenty-nine, Albuquerque, New Mexico.'

'This is the epitome of the *Jill* woman,' I went on. 'She's savvy, hip, independent, and interested in new music. She has disposable income, and she wants good suggestions on how to spend it.'

That was just the start. By the end of the meeting, we had won a giant new account.

'Congratulations,' Liz said begrudgingly. 'See, it's not all that hard, right?'

I didn't say a word. What I wanted to say was, 'If it's so freakin' easy why don't you just do it yourself?!' But I knew that she was having trouble getting meetings without guaranteeing I would be there too and I was playing nice.

Over the next five weeks, though, Liz played dirty. Imagine my surprise when she didn't show up at the airport for a 6 A.M. flight to Portland, Oregon, but one of her junior staffers did. 'Where's Liz?' I asked.

'She couldn't make it today,' the staffer said, 'so she sent me.'

Or my surprise when she decided for the trip to Detroit that we should 'divide and conquer.' She loaded my schedule with exhausting, back-to-back meetings at automobile companies from 7 A.M. to 7 P.M., but when I found her own itinerary, which she dumbly discarded in the pouch of her airplane seat, I saw that she had only two meetings that day: lunch and drinks.

Or my surprise when she made a pointed remark in Miami about my wardrobe in front of a liquor company rep. 'Real businesswomen don't show so much skin,' she said, obviously referring to my skimpy halter.

Or my surprise when on a visit to an accessories manufacturer in Texas, we found out after our schmoozefest, which, for the most part, involved me taking photo after photo with the manufacturer's daughters and nieces who just 'happened' to be visiting, the company was bankrupt and had no money to spend. That was the one time I lost it and was nearly moved to reach out and grab Liz by the throat. I blew up at her on the flight home. 'How could you not know that they're going out of business? What a waste of time!'

'I can't be on top of every little business blip for every little company,' she answered, before tuning me out by putting on her headphones.

It had to be the most exhausting, enervating five weeks of my life. I was relieved when it was over, knowing that I had gone above and beyond Ellen's call of duty. When I got home, I actually looked forward to the mountain of backed up copy that awaited me, not to mention my backed-up personal life, which now demanded, deserved, and craved my attention. After many unsuccessful attempts at making another baby, Josh and I were about to start our first round of in vitro. So it was the absolute wrong time to be doing two jobs. Hopefully, Liz would start doing hers – and she'd leave me to do mine.

10

Mindy Weiner, Formerly of New Jersey Lighthouses Magazine, Joins Staff of Jill

—mediabistro.com, November 2004

Remember your emotional state of mind when you were a teenager? The hours of dejection when you felt like locking yourself in a dark room until you turned twenty; and the manic highs of anticipation and unbridled excitement when you felt like running into the streets and dancing on top of cars like those free-spirited students in *Fame*? Magnify those ups and downs by about a thousand percent. Then imagine paying over six figures total for the pleasure. That's what it's like to be pumped up on fertility drugs and going through in vitro.

I've always hated needles. But now I was as blasé about sticking myself as a seasoned heroin addict. I was injecting myself in the ass two times a day, after all. Then I'd get jabbed by the doctor, so he could check my blood, or extract my eggs and then implant them again. I was more intimate with needles than I was with Josh, whose sex life had been relegated to jerking off into a plastic cup with skanky, dog-eared porn magazines. (He later learned to bring his own smut.)

When I was 'cycling,' as they call it, I'd spend hours every other day for two weeks in the doctor's office. Sitting in that waiting room was even worse than the procedure. I'd see the same women day after day. At first, I yearned to reach out to them, hoping for some advice, some solace, some kinship. But all we'd end up sharing were awkward conversations. Eventually, instead of bonding with them, I found myself gauging their varying stages of depression, wondering who I'd be on par with that week. It made the whole experience even more disturbing.

The only person at *Jill* who knew the reasons for my mysterious absences was Casey, who would be the sponge for my inevitable postdoctor depression immediately after. Casey had become a master at juggling my new, now even more complicated calendar, and at coming up with legitimate-sounding appointments to cover for me if I was at the doctor when Liz or Ellen called.

But no one got the brunt of my emotions more than Josh. He stoically weathered the cycles of hope and disappointment like a champ. Somehow, even that upset me.

During one of Josh's comforting sessions, I freaked out. 'Why aren't you as upset as I am?!' I screamed. 'How could you stay so goddamned even?! Don't you have any emotions?!'

Josh addressed my last statement by becoming the angriest I have ever seen him. 'How can I possibly get emotional?!' he shouted. 'Who's going to comfort *me*? You're too much of a basket case to see beyond your own misery!'

Josh's eruption shocked me into finally understanding him. I swallowed my tears, bucked up, and squeezed him as he finally let go and cried.

'I'm so frustrated I can't fix this,' he said to me then. 'I wish there was a way that I could.'

I was too involved in my own sadness to realize how this all took its toll on him, too. I realized, then, that he had shown it in his own way, by not writing as much, by losing a lot of his trademark energy. It was strange how something that was supposed to bring us closer together was making us come apart instead.

'This isn't fun. Maybe it's time to look into other options,' he went on, gingerly, like he had been considering the possibility for a while. 'Like adoption.'

'I want to give it a few more tries,' I insisted, though it sounded insane. The process was taking its emotional toll on both of us, and it was costing an arm and a leg. But I wasn't ready to give up – just yet.

'Okay,' Josh agreed. 'But I also want you to know that if we never become parents, it's okay. All I really care about is us being together.'

Those words not only comforted me; they suddenly spurred on a revelation about part of the reason I was so desperate to be a mom. I recognized a deep-buried fear that if I didn't produce a child Josh would leave me. After all, we had gotten married in the first place because I was pregnant. So deep down I felt that I wasn't delivering my end of the deal, and my crazy emotions had amplified that crazy fear. I was scared to death that Josh didn't want to be with me unless we had a child. And here he was, assuring me of exactly the opposite.

'Do you really mean that?' I asked him, still startled at my discovery.

'Of course, Jill. I want to spend the rest of my life with you,' he said, lifting his hand to stroke my face. 'Kids or no kids.'

It was a giant relief. But I still desperately wanted to become a mother and I still had my share of irrational emotions.

Like one weekend, shortly after, at Sarah and Taso's. Josh and Taso were playing basketball with the kids in the driveway as Sarah and I sat in the yard. Every time I heard Josh's laugh, I wanted to cry. His having such a good time with the kids made me feel like he was throwing our childlessness in my face.

I know, crazy.

But I kept it to myself because Sarah, for once, was going through her own stuff. She kept wistfully asking me about work.

'It sucks,' I told her bluntly. 'Every day I swear I hate this business more and more. If IVF wasn't draining my bank account, I'd be gone already.'

'Oh, yeah, right,' Sarah said.

'I'm serious,' I told her, and I was.

'There's no way you'd just walk away from all that you've created,' Sarah said. 'I know you. You've worked too hard. You've achieved everything you've set out to achieve. And you've earned every bit of glory that goes along with it,' she added.

'It's not all it's cracked up to be,' I confessed. 'Believe me. Lately, I feel like I'd give it all up and gladly trade places with you – to just say screw it all and raise a family.'

Sarah then emitted a rueful, 'Hmph.'

I cocked an eyebrow at her, I knew she had something on her mind. Then she spilled.

'I often would rather trade places with you,' she said.

I was shocked. I would never wish my life on dear Sarah. 'Please!' I said, outraged. Now this was crazy talk. Maybe she was just trying to make me feel good, for all of the things I had been going through. 'You can't have any regrets!'

Sarah looked over at Taso and the kids and lowered her voice before she proceeded confidentially. 'Of course I have no regrets about having a family,' she said. 'But I do wonder all the time where I might be right now if I hadn't given up my career. Would I be a high-powered, sought-after art director somewhere? Would I be the darling of seasonal art shows in Manhattan? I guess I'll never know.'

'But you've always gotten work –' I started.

She cut me off. 'I haven't progressed or grown at all. Whenever I do get work it's the same thing, over and over.' She sighed. 'I don't know, I'm thinking about going back fulltime. The kids aren't babies anymore . . .'

Though I still thought having a successful career wasn't all that fulfilling, especially in light of recent events, I wanted to encourage Sarah. 'Well, then, why not?'

'I've been out of the loop for so long . . .' she said. 'And I feel so insecure with my portfolio and the big gaps in my resume.'

'You're not alone, Sarah,' I said, finally making sense.

'Women go back to work all the time. No one is going to shun you because you stayed at home to start a family. And you've never lost your talent; I can vouch for that.' It felt good to be on the giving side of a pep talk for once, especially to Sarah.

'Thanks, Jill. That means a lot coming from you,' Sarah said. 'I mean, I admire how much you've accomplished over the years. You've really made a name for yourself.'

Yeah, I thought, just so the Stepford Twins could attempt to destroy it. But it felt good to have Sarah say that. My self-confidence not only was shot from all of the infertility drama, it was even more rattled from being mangled by Nestrom's corporate machine. I often had to remind myself exactly why I was putting up with all this crap in the first place. Oh, yeah, because of another round of IVF. And because of another monthly mortgage payment. My financial obligations were holding me hostage. I was literally being forced to watch years of hard work morph into something that was increasingly difficult for me to be proud of. And the worst part was that I was required to participate in the destruction of a magazine that not only bore my name, but was also supposed to encompass my values, my views, and my voice.

And while Sarah's confidence in me was rock solid, it seemed there was nothing I could do to reclaim my respect at Nestrom.

The first ego blow came, even though it wasn't unexpected, when we were finally moved off of *Fashionista*'s floor. We were literally, and unceremoniously, 'kicked downstairs,' to the eighth floor. Whereas we once shared real estate with the great Myra Chernoff, we now cohabited with the cafeteria, the various critters it drew, and the supply room.

Then my managing editor quit, leaving me for *Epicure*'s much more delicious pastures. Immediately after, I was handed a mandate and an unrealistic deadline for a redesign, while a new candidate for managing editor was being curiously shoved down my throat. In the middle of it all, I found out that my latest IVF didn't take.

Thankfully I was having an 'up' day when it came time to meet Mindy Weiner, Ellen's pick for managing editor. All I knew about her was that she was coming from some magazine about lighthouses. Talk about a niche publication. I had no idea why Ellen thought she might be a good fit for *Jill*, unless, of course, she was a member of the Stepford sisterhood as well. The more I thought about it, the more I worried that that might be the case.

But my Stepford-connection worries melted away when I finally met the woman. She looked like she had never seen a sweater set, never mind owned one, unless it was made of polyester knit and on the rack at Kmart. The navy blue stretch pantsuit she wore that day seemed to come off that very same rack. Even her hair seemed to be bought from a discount store: it was brittle and wiglike, sticking out of her head in a stiff, unmoving triangular mass.

Despite her fashion-challenged style, however, she carried herself in a self-assured way, and she exuded a motherly sort of aura. She told me that she spent years in the magazine trade in New York before her husband moved her down to south Jersey. But now that they were moving back to the area, she couldn't wait to get back into the game. '*Lighthouses* is a little . . . slow paced for me,' she confided.

She also seemed very energetic, and eager to take on

responsibility. 'I'll take the late nights so you won't have to,' she assured me, as she looked around my chaotic office. 'I can already tell that you're doing more than you should be doing,' she said.

She had no idea. I was glad that someone in that building could recognize that. 'I know I come from a small publication, but I can cut your workload in half,' she added confidently. If only . . .

Managing editors have a thankless job. It is their responsibility to kindly nudge everyone along to get the magazine ready for shipping on time without causing the staff to hate them. They had to be extremely organized, but it was even more important for them to be diplomats at heart. I got the sense from Mindy that she possessed those vital qualities.

She was very convincing, and if she would live up to her word, she was welcome aboard. So I decided not to judge her by her questionable taste in clothing, and give her the thumbs-up. Plus, we needed someone right away if we were going to pull off this redesign.

Mindy was hired and immediately saddled with moving along two issues at once: the current one and the prototype for the redesign. We spent a lot of exhausting late nights in the office together, though she frequently tried to shoo me off to go home. 'I'll handle it,' she'd often say. And though I trusted her, I couldn't let go of the details. Plus, the workload was a great mechanism to distract me from my depressing home life. Nothing against Josh, but our whole lives revolved around IVF. I found that the office was the one place where I wasn't constantly thinking about it.

The biggest demands on my time at *Jill* were working

closely with Sven on the look of the redesign; painstakingly going over every piece of copy to make sure the content was sufficiently toned down (i.e. redacting the word *penis* wherever possible, per Liz); and selling the changes to the staff members without making it seem that we were selling out, though we really were. I became a master of illusion and wiggly words, telling them that all the changes were just so we could 'take *Jill* to the next level.' And I think I convinced them, for a while, that all of this was actually a good thing. I think I even convinced myself, too.

I was impressed by Mindy's expediency the whole way through. And I was further impressed by the fact that she somehow raised two kids (ages ten and twelve), though it seemed that she lived in the Nestrom building. She kept her promise to keep me from working too many late nights, so much so I heard that she'd often be there until three to three-thirty in the morning. I was amazed at how she retained her high energy all along.

'Don't forget to look after yourself, Mindy,' I told her one late night as we shared Chinese food in the conference room. I certainly didn't want her to burn out too soon. She had made herself indispensable in a short amount of time.

'You, too,' she said to me tentatively. 'I don't mean to pry, but I noticed your eyes were red and puffy earlier today. Is everything okay with you?' Her question came with plaintive concern.

No one was around. And I was tired – tired of keeping in all my emotions. I needed to unload right then, and Mindy seemed like she would be receptive and compassionate. 'Things could be better,' I answered, deciding to confide in her. I laughed a little then. 'Everyone must think I'm a psycho with all of my mood swings. You see, I'm undergoing fertility treatments. And sometimes I have emotional moments, which could be about something important, or about absolutely nothing at all. So, yes, I was crying today. Today it was over absolutely nothing.'

'I know exactly how you feel,' Mindy said, surprising me. 'I went through six rounds of IVF. It was awful.'

'Really?!' I said, happy to have someone who could relate to what I was talking about.

Mindy nodded. 'The story has a happy ending, though. I had my second child via IVF. And let me tell you, all the agony you're going through now will be worth it in the end. So keep your eye on the prize.'

'Well,' I said, 'I'm trying not to get my hopes up too much. I always seem to end up being disappointed.'

Mindy put a supportive arm around my shoulder. 'I have a feeling it will happen for you. So hang in there.'

Our conversation, and her optimism, were extremely comforting to me, and I appreciated that. And she went on to gamely answer a ton of questions that I had about the process and her and her husband's emotional state. Some of the questions were quite personal, but Mindy didn't seem to mind the intrusion. 'Any way I can help, you just let me know,' she assured me.

Of course, though, I asked her to keep the information to herself. I didn't want anyone else to know, most especially the Stepford Twins. She swore up and down that it was our little secret. Ours and Casey's, in reality.

Through it all, the redesign was coming out wonderfully,

thanks especially to the hard work of Sven and his department. We had scored a big name for the cover of that issue: troubled teen actress Laura Lonagan. We had an incredibly difficult shoot with her, as her boyfriend was dumping her, via cell phone, throughout it. I thought we would have to airbrush the cell phone out of the photo since she clung on to it so desperately, either frantically redialing him or waiting for him to call back just so they could have another loud, foul-mouthed brawl.

I expected we wouldn't get one decent shot that day, but Sven worked his usual magic. When he unveiled the mockup, I was stunned. It had come out beautiful. Too beautiful almost. So beautiful I thought I was looking at a *Fashionista* cover. I brought the still out to the cubicle pit and laid it out for everyone to see.

A crowd formed to give Sven the 'oohs' and 'aahs' he deserved, Mindy among them. But she also took the opportunity to comment on the size of the coverlines, which pissed off Sven to no end.

Mindy's frequent design 'suggestions' caused Sven to breed a deep dislike of her. 'I won't be told how to design a magazine by a woman who wears stretch pants pulled up to her breasts!' he had snapped at me once. I just laughed inside, knowing that Sven never reacted well to criticism from anyone. And I reassured him that surely no one would ever take her opinion of the design seriously. Still, she always managed to get under his skin.

But as she bent over to examine the cover still that day, something else happened that upset Sven. 'Hey!' he shouted: 'You're bleeding all over my cover!'

I looked at Mindy, and she had a stream of blood running out of her nose. She put her hand to her face, and the blood continued to gush out through her cupped fingers. I grabbed a chair from the cubicle. 'Sit down and put your head back!' I told her. 'Someone get some tissues and paper towels!'

Casey was already on the job, emerging with a giant box of Kleenex and a wad of wet paper towels.

'Are you okay?' I asked Mindy.

She nodded. 'My allergies,' she mumbled.

Sven walked away in a huff, muttering under his breath. I stared after him, as I was certain I heard him say, 'Cokehead!'

Cokehead? That shocked me. Maybe I was naive, but how could this woman, this fashion-backward mother of two, be a cokehead? Cokeheads were rock stars or skinny models or moneyed Wall Streeters. Not Mindy Weiner.

But she did have an awful lot of frantic energy and didn't blink an eye at the all-nighters. And she wasn't the healthiest-looking person around. But a cokehead? I wasn't so sure. At least . . . I didn't want to believe it.

Mindy had become a very good front line for me during a time when I needed it most. She was a good shield, always seeming to have everything under control. The magazine was moving incredibly smoothly under her, despite the monkey wrench of the redesign. She never had any problem making budget. And she seemed to be as loyal as they came, even taking more than a few bullets for me . . . So I just couldn't believe it. I chalked the comment up to Sven's dislike for her.

After the bloody cover incident, Sven and I went on to have a very successful presentation to Ellen and Paul, who, in turn, expressed their approval for the redesign. Of course, Liz had to find something negative to say. Staring at the gorgeous cover, she mused, 'Maybe you could do some more work on this. Airbrush out her freckles and close that horrible gap between her front teeth.'

Before Sven could throttle her, I held up my hand. 'Everyone knows that signature gap is what makes Laura's beauty human,' I said firmly. 'And I love the idea of being the first magazine to show her as she really is – freckles and all.'

Thankfully, Paul and Ellen agreed, and I left that meeting relieved.

Now, all we had to do was sit back and wait for Liz to sell it.

We waited. And waited. And waited. Time was drawing perilously close to our presentation to T.J., where we would not only unveil the redesign, but present him with a brand new and improved ad page count, too.

But then I received a call from Ellen's office notifying me that the meeting had been postponed, and that she needed to see me right away.

So I did my perp walk up to her grand floor, expecting the worst, of course. Ellen never called me upstairs when she had anything good to say. These days, she never had anything good to say. When I arrived in her office, Liz was there, of course, standing next to Ellen's big chair, posing like she was Morticia Addams or something. The image cracked me up – Ellen as Gomez and Liz as Morticia. It wasn't a stretch, for some reason, to picture them as some kind of creepy cartoon couple.

'The ad page count isn't where we want it to be for the meeting with T.J.,' Ellen started before I even sat down.

I shot a look at Liz. 'I don't get it,' I said, frustrated. 'How can that be? We delivered exactly what you asked for. We delivered exactly what you said you could sell.' I had made so many compromises for this woman and my staff had worked ridiculously hard to deliver for her. It was a 'down day' for me emotionwise and I was out of patience.

Liz's face turned red; she looked down; and, for a moment, I thought she might cry. Maybe she was – as she should be – embarrassed. But when she looked up, her eyes turned to slits and her hands went to her waist. And when I heard the pinched tone of her voice, I knew she wasn't going to admit to anything. 'Again,' Liz said patronizingly, 'it would help if you were more available to go on a few more calls. Casey called to cancel several important meetings I had gone through a lot of trouble to get, citing your editorial workload.' Same old shit. Brand new day. It would never end. 'Now that you're finished with the redesign, what's your excuse?' she asked, a little too pryingly for my comfort. 'What's been taking up so much of your time?'

My excuse was twofold: (1) I had already done more than my fair share in terms of ad calls, and (2) I was going through, another round of in vitro. And that was none of their fucking business. So I sat smugly and silently before them as I sighed.

That didn't put Liz off one bit as she glared at me with her green cat eyes. 'It's just that you've been hard to get hold of recently. You seem to be out a lot,' she said. 'Is everything okay with you, Jill?' she asked, with fake concern.

'I've been out promoting the new look,' I said, scrambling to remember some of Casey's better excuses. 'Doing press. Pursuing high-profile cover possibilities, per your mandate.'

'Listen,' Ellen said, trying to play referee, and sounding just a tiny bit desperate. 'Jill, can you just try your best to help Liz in this push? It's crucial at this point. We need to get those numbers up before our meeting with T.J.'

'And what if we don't?' I asked, thinking their expectations unrealistic and the whole situation hopeless.

'Positive thinking, Jill, will get us there,' was Ellen's answer.

I relented, again, and the next few weeks I spent going on more calls with Liz. I had been going on so many calls lately that some of the advertisers would request to see me specifically, not wanting to deal with Liz at all. During this spell, I ended up running most of the show myself. The whole thing made me burn with resentment. What in the world was she so busy doing if not selling ad space? I couldn't believe I was even doing this because deep down I hated asking people for money. It made me feel like some kind of slick beggar, but I rose to the occasion even though it wasn't my job. I tried my best to help her sell the redesign, but at the end of the day, I was convinced that she couldn't even sell crack to Whitney Houston. She didn't have a clue and had already done quite the job of turning key people off at one too many accounts.

We miraculously landed a few new accounts, but not as many as Ellen was hoping for. And the excuse the ad execs clung onto infuriated me, especially if I made the time to fly across country somewhere – like Detroit for an upscale auto advertiser or Oregon for a sportswear giant – just to hear the same thing: 'We're spending our budget for this demographic on *Fashionista* and *Charisma*,' they'd say. 'We simply don't have the money for another publication geared toward the same audience.'

I tried in vain to explain how the readerships were actually very different, despite the fact that the magazines now looked very much alike. I sounded like a total idiot, and it just reinforced my belief that as beautiful as the redesign was it was inappropriate for the magazine. We were shooting ourselves in the foot by trying to horn in on a market that we weren't intended for in the first place. They were trying to make *Jill* something it simply wasn't. And something it clearly would never be.

Liz and I spent our time after each depressing ad call sitting in a town car in acrimonious silence. On our way back to the office one day, we came across a pack of school kids crossing the street in front of us. I laughed to myself and smiled at them. They were probably about seven years old, following their teacher like a flock of baby ducks. I fantasized about being that teacher instead of sitting two feet away from Stepford Liz at that moment.

'So overrated,' Liz muttered, snapping me out of my reverie.

I shot her a curious look.

'Kids,' she went on, being real for what seemed the first time since I knew her.

'You ever think about starting a family?' I pried, wondering if we could find some common ground there, at least.

She shook her head. 'No way. I don't have the time or the desire. It's best left to others. But not me, no way.' Then she gave me one of her famous catlike, sideways glances. 'And you?'

'Someday,' was my succinct answer.

'Yes, well,' she needled, 'someday when you have more time. Right now I'm sure that's not where your priorities lie. At least, it's not where they should be right now. The whole *Jill* team is counting on you during this crucial time.'

I had a creeping feeling that she knew something, something I really didn't want her to know. And she had the nerve not to be too subtle about it. But how? How did she possibly know? Certainly Casey would never tell anyone – especially Liz. The only other possibility was Mindy . . .

The meeting with T.J. loomed dauntingly on the horizon those few weeks. When the time finally came, Ellen called a hasty meeting in her office just prior.

'Hopefully, he'll give the redesign some time to sink in,' I worried out loud. 'Liz's sure to get more ad revenue once it's out,' I said, eyeing Ellen hopefully even though I really wasn't convinced she could do that at all. If T.J. poo-pooed the presentation, it could mean yet another redesign. Or worse. 'You should assure him of that when we give him the numbers.'

Ellen shook her head. 'We're not going to give him the numbers,' she said. 'At least, not the real numbers.'

I couldn't believe my ears. 'You mean we're going to lie? To T.J.?!' Was she out of her mind? T.J. Oldham wasn't the chairman of Nestrom Media because he was an idiot. As eccentric as the man was, he was sharp. Sharp enough to see through any ploy of Ellen Cutter's.

'We're not going to lie, Jill, dear,' she said, all saccharine.

Again with the 'dears.' 'We're going to give him the projected numbers, that's all. You know, the numbers that I'm sure we'll eventually reach.' Then before I could say anything more, she brusquely looked at her watch. 'It's time. Let's go.'

'Where's Paul?' I asked, realizing they had once again excluded him, as they often did in matters involving T.J. Now I had seen it all: a presentation of a redesign without the creative director present.

I had no ally and I had no time to think over what was about to happen: the three of us were just about to go into a meeting with T.J. Oldham and lie about the state of advertising.

I wanted no part of it. And I felt ill throughout Ellen and Liz's entire dog and pony show.

'We're extremely positive about the redesign,' Ellen said, as she unveiled it to an unmoved T.J.

'It was a long time coming, but I think we finally got it right,' Liz said, always one to put my previous efforts down. Couldn't she just restrain herself once in front of the chairman?

'Well, judging from the numbers, it certainly seems so,' Ellen said. I was amazed at how easily the bullshit flowed out of her mouth. And she didn't seem to be the least bit nervous that T.J. would detect it.

Then Liz started to talk numbers. Fake numbers. Numbers I couldn't imagine us achieving as long as Liz Alexander had the job.

I sat there in silence, stunned, the whole display making me so angry. If they could lie right in the face of the chairman, then what in the world must they be doing to me? I couldn't even begin to imagine. Then I started to feel incredibly, incredibly sad.

I felt like a total fraud. By even sitting there in silence I was cheerleading for something that I created yet no longer fully recognized. And I felt sick to my stomach as Ellen and Liz pumped up numbers and blew smoke up T.J.'s ass, while he in turn clipped his fingernails right at the conference table.

It was all so disgusting in so many ways.

I don't know if T.J. bought any of the bullshit they fed him. He was always cryptic in these meetings. He sat there quietly clipping his nails, the clicking of the clipper sending chills of revulsion down my spine. At the end of it all, he just looked up at Ellen and said, 'I trust you. Do what you have to do.'

But the truly sickening part followed, when T.J. stopped Liz on the way out and said, 'I've been meaning to tell you what a great coup landing KewlTunez has been. They blew up right after you brought them on, and now they have about fifty times that buying power. Make sure they spread that wealth.'

'Thank you, T.J., I will,' she said, all dutifully, as I shot her one of the deadliest looks I could muster. I was clearly the one responsible for landing them. But she just stood there basking in the praise and taking all the credit.

What was the point of doing two jobs if I wouldn't even be given credit for one?

I followed Liz out of the conference room and into the elevator. I was tired of being stepped on by her and I needed to stand up for myself. I didn't want to start an angry confrontation, but I wanted her to know that I was on to her, and that I wouldn't let it slide. 'I wonder how T.J. got the impression that you were the one who landed the KewlTunez account?' I said casually.

'What do you mean?' Liz angrily shot back, despite my gentle approach.

'Well, it's just that I was the one who pitched them that day, that's all,' I said, keeping the casual edge to my tone.

Liz looked at me like I had five heads. 'I don't know what you're talking about,' she said.

'Really?' I answered. 'You should look into that, then – you know, your memory loss situation. It could be early Alzheimer's.' Okay, so the bitch in me came out after all. I just couldn't resist.

Liz just shook her head tensely and sighed. 'I'm the publisher, Jill. I got the meeting and the account. I think you're the one who is having a problem with her memory . . . and her ego,' she huffed before conveniently slipping out of the elevator just as we reached her floor.

I slunk back to my office then, exhausted and repulsed. I flopped into my chair and absentmindedly sorted through my e-mail. I saw Casey's roundup of the monthly letters from readers waiting in my in-box.

I opened it, hoping reading it would distract me for a while. There was a lot of the same stuff as usual: compliments, complaints about ads. But one particular letter stood out, sending me right back to the last days of *Cheeky*.

Dear Jill:

What is up with the magazine these days? I was flipping through the latest issue and I had to check the cover – I

thought I had mistakenly picked up Cosmo. Et tu? You're clearly selling out. I'm so disappointed in you.
Kathy, 32, Chicago

I minimized it and sighed. Maybe it was a sign. Maybe it was time for me to think about letting go of *Jill*. Maybe it was time for me to start exploring other opportunities.

So right then, I picked up the phone and decided to call a few old friends, notably *Jill*'s former publisher Lynn Stein, who had, as I predicted, landed on her feet (and then some) as the CEO at Nestrom's biggest competitor – *and* who was rumored to be looking around for new magazine ideas.

11

Buxom Blonde Penny Doherty to Pen Column for Jill

— Entertainment Weekly, December 2004

One of the first lessons you learn in the business is that two things make the world of magazine editing go round: celebrities and swag.

A great celebrity 'get,' for example, could save a waning magazine from bankruptcy or pull a start-up out of obscurity, while the swag baits bright young things into the business, then buys their patience for low-paying jobs. Even though our circulation was higher than ever before, I felt increasing pressure from the suits upstairs to keep bettering each month's rising numbers. And despite our success both with subscriber renewals and at the newsstand, Ellen instituted a hiring and salary freeze that left my talented, sought-after staff ripe for poaching. So, in order to keep my staff from jumping ship, without any promise of a raise in sight, both celebrity and swag came in handy.

Trying to come up with some 'selling' ideas, I decided to do more offbeat and fun things with celebrities, letting them show off hidden talents and show our readers who they were as people, and even did an entire issue completely produced by celebrities. Richard Ruiz photographed a fashion spread, famous authors served as models, Serena Sax donated some decorating tips, Jay Z handled the music reviews, and Tom Cruise gave advice on buying a car. Our numbers skyrocketed. But it was one unlikely celebrity who committed to a monthly column who really grabbed the attention of readers – and the media.

Penny Doherty was a blond, B-list television star known more for her large breasts, sex tapes, and troubled marriage than her acting ability. When I ran a revealing interview with her on just why she hung on to her poisonous, washed-up rock star husband, I received a phone call the day after it hit the stands. I was used to such phone calls, but they would usually come from publicists. So I was a little taken aback when I heard Penny Doherty's own whispery voice on the other end of my line that day.

'There's more to the story,' she said. 'You only asked me certain types of questions about my relationship and we had limited time. I didn't think you would be focusing only on that.'

'But you can't have any issue on what was printed,' I gently argued. 'We printed exactly what you had said.'

'Yes, but I'd like a chance to elaborate,' she pressed, as polite as could be. 'Would you give me that chance?'

I found the idea interesting and told her that I'd have to give it some thought. And after mulling it over for a few days, I decided that, yes, I would give Penny Doherty that chance. One thing I did learn in that interview was that she wasn't the bimbo she appeared to be – she was anything but dumb and she had solid opinions and some interesting things to say. She knew exactly how to turn her dumb-blond image into a moneymaking machine and was really honest about how she had leveraged her assets. Plus, she was devoted to several causes, like PETA and Habitat for Humanity, and despite it all – her husband's drug habit, the sex tapes, the bad TV – she was trying her best to be a good mother. And I especially respected the professional way she disagreed with our portrayal of her.

I called her back, and she sounded thrilled when I proposed not only a chance for her to respond, but a monthly column, if she was up to it. She snapped up the opportunity, turning in a surprisingly candid piece just a few weeks later. In it, she defended her decision to stay with the father of her children, having been the product of a broken home herself. But she also dropped a bombshell, revealing that she had picked up an STD from him that would prevent her from ever having children again. I applauded her bravery and decided that she should also be our cover girl when the column debuted. The coverline she approved, 'How I Live with My Husband – and My STD,' was sure to grab attention. But what was even more shocking was the complete makeunder we gave her for the shoot. Though Penny was a naturally beautiful woman, so much of it was hidden under her bleached, heavy-metal hair and make-up only a drag queen could love. A stripped-down photo of her would show the Penny behind the brass.

The response to the story and the magazine in general was amazing. Every gossip column, every entertainment television show, and every morning radio show host talked about *Jill* for weeks. We also received a ton of supportive letters for Penny. She reveled in the validation it all gave her. We reveled in our increased exposure and sales. It was *Jill*'s best-selling issue ever. Of course, Ellen and Liz continued to find reasons to complain about the content and, despite all our positive press, would wonder aloud why I couldn't get Jennifer Aniston or Gwyneth on the cover. I decided in frustration that no matter what I did it would never be good enough for them and that I would always be held responsible for Liz's failure to raise the ad count.

But after our Penny cover, the 'gets' got somewhat easier, as celebrities started to notice how much publicity the magazine was generating. Pretty much every magazine had followed our lead in terms of putting actors rather than models on their covers, and snaring the big stars had gotten pretty competitive. So although we still would lose Jennifer and Gwyneth to more prestigious mags like *Fashionista* and *Bazaar*, Rosario was deluged with calls from publicists pitching their celebrity clients, and it seemed like a day couldn't go by without a major gossip item that began with 'Actress tells *Jill* magazine,' and the like. So as *Jill*'s profile and circulation numbers grew, more A-listers clamored for our cover. Some celebrities loved our unorthodox approach to interviews. It would have benefited some others, however, to actually read the magazine before they begged to be in it.

Like the pop/country singer who refused to sit next to me at the Grammy's because she came off like a raving bitch in an interview during which she was, quite frankly, a raving bitch.

The question that set her off was, 'Is this song about oral sex?'

Instead of responding with honesty, or even humor, she grew furious. 'Why would you ask me that question?!'

'I'm surprised that no one had asked you that before,' the reporter responded, citing some very suggestive lyrics. The singer threw a tantrum, then threw our reporter out of her car.

When the reporter finally made it back to the office, she came to me defeated, saying that she didn't think she had enough for the story. I calmed her down, then listened to her tapes. 'We have a great story,' I assured her. 'We're going to print everything she said – tantrum and all.' And we did. Which led to the Grammy tantrum. After finding her a suitable new seat (I certainly wasn't moving), her boyfriend came back to curse me out during the ceremony, then tossed a drink at me at the after party. I stepped out of the way just before it hit me, causing the spill to land on an important record industry exec, and making the boyfriend look like an even worse ass than he already was.

Some celebrity disasters weren't our fault. Like the shoot with the diva singer who told us she was a size eight. We were shocked, then, when after ordering an entire wardrobe for her, she showed up more like a fourteen. Nothing fit her bulging body, and there was no way we could justify a reshoot because of her delusional downsizing. So we crammed her size fourteen ass into size eight clothing by literally slicing shirts, skirts, and dresses open in the back to accommodate her figure.

Sometimes we were plainly in the wrong, though. There

was the freelancer who interviewed an English model turned Bond girl who ostensibly complained that her heart-throb ex-boyfriend was 'bad in bed.' Of course, we highlighted that quote, only to face wrath that I never realized the English could muster. After a series of hostile phone calls and threatened lawsuits, the giant cosmetics company for which she was the spokesperson joined the fray, vowing to pull its ads from every Nestrom publication it advertised in (which was nearly all). After fielding some frantic calls from both Liz and Ellen, I had to ask the writer to produce the interview tapes, which she did. But on them I couldn't find any complaints about the model's sex life whatsoever. We ended up with egg on our face, and I printed a retraction. Thankfully that was enough for the model to pull the lawsuit, spare me the wrath of the Stepford Twins, and satisfy the cosmetics giant. Needless to say, I never hired that freelancer again.

For every celeb disaster, however, there'd be an equally fun interaction, like the rock star who let us photograph his medicine cabinet, and the model who let us shoot her fridge knowing that it had nothing in it and willing to poke fun at herself for it. Or there would be the odd occasion when you realized that celebrities were people, too, like the young actress I once interviewed with the scars on her arms. Of course, I knew just what they were from, and I felt horrible for her. I started to talk to her off the record. She pretended to not know what I was saying at first, but then she finally fessed up when I shared my own experience with cutting.

'I don't even know why I do it,' she confided to me, her eyes welling up with tears.

'It's because the pressure is too much and it feels like a release,' I told her. 'But do yourself a favor, and stop. Just go cold turkey. You can do it. If you ever feel like cutting, just call me. Okay?'

She not only stopped cutting; she was nice enough to tell the world that I was responsible for her recovery.

But enough about the celebrities; now on to the swag. *Swag* was the industry term for the glamorous giveaways that would come through the office. They'd be everything from clothing samples to electronic gadgets to front-row concert tickets with backstage passes. But the best swag was always served up at Fashion Week. I'd come back from shows all over the world with bags full of gifts to bestow on the staff like I was some kind of runway Santa Claus, the real choice items reserved for underpaid assistants and junior editors. How else were they ever going to get their hands on a Prada bag? But leave it to Liz Alexander to be the giveaway Grinch.

It started in Paris at a John Galliano show. Liz's eyes lit up like the headlights on a hummer when she slipped in the seat behind me and spotted my shiny new Chanel boots. She whispered my name, but I wouldn't turn around. I didn't want to take my eyes off John's new line. Before long, I felt a persistent tap on my shoulder. 'Where did you get those boots?' she leaned in and hissed. Liz and Chanel went together like chocolate mousse and whipped cream.

I reluctantly turned around, then. 'They were in the gift bag in my room,' I explained nonchalantly, as I clapped for a fabulous embroidered skirt.

'What gift bag?' she asked testily. 'I didn't get one.'

I just shrugged innocently. 'There must have been some kind of mix-up,' I said. 'They shouldn't overlook a Nestrom publisher like that.' I knew full well, though, that they didn't give the good stuff to just anyone. If your name was on the cover of a magazine, though, you pretty much had first pick.

'All I got was a bouquet of flowers and some perfumes,' she huffed.

'I thought I smelled something nice,' I said, trying to throw her off the scent of my swag.

It didn't work. When we got back to New York, I had this pointed e-mail waiting in my in-box from Ellen.

To: Staff
From: Ellen Cutter
Re: Gifts
Effective immediately, it is now editorial policy that we not accept any gifts offered, either domestically or abroad, for staff. Receiving gifts reflects poorly on editorial integrity. If you do receive a gift from any advertiser, vendor, or potential advertiser or vendor, you must return it immediately. Please let these accounts know of our new policy.
Ellen

Liz's obvious reaction was that if she wasn't getting good swag then no one would. But I wondered, did anyone at *Fashionista* – or any other Nestrom publication, for that matter – receive the same mandate? I knew the answer to that was no, as I knew for a fact that Myra Chernoff swathed herself in swag. I didn't mind the mandate so much for myself – I had everything I wanted and there was only so much clutter I could take anyway. But to take it away from my hard-working staff seemed just plain mean.

So I wasn't going to let it go so easily. I went to bat for my staff, writing Ellen a return e-mail, ccing Liz as an 'I know you're responsible for this' measure.

To: Ellen Cutter
cc: Liz Alexander
From: Jill White
Re: gifts
Ellen –
While I agree that senior staff members need not accept gifts, I wanted to make a plea to allow junior staff members to keep gifts or at least be able to purchase them at an in-office auction at a very low price. We could donate the proceeds from the sale to charity. Since there is a current budget freeze on raises, taking this away from them would be taking away one of the attractive aspects of the job, a nonmonetary bonus that saves the company money in the end and boosts staff morale. Allowing them giveaways is much more economical than giving raises, don't you agree?
Jill

It didn't take even two minutes for my plea to be poopoohed:

To: Jill White
From: Ellen Cutter
Re: gifts
While I appreciate your concern for your staff, I'm afraid that no matter who accepts the gifts, it is still a poor reflection on editorial ethics. The policy stands.
Ellen

And then it didn't take Liz another two minutes to send a kiss-ass response in support:

To: Jill White, Ellen Cutter
From: Liz Alexander
Re: gifts
Thank you, Ellen! I wholeheartedly support your new mandate. On the business end, the last thing we want to happen is for the editorial and advertorial lines to blur. If the junior staff members can't accept it, they are welcome to work at less ethical publications.
Liz

Coming from the queen of editorial/advertorial blurring, that e-mail was a total joke. But it was yet another unfightable battle, and like every unjust policy, we figured out ways to get around it. I told my staff members that if their contacts decided to send things to their home addresses, how was I ever going to control that? And if a gift bag was grabbed at a party and no one was around to see it, surely, then, no one would make a sound.

It worked, and the order was soon forgotten as items

began trickling in again and even Ellen started to look the other way. So despite the scare, *Jill* magazine entered the mainstream and my staffers stayed put, thanks in no small part to the swag, and the celebrities, of course.

12

Ellen Cutter Hosts Lavish Benefit at Park Avenue Home

—*New York Magazine*, January 2005

Is it possible for a full moon to last several months? Because if it is, it had to be the case at the turn of the new year. Or maybe my stars weren't aligning right or my planets were in retrograde . . . This was the type of stuff that Sarah knew all about. All I knew was that something extraterrestrial and strange was going on. Nearly everyone around me was acting out of character. There was an eerie sense of calm in the air, the kind of calm that you know is preceding one bitch of a storm.

While in this bizarre state of limbo, I played a lot of phone tag with Lynn Stein. We arranged to meet in L.A., as I was going out there to wrangle some A-listers for covers, and she was going to be doing business there as well. Plus, we both thought it would be best for our meeting to be out of view from prying eyes. I had to wait an anxious month, though, before it happened.

Meanwhile I kept waiting for the shit to hit the fan at *Jill*.

The state of affairs there was curiously calm, at least on the Stepford end. Liz wasn't bringing in any big, new accounts, yet Ellen hadn't called me in for a dress-down session in weeks. I wasn't harassed into attending ad calls any longer, much to my relief, but I was being prodded – politely so, but prodded, nonetheless – into doing more PR for the magazine to talk up its 'hot, new' look, which was definitely one of my strong points, even if I felt that the magazine I was out there pushing wasn't really mine anymore. 'Jill keeping a high profile can only benefit *Jill*,' Ellen chirped to me on the phone one day.

As the Stepford Twins were keeping an unusually low profile, Mindy Weiner's erratic behavior magnified hers. She was keeping tight control over the magazine, at least, and it was moving along smoothly, without any glitches. Yet she still seemed to spend many completely unnecessary late nights in the office. It occurred to me that Mindy might be a workaholic. But it was becoming clearer that the workplace wasn't her only addiction.

The one thing that drew more and more attention to Mindy's behavior was her growing mistrust of everyone. No one could ask her a question anymore, it seemed, without her interrogating the asker on why exactly he or she needed that piece of information. She was increasingly secretive, and controlling, desperate not to share too much. Even little things like asking her to let the staff know when drop-dead deadlines were would make her act as if she had to open an underground iron vault to get the answer.

But the worst thing was Mindy's increasing paranoia. For example, it seemed like any time Casey and I would have a conversation, Mindy would rush out of her office, which was diagonal from Casey's cubicle, and anxiously ask, 'Are you talking about me?!'

Casey and I would just exchange freaked-out glances when that would happen. Of course we hadn't been talking about her. We'd be talking about anything from my schedule to who we thought should win American Idol, and we reassured her that, no, we had not been talking about her. But with such behavior, Mindy could be certain that we would be talking about her later.

That's when I realized that Sven's 'cokehead' accusations might actually be true. It all came together one night when I left the office and saw Mindy having a very quiet, very guarded conversation with Mike from the mail room. Mike had worked at Nestrom for a few years. And he was pretty good at his job. Only pretty good, though.

The problem with Mike was that he was always stoned, and quite often forgetful. He frequently reeked of pot when he'd breeze by with his cart. For some reason, people looked the other way. I personally didn't care what he did as long as I got my mail. But rumor had it that others ignored his habits because he was supplying their own . . . alternate lifestyles, shall we say. That's why I grew exceedingly curious when I discovered that he and Mindy were 'friends.' What could a middle-aged mother in a Jaclyn Smith pantsuit have in common with a dreadlocked twenty-five-year old? Hmmm?

One night when Sven came to show me a layout, Mike walked into Mindy's office, which was right next to mine, and closed the door behind him. I couldn't help but stop what I was doing and rush over to the wall to see if I could hear anything.

'So, it's true, then,' I whispered to Sven as I had my ear pressed up against the wall. 'You weren't joking. Mindy *is* a cokehead?' It was more a statement than a question.

'No,' he answered sarcastically. 'I think Mindy and Mike belong to the same sewing circle. That's why they hang out together.'

'But do you have any real evidence?' I pried.

'Let's see,' Sven went on, in his 'duh' tone of voice. 'No, unless you count nosebleeds, paranoia, constant sniffing, and bags under her eyes the size of Bloomie's big brown ones. The only symptom she doesn't seem to have, unfortunately for her, is weight loss.'

I found the realization sad, and troubling. But I decided that as long as she got her work done it was really none of my business.

And it stayed none of my business. Until her paranoia blew completely out of control. And until she inexplicably turned against me.

'I need a raise!' she demanded one day after storming into my office and slamming the door behind her.

I wanted to ask her what she had against knocking and asking nicely, but I didn't want to agitate her even more than she was. 'Have a seat,' I said soothingly, hoping to calm her down in the process.

'Do you think I'm doing a good job?' she asked, leaning on the edge of the chair, her wig-do a scattered mess. In fact, all of her was a scattered mess: she didn't have a stitch of make-up on, black circles hung from the bottom of her eyes, and she was noticeably twitching.

'Yes,' I assured her. 'You're doing a great job, in fact.' And that was the truth. 'But the reality is that our budget is frozen right now.' Also the truth.

'I'm sure you can find the money somewhere,' she insisted, jumping out of the chair to frantically pace around my office. 'The cost of living here is killing me.'

'I know this city, especially when you have a family, can be tough,' I said, trying to be as much on her side as possible. 'But you are nicely compensated compared to most managing editors in town . . .'

'But I go above and beyond the duty of most managing editors in town,' she said. 'And I want to be justly compensated.'

I knew there was nothing I could do but put her off for the moment, and luckily I was about to leave for L.A. 'Listen, I'll look into it – I promise you. But I'm about to leave on a business trip. Can further discussion wait until my return?'

She assented, though she seemed annoyed by the delay.

So I went to L.A., and in between the schmoozing and the parties, I caught up with Serena Sax, who I hadn't seen in a while. And coincidentally, as I visited with her and played with her toddler, Alexis, I realized that my period was late. I remembered all that she and Kevin went through to have their beautiful daughter and it filled me with hope. Could I actually be pregnant? Would Josh and I be playing with our own little bundle within the year? I decided not to obsess about it until I got home, when I'd take a pregnancy test.

The meeting with Lynn was the perfect thing to keep my mind off a pregnancy possibility, and I felt so hopeful as we discussed plans for potentially working together again. She told me to start thinking of my next great idea for a magazine as soon as I got home. In the meantime, we had a nice, long lunch and I filled her in on all the Nestrom gossip.

'Ugh,' she said. 'How's T.J. Eckelberg?' she asked.

'Eckelberg?' I questioned.

She laughed. 'You know, from *The Great Gatsby*? There was that billboard for the optician T. J. Eckelberg with the big eyes watching over everything? That was my nickname for Oldham, with those big glasses of his. Not to mention, Nestrom does have a bit of a "Big Brother" atmosphere.'

'Yeah,' I agreed. And I told her I was starting to feel it more and more.

Little did I realize, though, that T.J. wasn't the person watching me most. It was Mindy, I discovered, right upon my return from L.A.

The day of my return she stormed into my office the second I got in. 'Can we finish our conversation about the raise now?' she asked urgently.

I hadn't even finished my decaf. And I hadn't even had a chance to go buy a pregnancy test, which was the first thing I really wanted to do. And here Mindy was, hounding me the second I planted my butt in my office chair. 'I promise you I'll look into it,' I told her. 'But I've just gotten back, and I haven't been able to talk to anyone about it yet.'

She nodded somberly. 'It's just that moving back to the area has been more costly than we thought,' she pressed. 'Our expenses have been piling up.'

I tried to stave her off by letting her know that I would follow up, but that it didn't look promising.

She nodded again, impatiently, then rose to leave. Before she stepped out of my office, though, she turned back to me. 'How was L.A., by the way?' she asked. She was trying so hard to sound casual that her question came off as anything but. She definitely had something up her sleeve.

'Fine,' I answered, shuffling papers to signal that I had a lot of work to do and that I really didn't have time for idle conversation.

'Any good new covers lined up?' she went on.

'There are a few possibilities. I had a few good publicist meetings,' I said.

'Who else did you meet with out there?' Her nosy question startled me, even though I had gathered that something was up from the way she had asked so pointedly about L.A. 'Did you see anyone else interesting out there?'

'No,' I answered shortly, then logged on to my computer. 'Just some friends.'

'Is Lynn Stein a good friend?' There it was – the bomb she had been waiting to drop.

I paused. 'What does she have to do with anything?' I muttered my response as if she was downright crazy to even ask such a question. But inside, I was pissed. Where did she get this information from? Casey was the only person in the office who knew about my meeting with Lynn. And I was confident that my secrets were safe with her.

Mindy stepped over to my desk, then, and folded her arms across her chest. Her eyes got all slitty and her expression became menacing and distorted. 'I know what you were really doing in L.A.,' she whispered. 'And I'm going to tell Ellen. I'm sure she'd agree I deserve a raise if she knew that while you were flitting around trying to further your career I was here holding fort – not just doing my own job, but yours too! Unless, of course, *you* want to approve my new salary. Then I might forget all about your meeting with Lynn Stein.'

I made my eyes equally slitty and tried to make my face equally menacing as I said plainly, 'I have no idea what you're talking about. And if you're burning through your cash so quickly, maybe you should think about dropping some of your bad habits.' I smirked as I saw her catch her breath. She seemed surprised that I had it in me. *I* was surprised I had it in me. 'Now, if you don't mind, I have a lot of work I need to catch up on.' I left her with that, and she speechlessly stalked out the door.

How dare she threaten me? Did she really think she could blackmail me into giving her a raise, especially with such a lame piece of information? She could certainly kiss any possibility of a raise good-bye, now. But the interaction still bothered me. How, I was dying to know, did she possibly find out that I met with Lynn Stein while in L.A.?

I immediately called Casey into my office to get to the bottom of this. 'Close the door,' I said when she came in. I got right to the point. 'Do you have any idea how Mindy Weiner could have caught wind of my meeting with Lynn Stein?'

Casey looked shocked, and a little hurt, but I raced to reassure her.

'I'm not saying that you told her – I know you would never. But she just came in here and tried to blackmail me. She said she'd tell Ellen about my meeting if I didn't get her a raise.'

'Blackmail? You've got to be kidding me!' Casey said.

'I kid you not,' I answered.

'What does she think this is? Some kind of bad rerun of *Melrose Place*?' Casey half joked.

'She is a bit delusional . . .' I joked back. 'But seriously, did you happen to put the meeting in your Outlook calendar? Or document it anywhere where she could have snooped? Could she have overheard you setting up the meeting?'

'You know me better than that,' Casey said. 'I can't imagine where she got the info. I only traded a few phone calls and one voice mail with her assistant, making absolutely sure that no one was around and the conversation was minimal; then I gave the info directly to you. I even marked it as "personal time" on your L.A. schedule.'

Yes, Casey was way too careful, and discreet, for the info to have gotten into Mindy's hands via neglect.

'I mean, unless someone in Lynn's camp told her, which I highly doubt, the only way she could have found out was by somehow listening to my voice mails . . .' she said, as if something was dawning on her.

'Actually,' she went on, 'now it makes more sense. Lynn's assistant mentioned leaving me more than one message, and I was confused because I had gotten only one. It didn't seem like a big deal at the time . . .'

'She's accessed your voice mail, then,' I said, not putting it past something a paranoid cocaine addict would do.

'How do we find out for sure?' Casey asked.

'The only way to find out if she's spying on us,' I said, 'is to spy on her. Do you have any friends in the facilities department?'

'A few good ones,' Casey said.

'See if they can find out if anyone has been logging into your voice mail besides you,' I said.

That night, I found out some answers to lingering questions of my own. First, when I came home, I rushed to the bathroom to take a pregnancy test. Much to my shock, it was positive. I knew better than to get too excited too early, but it was hard not to feel crazy happy and . . . totally exhausted. I usually dealt with jet lag much better than I had that day. But I had to pep up because that night was also the night of Ellen's UNICEF benefit at her home. Anyone who was anyone at Nestrom had to show. And I knew that no excuse I could come up with would be good enough to get out of it.

I told Josh the news just as he was putting on his tux. He was thrilled, but cautious too. After all, we had gotten our hopes up too high with my first pregnancy. But still, we were holding hands and beaming as we rode in the town car uptown to Ellen's. Josh looked so polished, so proud in his tux. I felt like a starlet in my custom-made Gerard Gautier gown. The sky was so clear that night that the moon seemed to throw more illumination than the streetlights. We stepped onto Ellen's Park Avenue stoop, and as I looked up, I saw some stars twinkling overhead. Maybe they were finally lining up for me . . .

Ellen's benefit was everything I dreaded it would be: a glam, celebrity-studded, high-profile, $5,000-per-plate event, which Nestrom was kind enough to shell out for her senior staff. So despite my exhaustion – and delicate condition –

there was no way I could slip out early and unnoticed.

I had never been to Ellen's town house before, but I had heard plenty about it. It was just as fussily lavish as I had expected. It was a Greek Revival number just off Eighty-fourth Street with a shocking amount of space for a couple and their two small children. A white marble staircase lined with a mahogany banister led to the three sprawling levels. The ground level, where the benefit was held, was also attached to a spacious garden, which some partygoers braved in the winter chill, their furs in tow, of course. Josh and I stayed in the parlor, which was full of all sorts of glamorous, old-fashioned details: antique moldings, ceiling rosettes, wide-slat wood floors, shiny chandeliers, meticulously carved mantelpieces, and priceless furniture outfitting it all. Ellen was definitely living very, very high on the Nestrom hog.

It was the type of party that was going to make the papers, with its white-glove service, string quartet, fine champagne, and every gossip columnist in town in the house. Ellen knew that this was just the type of affair to pander to the press. If it was for a good enough cause, and if there was enough glam and expensive champagne, no one would dare write a nasty word about her, or Nestrom, at least for a little while.

And they all looked as if they were having a great time, and ready to sing Ellen's praises. I chatted with Liz Smith, who I actually quite liked. She was a friendly, down-home type of gal, like someone who would be a good companion to belly up to a bar for a scotch. Then there was Cindy Adams, the gossip doyenne of the NY Post holding court, while Page Six honcho Richard Johnson cutting quite a fine figure, was cuddling up to anyone for a sound bite. The Daily News Rush and Molloy were there, though they spent so much time apart it was hard to believe they were actually a couple.

Ellen spotted me and made a big show of greeting me in front of the reporters. She was wearing a long, tight, ivory gown, probably a Vera Wang. 'It's a true party now!' she bellowed, rushing over to give me an awkward hug. 'Jill White is in the house!' Her attempt at hip lingo made me inwardly cringe. Outwardly, I smiled for the photographers as I was introduced to Ellen's husband. Josh had chosen the perfect moment to wrangle up drinks.

Ellen's husband was also everything I expected, and a bit more. He actually looked like he could be Ellen's twin brother. He had the same coloring, the same blandness. Even the same shade of blond hair. Except whereas Ellen was a power WASP, Carson Cutter had a very effete, effeminate way about him. It was almost hard to believe he was the CEO of a bank.

Ellen's kids – six and eight – were like a set of Hummel figurines in their matching outfits. I didn't see much of them, however, as they were quickly trotted out to be shown off before being put back on their respective shelves.

T.J. was there, of course, and for once, he looked like a power player, because he had donned a polished tux instead of his usual raggedy old sweaters. And Myra Chernoff was practically covered head to toe in fur, so much so that I would have fired at her if I had been on a hunting trip. And Liz, clad in a black backless Donna Karan, dragged her bored-looking husband around like he was some kind of lap dog. Though I had been trying to avoid her, we ended up standing right next to each other at one point, right in front of a photographer, as luck would have it. Ellen joined us, suddenly, and we were forced to give each other the fakest air kisses this side of Hollywood. Cindy Adams saw an opportunity and grabbed it just as the photographer started to snap away. 'Can I get a picture of Ms White alone, please?' he asked, motioning Ellen and Liz to step out of the way.

Ellen plastered on a phony gracious smile as she stepped out of the frame. Liz mustered one of her evil glares as she also stepped aside.

'How could you separate Nestrom's power trio?' Cindy Adams chided the photographer. 'Let's get some more shots of them together.'

Ellen and Liz came back into the frame, flanking but barely touching me. The tension among us could have shattered glass.

'Are you gals pals outside of the office as well?' Cindy asked, her notebook at the ready.

What a question. Liz and I stayed mute while Ellen fielded it. 'Oh, yes,' she said, the phoniness oozing right out of her mouth. 'We're quite the inseparable trio.'

I saw Josh out of the corner of my eye, who had returned from the bar. He appeared to be choking on his champagne. He moved in to save me from further questions and to bring me a club soda. As he pulled me aside, Liz stepped out of the fray, too.

'Is this your husband?' she asked, definitely more out of curiosity rather than sociability.

I nodded, then realized the polite thing to do would be to introduce them. 'Liz, I'd like you to meet Josh Andrews. Josh, Liz Alexander.'

Josh was his usual charming self, shaking her hand as she looked him up and down. 'I've heard so much about you,' he said. He had heard way too much about her, in fact.

'Right. I've heard about you, too. You're a Broadway actor or something,' Liz dismissively stated.

'I'm actually a playwright,' he corrected.

'Oh, well, I never have time to get to Broadway these days. Sorry,' Liz said.

Josh set the record straight again. 'My plays are produced off-Broadway, actually.'

'Oh! Off-Broadway! How quaint! I just love those tiny little theaters downtown,' Liz said condescendingly.

'Thanks,' Josh said. I could tell that he wasn't sure if she was actually complimenting him or not.

She leaned in conspiratorially, then, like she was about to share some kind of great secret or illustrious piece of wisdom. 'Let me know if you need some ideas for backers so you can get to Broadway one day,' she said. 'I know some people.'

Josh looked like he might burst out into hilarity. I wanted to pull her down by her rhinestoned décolletage. 'Thanks, I'll keep that in mind,' he said politely, being the class act that he is. Then he gently took my hand, excused us, and we both stepped off into the crowd.

'So that was the famous Liz,' he snickered. 'She's everything you described – and more!'

'I'm sorry,' I said, loving, of course, that he hated Liz at first sight. 'I'm sorry we're even here, and thank you for putting up with this overblown bag of bullshit.'

Josh planted a kiss on my cheek right then. 'You've done your share of dull cast parties. This is my payback.'

I did my part to schmooze. But I was so tired. And like a prince, whenever Josh noticed that I looked fatigued, he came to rescue me from whoever drained my energy at the moment.

At one point, we stole away to the library, where only a few guests had strayed. It was probably the most elegant room in the house, with its rich mahogany paneling. I rested my elbow on a mantelpiece there, while Josh pointed out Ellen's wedding pictures.

'Definitely written up in the *Times*'s style section,' Josh said dryly. We often made fun of how dull the couples they chose always looked, as if the perfect looking pairs had binged on Prozac right before the photo was taken.

There was a picture of Ellen, a vision in white and pearls, surrounded by her adoring attendants, like angels in their silk ivory gowns. I hated to admit that nothing much had changed about Ellen, though the photo had to be about fifteen years old. But it wasn't just her age. She had the same bob haircut; the same taste in jewelry; the same overcomposed expression.

I inspected the photo closely as Josh walked off to grab me a Perrier.

'Let me guess,' he said quietly when he came back. 'Large affair, at the Club, somewhere in Connecticut.'

'Bingo,' I said.

'The bridesmaids look like they just got out of finishing school,' he cracked. 'But where are their white gloves?'

I chuckled as I took a close look at the bridesmaids. There were a lot. I saw a few familiar faces. The maid of honor – who wore a slightly different dress than the others, didn't surprise me at all – Liz Alexander, with her fake smile. I knew she and Ellen went way back, and this just affirmed their unbreakable bond. It confirmed why Ellen was always going to bat for Liz, and why Liz eventually followed Ellen to every publication she worked for.

There was Barbara Sterling, Nestrom's vice president of human resources. I knew they were close.

But there was another recognizable face that came as a total shock to me.

'What?' Josh asked, knowing that I noticed something strange.

'I can't believe it,' I said, stunned. 'That's Mindy. Mindy Weiner. Third from the left.' And it was. Much younger, with different hair, but managing to look frumpy just the same – despite the elegant dress. I almost might have missed her had I not studied the picture. 'Is she here? At the party?' Josh asked. He was strangely fascinated by all the wild stories I had told about her.

'I haven't seen her,' I said, shrugging. 'Strange that she wouldn't have been invited, though. Especially if she's Ellen's former bridesmaid!'

I spotted Paul, then, mingling in the corner, and called over to him. Even though he had pretty much been stripped of his creative director responsibilities at *Jill*, he was still in charge over at *Profile* and much admired in the industry for turning it into a serious competitor to *Fashionista*, the crown jewel of Nestrom. In fact, I had heard from a reliable source that Myra was so threatened by *Profile*'s success that she had walked out of Prada's most recent show in Milan because she had been seated next to Paul. She was truly the devil.

Because of the insanity of our work environment, I interacted with Paul less and less in the office these days, but I still enjoyed hanging out with him socially. He dutifully obliged my beckoning.

'Am I totally losing my mind or is that Mindy Weiner?' I asked him, just to be sure.

Paul squinted at the photo, too, and nodded. 'Yep. That's old wig-head. But I'm not surprised. I heard a rumor she was an old, discarded friend of Ellen's.'

I started to feel a little duped, and a lot like Mindy right then as paranoid delusions filled my head. Was Mindy deliberately put in my department just to spy on me? I was aware Ellen knew her, but I never realized they were that close. I wondered, with Liz replacing Lynn Stein, and Mindy conveniently swooping in when there was a vacant managing editor post, would I be next to be replaced? Even with all of the concessions I was making? It sounded insane, but I couldn't discount the possibility.

I studied some of the other faces in the photo. Who were the others? I wanted to know. And which one was in line to replace me?

'Want to hear some good party gossip?' Paul then devilishly said.

'Bring it,' I encouraged.

'I walked into the solarium, earlier, you know, to snoop around the house. Well, I heard all sorts of giggling going on inside. Ellen and Liz were there, and when they saw me they got all flustered . . .'

'You don't think!' I said.

'Well, I didn't catch them in the act, but I wouldn't be

surprised if some hanky-panky was going on between them,' he said.

'Stealth dykes,' Josh added, in mock horror.

'I'm just telling you the situation as I saw it,' Paul said.

The notion was so preposterous, and so horrifying, I shrieked. 'The Lesbian Vampires of Nestrom,' I said to Josh. 'Now that's fodder for some campy off-off-off-off-Broadway play.'

'Hmmm,' Josh said, mocking thoughtfully. 'I'll get right to work on that.'

I spent the rest of the party laughing inside.

The next afternoon, Casey walked into my office, smiling triumphantly.

'What's up?' I asked.

She simply laid a printout of calls made from Mindy's desk.

'You do have friends in Facilities!' I said, impressed. I was also reminded of Lynn's 'Big Brother' comment. She wasn't kidding.

'Look here,' Casey said excitedly. She pointed to a line where it looked like Mindy had dialed voice mail. 'On this one, Mindy enters her mailbox number. But here, she enters mine. And here, she enters yours. Proof! Mindy has been hacking into our voice mail!'

'The nerve!' I said, not surprised, but amazed nonetheless.

'But wait – there's more!' Casey said. 'I have friends in Finance, too.' She held up a photocopy of an expense report. 'Remember when we had that off-site in Boca?'

'How could I forget,' I said. We had these dreadful

corporate team-building retreats every year – a Nestrom thing, not a Jill White thing.

'Well, here's Mindy's expense report from then that she had some poor unknowing assistant in accounting sign off on,' she said, producing a copy. 'What's all this? For a hotel in Disney after. And what about this? A business dinner at freaking Sea World. Doesn't sound like business to me,' she said.

'We were footing the bill for her vacation with her kids, too,' I said.

Now I had all the ammo I needed should Mindy ever dare to threaten me again. I'd just wait until the perfect moment to use it, especially now that I knew she was much more firmly ensconced in Ellen's pocket than I'd ever imagined. 'Good job, Casey!' I said. I knew I could count on her.

But it turned out that I never had to use the ammo, because Mindy did herself in.

The following week, on one of Mindy's most frazzled days ever, she was scampering around the office like a cornered mouse. And on her way to the art department, she walked – smash! – right into a wall. It was so crazy, even slapstick, that for a quick second I thought she was joking. Then she had a seizure before she passed out unconscious.

Casey promptly called 911. EMTs came and revived her, saying she had ODed. Mindy was then brought to the hospital to detox.

It was sad to see her completely unravel, and I felt bad for sometimes making a joke about her habit and then completely ignoring it, like it wasn't my concern. When the people around you don't reach out or care, that's what leads to self-destruction. And Mindy self-destructed, right there in front of everyone in the office.

I wondered, then, what about her husband? Why hadn't he helped? Perhaps he was fed up?

That was the case, it turned out. Mindy and I had a heart-to-heart when I went to visit her in the hospital. 'I drove him away. He took the kids,' she told me between sobs. 'I'm ruined. My whole life is over. I keep messing things up. I don't know why. Ellen gave me this job as a favor, but she hasn't even called to see how I'm doing. I guess I'm out of a job, now, too.'

I shook my head. I couldn't believe it; maybe it was the pregnancy hormones zipping through my body, but my heart went out to Mindy. I wanted to give her a chance, thinking that perhaps the paranoid monster who stalked the halls of Nestrom Media wasn't the real Mindy. This poor, broken woman lying in the hospital bed might be the real one. And she deserved another chance.

'You're a good managing editor,' I told her, which was the truth. 'But you need help. You need to clean up. And I want to help you.'

Her eyes opened wide then, as if she had spotted a miracle. 'But I've been so awful to you.'

'I would hope your recent behavior was because of the drugs,' I told her. 'So you can keep your job if you go into treatment and if you bring the real Mindy back to *Jill*.'

Mindy was grateful to the point of more tears. She kept to her word and checked into rehab. But as she slowly began to rebuild her world, mine began to crumble.

I was eight weeks along in my pregnancy, and all I wanted

to do was stay home and sleep. But I was still editing the magazine, doing press, attending fashion shows – all because I was afraid to incur Ellen's wrath if I were to ease up on my social schedule at all. But it wasn't just because of Ellen. Now that I was going to have a child, I wanted *Jill* to become more successful than ever.

But I didn't have a managing editor for the time being; the deputy managing editor was doing her best to juggle Mindy's workload until her thirty days of rehab were up. And the stressful pace was taking its toll on everyone.

I often wonder if I had done things differently – if I had just put Jill the person before *Jill* the magazine – if things might have turned out differently. The doctors say no, there was nothing that could be done. Still, I couldn't help but blame myself.

One morning, as soon as I got out of bed, I encountered a staggeringly sharp pain in my pelvis accompanied by a frightening dizzy spell. I fell to the ground, still conscious, thankfully. I called out to Josh, who was in the bathroom.

He rushed me to the hospital, where they discovered that my pregnancy was ectopic. My left fallopian tube had ruptured, I was bleeding internally, and I had to be operated on immediately because I was losing blood at an alarming rate.

At one point, Josh told me later, he feared that I wouldn't make it.

I know that this part will sound crazy, but I do think that I did die for a little while. I remember the white flashing pain, which then melted into a soothing calm that I had never felt before in my life. Suddenly, I was in Georgia on the lake fishing in my old rower with Alex, Mom, and Dad. We were all happy and peaceful, and it was a beautiful, sunny day with a comforting warm breeze stroking our cheeks.

As we approached the dock, I went through a whirlwind of emotions for the people who waited to receive me. I felt tenderness when I saw Josh reaching out for me; I felt laughter when I saw Sarah dancing; I felt comfort when Walter Pennington opened his arms, and beckoned me for a hug; I felt excitement when Richard Ruiz waved and winked at me. 'Everything's going to be okay, don't you worry. Things will turn out in your favor, sweetie,' Mom said to me as we rowed into the sunshine.

Then I woke up. Josh was gripping my hand. It was late at night. The room was full of baskets and flowers and good wishes. He told me about all the real visitors I had had.

And I felt a few intense emotions. I was happy to be alive, yet unafraid to die. I felt the love, comfort, and support of my family and friends. But there was also an overwhelming sense of relief and acceptance that my life would be a good one, even if I never did become a mom, and even if I had never heard of a magazine called *Jill*.

13

Friends Concerned for Jill White

— 'Page Six,' The New York Post, March 2005

I was a sucker for all of the attention lavished on me while I was in the hospital. But it was still frustrating knowing that the world was turning – life was going on without me – while I was lying in that Lysol-smelling bed. After the operation, and several blood transfusions, I was trapped there for a week. I tried to be upbeat, to convince the doctors each day that I was improving in leaps and bounds and that I was well enough to walk out of there any minute. I felt like a prisoner who was angling for parole with good behavior.

Still, it was good to have a mandatory rest, just sleeping whenever I felt like it, swaddled in blankets like I was a baby. And I did enjoy the visitors. My parents came – yes, both of them – which was a little awkward since they hadn't seen each other in years. It was nice to see them put on their best faces for my benefit, however.

Dad had the good graces to leave his cohabitator of the month in upstate New York, where he was currently residing.

And I especially appreciated his visit because I know how much he hated the city. He always said he felt like he was wearing a stifling, ill-fitting suit when he was here. 'You came,' I said to him, smiling, as he took my hand.

'Of course, pumpkin,' he answered tenderly. I was shocked at how old he looked, and how clean, with his beard neatly trimmed and his hair pulled back in a short ponytail.

'You're looking a little establishment, there,' I teased.

He laughed his still-charming laugh. 'I was hoping you'd say I looked wiser,' he said. 'But that's okay. I know you're probably a little delirious.'

He actually did look wiser to me. 'Then tell me, Oh Great Wise One, when does life get easier?' I asked, only partially kidding.

He sighed, but it was kind of a laughing sigh. 'It doesn't, sweetheart. Who ever told you that it does?'

I shrugged.

'The Whites weren't meant to live easy lives,' he said. 'Easy lives are for the dull witted.'

'Great, just great,' I answered, smiling the whole time. It was nice to have him there.

Mom, meanwhile, hovered a lot, as moms do. She fussed constantly to make sure that I was always comfortable, and that I had everything I needed, or wanted. She was making up for years of being so conscious of never spoiling me as a child. Mom was essential in getting hold of things that Josh didn't have the wherewithal to think of. 'Bring her her favorite pajamas,' she'd instruct him. 'And her comfy slippers. And bring better pillows. These things are like rocks,' she observed, while attempting to fluff the hospital-issue boulders under my head. Both my parents' reassurance made me feel like a kid again. They made me want to regress, to let someone else do all the worrying. Someone besides Josh, for once.

Poor Josh. He was ever the dutiful husband. But it was taking its toll – he looked exhausted. I was constantly trying to send him away to get some rest, but he was always reluctant to leave my side. I couldn't help but feel guilty. He had experienced a loss, too, but once again everyone was focused on me.

I also received visits from countless friends and co-workers, like Casey, who refused to talk about work for fear of making me even more stir-crazy; and Paul, who brought me goofy puzzles and kitschy toys to keep me amused; and Gerard, who brought me the softest, warmest, fuzziest pajamas he could find. His visit especially meant a lot to me since he was spending most of his time in Paris these days. Ellen, T.J., and Liz filled the room with fragrant flowers, overflowing gift baskets, and the guise of well-wishing. And I even received a surprise visit from a postrehab Mindy, who had visibly pulled herself together.

Sarah, though, was the best. She immediately cheered me up by smuggling in a cake for me. When we lived together, our guilty pleasure was to get an Entenmann's cake at the grocery store, drizzle the icing with nonpareils, and pig out. I laughed my head off when she arrived with her own homemade version of just that. Sarah played lookout for the nurse as I cut myself a giant piece of the cake and shoved it in my mouth. It was just as disgustingly sweet as I remembered it to be. It was heaven.

We also rediscovered the charms of soap operas, laughing about how we'd arrange our class schedule around *General Hospital* while at Bennington. Watching it together after all these years brought back so many memories, especially since the cast hadn't changed much in twenty years.

It was great to see Sarah so especially cheery; her desire to work more spurred her creativity, and she had written a children's book that I thought was terrific. She had submitted the manuscript and her portfolio, to the top publishers and had actually landed a book contract. That had boosted her confidence tremendously. So she took the time while I was recovering to crash at a friend's studio to work on it and visit with me each day. 'Taso and I are getting on each other's nerves,' she had told me. 'A little absence will make us both a lot fonder, I think.'

So Sarah was essential in keeping me in a bubble of girly comfort for most of the week, and making sure that I rested. I did check in with Casey every day, and though she said everything was 'business as usual,' I decided after day five that it was time. I told Josh: 'Bring me the laptop.'

He was hesitant, but he knew better than to defy me when I was in such a state. As much as I didn't want to do it, I had to check my e-mail and make myself feel like I was keeping at least one foot in the goings-on at *Jill*.

At first, I was comforted knowing that Casey was right – absolutely nothing seemed to be going on as I scrolled through my e-mail. But then a new one from Ellen appeared in my inbox – causing my eyes to bug out of my head. The subject line:

Liz Alexander named publisher of *Sweetie Pie*, a new magazine for upscale moms

I thought I was seeing things. But I read on:

Effective immediately, Liz Alexander will be leaving her post as publisher of Jill and taking the reins of Nestrom's newest publication, Sweetie Pie. 'Alexander was instrumental in the creation of the magazine,' says chairman T. J. Oldham, 'so it made sense to install her at the top of the masthead.' The staff of Jill is grateful for her contributions over the years, and we will surely miss her, but we are equally happy that Liz is remaining in the Nestrom family. Please join me in congratulating Liz on her deserved new position. Ellen Cutter

First, I thought the announcement was kind of funny – no, actually, really hilarious – since I knew that Liz not only wasn't a mom, but that she out and out hated kids. Suddenly elation set in: Ding dong the witch is dead! I realized. Liz Alexander had been moved away from the ad sales mess that *Jill* had become. T.J. must have finally seen the light.

I immediately called Casey. 'You heard the news?' she said, in her famous deadpan way.

'Yes!' I answered. 'But how long did you know? I can't believe you were able to keep it from me,' I said.

'I didn't know until just now,' Casey said. 'This was completely under wraps. No one knew. But we're all going out for champagne tonight.'

We chatted then for a few more minutes about all the possibilities for Liz's replacement. And when I hung up with Casey, I was hell-bent on coming up with a great 'get' list for Ellen. I was convinced it was a great opportunity for *Jill*. I spent hours on my laptop surfing the net to jog my memory and listing any possibility I could think of. There was that slick *Spy* alum, for example, and that woman who oversaw fashion advertising at *Talk*. I spent the whole day gathering any appropriate name, then shot off this e-mail to Ellen:

To: Ellen Cutter@nestrom. com;
TJ Oldham @nestrom. com
Re: Jill's new Publisher
Hello Ellen and T.J. –
First, thanks for passing along the news about Liz's new appointment. Though I am surprised at her decision, I think the move is a good one for her. I only have a few days left here, as my condition has improved tremendously. Thanks so much for all of your kind thoughts and good wishes to get well.
Here is a list of people who I think we should consider in replacing Liz . . .
Tom Kelly, formerly of Spy's on the market, as is Lily Cohen, ext-talk exec. Kathy Hunt, who is the number two at Joy, is an up and coming talent. I'm looking forward to talking further about these possibilities and other as soon as I'm back in the office.
Jill

All that work was for nothing, though, because the next day I received another e-mail, with this earth-shattering subject line:

Re: Roger Reynolds named publisher of *Jill*

My first reaction was, *Who?!* Then I read the short bio that followed. Reynolds came from a news weekly. Could they have found anyone more dull and inappropriate? Even worse, why didn't they bother to consult me? I was furious. I immediately got on the horn to Casey.

'What's the deal?!' I screamed. 'Did you forget to call me? Did anyone leave me any messages about needing my input on this? How is it that I'm finding out about my new publisher via mass e-mail?!'

'Good question,' Casey said. 'I'm stunned, too, Jill. I don't know what to say. They're not keeping us in the loop for some reason.'

'I'll say!'

Josh calmed me down before I could put in an even more hysterical phone call to Ellen. 'You'll regret it,' he cautioned. 'You need to cool off before you talk to her.'

'See why I need to get out of here?' I told him. 'Look at what they're doing without me! They're taking advantage of my absence . . .' I was jumping out of my skin, but the doctor, unsurprisingly, insisted that I finish my term in the hospital, which would be at least another day. After a Josh-ordered round of sedatives, I had calmed down significantly, realizing there was nothing I'd be able to do, at least right then.

I tossed and turned that night, preparing myself to give

Ellen a piece of my mind. But the worst, unbelievably, was still yet to come.

On the morning of my last full day, Josh came in with our usual morning accoutrements: a bagel for Sarah; a hot cup of herbal tea for me; and two copies of the *New York Post*, one for me and one for Sarah. He went back home to ready the apartment for my arrival later on – they were hoping to release me in the early evening and I was expected to be home for dinner. Sarah was going to spend the rest of the day with me at the hospital and prepare me for release.

Right after Josh left, Sarah turned immediately to 'Page Six,' which was her habit. I always liked to save the gossip for last, like it was a reward for getting through the real news.

I heard Sarah draw in her breath, though, as soon as she found the column. 'What? Good dirt?' I asked.

She just looked at me, spooked.

I didn't like that look at all. 'What is it?' I pressed, damn glad I had my own copy. I frantically flipped to the column as she closed her paper.

That's when I saw it, with a big bold headline:

Friends Concerned for Jill White

After an ectopic pregnancy landed her in an extended hospital stay, friends – and industry leaders – are wondering how the health – both physical and mental – of the perky editor-in-chief will affect the future of her magazine. With recent changes on the masthead, one can't help but wonder: Is the health of the eponymous women's magazine at risk, too?

'What the hell is this?!' I demanded, throwing the paper down. 'What the hell??!!' I screamed so loud that I must have woken up the entire wing. 'How did this end up here?! And why?!' I was beyond hysterical. After I had spent so many days of trying to feel better, *Jill* had to creep up and upset me even more. I was starting to hate that bitch – and the bitch who was in charge of it even more. 'This is why I have to get back there as soon as I can!' I told Sarah. 'I need to be there, like right now. I need to put a good face on everything, prove to the world that Jill, and *Jill*, are just fine!'

'Shh,' Sarah said, coming to my bedside to calm me. 'Don't pay attention to it. It's just gossip.'

'But look at this!' I hollered.

'Yes, it sucks,' Sarah agreed. 'And whoever is responsible for this is reprehensible. But you have to stop caring what other people think. Don't let this get in the way of your recovery. You need to put yourself first. You and Josh.'

Sarah then proceeded to give me the best pep talk in the world. 'Don't forget that Liz is out. This is your chance to reclaim the magazine. And don't let that Ellen intimidate you. She won't be as strong without her ally.'

'It doesn't matter,' I said. 'Ellen has it in for me, with or without Liz.'

'Don't be intimidated by her,' Sarah went on. 'You're stronger than that. You're your own person. She's an insecure woman who is not good at her job and is threatened by you. She just tries to keep you down so she can stay on top,' Sarah said.

'From the day we met she's tried to ruin me. Why does this feel like Hillander all over again?' I whined.

'It isn't,' Sarah said. 'This isn't prep school. Life isn't prep school. People like Ellen find that out the hard way. And don't forget whose name is on the cover,' she added.

'Yeah, right!' I said. 'Like she cares. I worked so hard to build that magazine, to make it what it is, just so she could destroy it! It's not fair!'

Sarah sat back down. 'Build anyway,' she said.

'What?'

'There's this great thing that Mother Teresa once said,' she said. 'It goes something like, "If you are successful, you will win some false friends and some true enemies; succeed anyway. What you spend years building, someone could destroy overnight; build anyway." '

'I like that.' It really resonated with me at that moment. 'Succeed anyway; build anyway,' I repeated. Sarah somehow always knew the right things to say – and do.

She picked up her copy of the *Post* right then, ripped out 'Page Six,' and ceremoniously tore it into little bits. She then threw them up in the air, like confetti. 'Fuck them!' she said. 'Succeed anyway! Build anyway!'

She was right. And I made my own confetti, too. 'Fuck them!' I echoed, tossing the little pieces into the air, just in time to earn a stern glare from a passing nurse.

I went home later that day, and I decided that I was going to take a few more days so I could fully recover and make sure Josh got the attention that he needed. Sarah helped me get settled in the loft, and then she went back home to Jersey. The break seemed to do her good; she was excited to get back to Taso. I know having her around was great for me.

'I'm going to miss you,' I said, as I gave her a strong farewell squeeze.

'Me, too,' she said, returning the embrace. 'Take care of yourself. And don't let the magazine get you down.'

'Thanks,' I said, not so sure that would be possible.

I was right, because the next morning I got a call from Casey. I hadn't even talked to her about the 'Page Six' item yet. I was still fuming and collecting my thoughts on how to deal with it. 'I need to see you,' she said. 'Can I come down?'

Something had to be terribly wrong. 'Sure,' I said. 'Is it about "Page Six"?'

'I'll talk to you there,' she hedged. 'Is there anything I can bring you from the office?'

'Ellen Cutter's head,' I joked.

She arrived about an hour later, looking worried and concerned. I made some tea and Casey didn't waste time getting right to the point. 'The "Page Six" item was planted from in-house; it came from someone at Nestrom,' she said.

'Ellen,' I said.

'I didn't say that,' Casey said, with a confirming look. Now I understood why she needed to tell me this in person. Big Brother was always watching at Nestrom. And this was one explosive piece of information.

'Why?' I asked. 'I don't understand why she would do something so awful, so cruel. And how in the world did you find this out?' I was always amazed at Casey's resourcefulness.

'Turns out Michelle is quitting because she says they stole the idea for *Sweetie Pie* from her. She pitched it to Ellen and, next thing she knew, Ellen gave it to Liz – poor Michelle wasn't even offered a position. Anyway, we had drinks last night . . . She told me the item was deliberately planted, but she didn't tell me by whom, though I'm sure your guess is accurate.'

'But why? I still don't get why she did it,' I pressed.

Casey tried her best to proceed delicately, but she had no choice but to be blunt. 'My best guess is that they're setting you up, Jill. Let's look at what's been going on. Paul's been rendered pretty much useless. They may still call him creative director, but all he is really directing these days is *Profile*. Liz has continued failing up. They brought in a new publisher without consulting you. Now this item. About "how the health of the perky editor-in-chief will affect the future of her magazine," I'm wondering, as crazy as it sounds, if they are setting up the perfect excuse to push you out.'

Could it be true? It sounded so . . . so evil. But I was Jill! How could they push me out of my own magazine?

'That doesn't make sense,' I said after a few moments of thought. 'I mean, if the magazine is doing so poorly, which it's not, why wouldn't they just fold the damn thing? Give me my name back. Bury it.'

'That's the thing,' Casey said. 'It's not doing poorly, like you said. It doesn't make sense to fold it. But if you were gone, Ellen could turn it into whatever she wants it to be.'

'A *Charisma* clone?'

Casey nodded. She always had my best interests at heart. And I had no reason not to listen to her. 'The funny thing is,' I said, with a bitter laugh, '*Charisma* keeps trying to look and sound more like *Jill*!'

'I know *Jill* is yours,' Casey said seriously. 'But it might not be a bad idea for you to walk away from it and let them crash and burn without you.'

I sighed. 'I'm going to take a few more days at home,' I told Casey. 'I'm going to think this over. In the meantime, do me a favor. Call my attorney and find out what the status of my contract with Nestrom is.'

I spent the next four days spending time with Josh, doing fun, coupley things to take my mind off the mess at *Jill* and so the two of us could just move beyond the whole pregnancy fiasco. We took long walks around the city. We cooked. We saw matinees of foreign films. We shopped in Chinatown. I even felt up to bowling one afternoon. It was like we were on an extended date in a happier time, and we were rediscovering ourselves after all of the in vitro, the hormones, and the baby strain. If our relationship could survive all that, I was convinced we could survive anything.

One night, Josh and I had a heart-to-heart about my work. 'Screw them, once and for all,' he said. 'Quit. You don't need this shit. All it does is stress you out. I don't even think it gives you satisfaction anymore.'

He was right. 'But, our expenses,' I countered. That was always in the front of my mind. The loft. Our car. Our penchant for fine restaurants.

'We'll be fine,' he said. 'We're done with all of this fertility crap. You're not going to risk your life again to have a child. As for the bills, I'll take on work script doctoring. I'll do anything, for crying out loud – I'll work my ass off. You have for all these years and you should take a break. Worse comes to worse, we'll sell the loft. Scale down a little. It's not the end of the world.' He shook his head. 'But if I know you, there's no way you're going to stay idle for long, that's for sure. You're way too creative not to have something in the works.'

He had a point. So I started to think a bit about divorcing myself from that stress-inducing bitch named *Jill*.

Everyone gave me a warm welcome when I sauntered back into the office. Sven had made a giant card, a mock-up of a magazine cover, with a photo of me on it. 'Welcome back, Jill,' one of the coverlines said. When I opened it, I got a bit teary eyed reading it.

'It hasn't been the same without you here,' wrote Rosario.

'You're my inspiration,' wrote Jocelyn, the *Fashionista* refugee.

Mindy signed it, 'I missed you!'

Everyone signed it – Paul, T.J., even Ellen. Her consequential, 'Welcome back!' made my blood boil.

Casey had let me know that she had heard back from my lawyer and that Nestrom's lawyers hadn't contacted him yet about extending my contract past its July expiration date. So now was the time to decide whether I would renegotiate or flee. I had thought about Lynn Stein's offer a lot these past few days, but I wasn't sure I had the energy, or the stamina, to start a whole other magazine at the moment.

I decided to buy a little time and fight, for now. My first line of battle: get that new publisher on my side.

I knocked on the door of his new – and Liz's old – office, finding him as he was unpacking a box. Liz's old office looked so strangely bare without the priceless works of art and feng shui furnishings. 'Sorry to interrupt,' I said, 'but I've really been looking forward to meeting you.'

A friendly, flattered smile crossed the man's face. He was in his late forties, early fifties, I guessed, with thinning light brown hair that betrayed his more youthful face. At first glance I would have pegged him for a corporate attorney, or a politician, rather than a magazine publisher, in his plain navy blue suit, white shirt, and striped tie. But though his wardrobe wasn't charismatic, he was welcomely warm and seemed very approachable.

'You're Jill White,' he said, walking over to shake my hand.

'I am,' I answered, returning his hearty grip.

'My daughter really loves your magazine,' he said. 'She's probably a little young for it, as she's eighteen, but she's always been a little too grown up for her age. She just packed a stack of back issues to take back with her to college, in fact.'

I pictured him as a suburban dad, the type who barbecued on weekends and went to cheer on his kids at Little League games. 'Thanks,' I said. 'I hope to make you a fan of the magazine, too.'

'Already am,' he said. 'And I'm really excited to be working with you.'

It was a great start, and I trusted this man would do his best in his position and I wanted to give him a shot to show me what he might be capable of. Maybe he could sell well, placate the higher-ups, and they'd let me be, finally.

I left his office with a get-to-know-you lunch date secured. And I went back to my office with a renewed sense of security. The clouds had lifted now that Liz was gone. Maybe *Jill*'s future would be rosy again, after all.

The thought put me in a great mood, so later on, when I got a somewhat surprising lunch invitation from Mindy, I didn't hesitate to join her, even though there was a lot I needed to do.

She looked great. 'I know you have a lot to catch up on,' she had said, 'but if you want to grab a quick bite . . .'

We had a very nice lunch over in a Caribbean place in Hell's Kitchen, where very few Nestrom workers dared to tread. Mindy was like a different person as she told me about how she was patching things up with her husband, and how being with her kids was keeping her strong, and straight. It was so nice to see her so unusually sunny. Her instinctual motherliness, the reason I was drawn to her in the first place, was coming through again.

'I can't thank you enough, Jill, for believing in me and giving me another chance,' she said. 'And again I'm so sorry for everything that happened.'

I reassured her. 'Like I said, you're a good managing editor. I didn't want to let you go.'

'It's just that Ellen always had this strange control over me,' she chattered on. 'I'm finally working this out in therapy. In college, it was doing her papers so she could spend more time with her boyfriend and the sorority. When we worked together for the first time, it was taking the rap for her wrongdoings. Then she made me the axe woman for her nannies. Next thing I knew she helped me get this job and was pressuring me to spy on you. It's crazy. Even as a full-grown adult, I'd do anything to be her friend and to fit into her clique.'

Finally I understood. Mindy was me at age fourteen at

Hillander, trying desperately to fit in with Alissa Ford and her crowd, even though I never could. I found myself paraphrasing some good advice just given to me. 'You're not in college anymore, Mindy. You're your own person and you shouldn't be intimidated by an insecure woman who is threatened by your intellect. She tries to keep you down so she can stay on top, so she doesn't end up exposed for the fraud she really is.'

'I'm starting to learn that,' she said, scooping up some callaloo with roti bread.

'A great woman once said,' I went on, ' "If you are successful, you will win some false friends and some true enemies; succeed anyway." '

'Wow,' she said, nodding thoughtfully. 'Who was that great woman?'

'My friend Sarah,' I answered.

14

The Wunderkind Has Wanderlust
— Crain's, April 2005

My parents tried so hard to make sure that my brother and I never got too attached to people or things when we were growing up. As a result of such well-meaning parenting, I've never had an easy time letting go of anything.

One childhood trauma in particular comes to mind as an example of how my instincts went completely against my parents' teachings. I was seven years old when Bay came to stay at the commune. He had to be in his early twenties; I remember thinking he was quite old, almost as ancient as my parents. Despite our age difference, though, I developed a whopping crush on him.

Bay used to jokingly call himself 'the mad nomad' because he could never stay in one place too long. He remained at the commune for a year, though, which I think was a long time for him.

Alex and I adored Bay because he would talk to us like we were grown-ups, not just kids, and he always found ways to make us feel special. I remember him telling Alex that he would be a great thinker one day. And I remember him telling me that I would be a great heartbreaker because of my beauty. I didn't really understand what he meant, but I liked what he said. I was such an awkward stick figure of a girl and, back then, no one would ever have described me as 'beautiful.'

Bay seemed to truly enjoy spending time with us, whether we were playing checkers or hide-and-seek, or whether he was just telling us about his travels. Those were my favorite moments – the travel stories. He'd tell us about how he learned to sail in Greece, or about what it was like to hike the hills of Switzerland, or about the time his motorcycle broke down on the back roads of Patagonia. All of his stories sent my imagination reeling about the big world beyond rural Georgia. And I could never hear them enough.

What I remember most about Bay, though, is how incredibly handsome he was. He had this windswept, sun-streaked light brown hair; a healthy golden tan; aquamarine eyes; and dimples so pronounced you could see them under his perpetual blond stubble. He looked like someone out of a magazine ad. I found it hard to take my eyes off of him.

Yes, I knew what 'nomad' meant, so yes, I knew from the beginning that Bay would eventually leave. Still, on the day that he announced he was moving on, my heart was broken. I couldn't stop crying and I remember hoping there was something I could do or say to make him stay longer. 'Remember, I'm a nomad, sweetie, and nomads gotta move,' he said to me, wiping the tears off my face. 'There are a lot of stories about you that I'd like to tell around the world. How am I gonna do that if I stay here?'

Dad consoled me by giving me a lecture about not getting too attached to people 'because eventually they'll either leave or let you down.' It was his skewed idea of self-reliance more than mistrust. 'The only person you can really count on is yourself,' he always said.

Bay left me a parting gift that I treasured. It was a Raggedy Andy doll, which I promptly renamed after him. Bay the doll then became my constant companion. He sat next to me at every meal and kept me warm in bed at night as I snuggled him.

Because I dragged him everywhere, Bay was one dirty doll. His eyes popped out and he lost so much stuffing that he was nearly flat. One hole on his neck grew into a full-blown tear. It got to the point that I couldn't keep his head upright anymore.

Mom spent more time sewing up Bay than fixing our clothes. Finally, she got so sick of resewing his neck that she just wrapped it in electrical tape. He looked ridiculous, but as long as he was in one piece, and with me, I was happy.

One time we went into town to have a picnic near the university. Of course, Bay came along with me. When I had to go to the bathroom, Mom brought me to the public toilets while Dad and Alex played Frisbee.

We returned to our blanket, and I panicked when I saw that Bay wasn't in the spot where I had left him. Needless to say, I freaked out. Everyone searched frantically – until Alex spotted a trail of stuffing. Our eyes followed it to a dog that had a mangled Bay clenched in his mouth. While Mom comforted me in my hysteria, Dad unleashed a treatise on why we shouldn't become too attached to our possessions.

So maybe it's the rebellious part of me that emerges, thumbing my nose at my father, when I become so attached to people and things. It was hard for me to let go of Joe Dryer, for example, even though he wasn't really a friend anymore. It was difficult for me to let go of Richard Ruiz, even though he wasn't what a boyfriend should be. The thought of letting go of my loft – the first important thing I ever bought – agonized me. I even find it hard to let go of ideas. If I'm convinced something can work, I refuse to let it die.

Dad would cringe if he saw what a princess of amassing I had truly grown into. So I tried my damnedest to channel him when I entered into a whole era of letting go.

I let go of IVF and the whole idea of becoming a mom, at least for a while. Josh and I did want to look into other options, particularly adoption, but we granted ourselves a break from any decisions, and any kind of thought on the matter, for one year.

And I had to let go of anger at the workplace and do my best to pick up the pieces of *Jill*. Now that Liz was out of the picture, I decided to even try to bury the hatchet with her by showing up at a party celebrating the inception of *Sweetie Pie*.

She strode over to me minutes after I arrived on the roof at Soho House, the private members club where the celebration was taking place.

'How nice of you to come,' she said, offering me nothing more than a nod and a weird, half smile.

'I wanted to wish you luck,' I told her, which was the truth. I didn't see the use of hard feelings anymore, but I also wanted to seem supportive of Nestrom. 'There's really nothing like the rush of launching a new magazine.'

'I will soon find that out,' she said.

'Listen,' I said, 'I know we weren't the best of friends, but I want you to know that I mean it – I do wish you the best.' I don't know what possessed me, but I did feel the need to clear the air with Liz Alexander. I was one of those people who couldn't stand the thought of someone not liking me, no matter how much of a ruthless bitch she might be. I was hoping that she'd let bygones be bygones, too.

'And I wish you the best, too, Jill. Hopefully, soon you will also experience that rush again,' she said, giving me a cryptic look.

I responded with an uncomfortable smile. What was that supposed to mean? Was I reading too much into that comment, by thinking that she might know something that I didn't know? Or was it just a typically bitchy/strange thing for her to say. 'Who knows?' I said, laughing a little. I wouldn't let her see the insecure rush that her statement brought on. 'Oh, look – an old *Cheeky* staffer is here. I'm going to say hi,' I said, trying to gracefully get out of the moment.

'See you around,' Liz said, as I slipped away.

I, of course, obsessed over Liz's comment for a few days, but then I realized her words shouldn't mean anything to me anymore, and that I should put all of my obsessive energy into undoing all of the damage that she had done to *Jill*. Again, I looked at her departure as a fresh start, so I quickly got to work on winning Roger Reynolds as an ally so I could rein back some amount of control. So when it came time to present the new issue to the Nestrom higher-ups, I felt rejuvenated, and ready to knock them dead.

I put on my best face and felt particularly on top of my game that day. It wasn't hard – I usually enjoyed these monthly meetings, when we'd not only receive feedback on content but brainstorm publicity opportunities, like which stories could provide talk show fodder, or which celebrity profiles were juicy enough to garner a mention on *Entertainment Tonight* or *Inside Edition*.

Roger shared some refreshingly encouraging ad news; the publicist had some really terrific pitches at the ready; results from a recent focus group were in, and quite positive; the head of circulation presented growing numbers. It should have been all good.

So why, then, did I feel like I was just taking up space and time as T.J. yawned and rubbed his feet and Ellen sat there like she was made of marble? Why did I feel like they were there just to humor me? This apparently upbeat meeting had a strangely tense undercurrent.

I shouldn't have been surprised, then, to find Barbara Sterling, VP of human resources, waiting for me outside the conference room when the meeting was over. 'Could you come with me a moment, Jill?' she asked, with a saccharine smile.

Barbara was the very same woman I had spotted in Ellen's wedding photo. A satellite Stepford, so to speak.

'I don't know if I have much time right now,' I answered, just to toy with her. 'What's this about?'

'It's concerning your contract,' she said.

Oh, that. I knew it was coming.

Right then, Ellen stuck her head out of the conference room. 'I'll be there in a few, Barb,' she said, before she closed the door, staying behind for a secret pow-wow with T.J.

As Barbara and I headed into the elevator, I mentally prepared myself for the negotiation. I was anticipating a bunch of back and forthing, a new term, probably no new money. Surely some mumbo jumbo about making certain goals. I had my own demands at the ready, too.

Barbara made small talk as I followed her to her office. It was so phony and forced that I wanted to knock her off her four-inch pastel pink Manolos.

When we arrived, she offered me a seat.

'So, then, what about my contract did you want to discuss?' I asked, checking my watch and hinting that I wanted to cut the bullshit and cut right to the chase.

'I'll tell you in a minute. It's important that everyone be here, first,' she answered, in a placating way, like I was some kind of impatient schoolkid. Then she excused herself to check voice mail.

The door opened a minute later, and Paul stepped in. He pulled out the seat next to me, nodded, smoothed his Prada jacket, and sat. I shot him a curious glance. Usually he was never a part of my contract talks. Strange.

The next minute, Ellen brusquely marched in, all business, and still stony, too.

Barbara greeted them both, then got right to it. 'Jill,' she started, 'Nestrom Media has decided not to renew your contract.'

Wow.

Not what I had expected her to say at all.

'Nestrom Media has decided not to renew your contract . . .' Just like that.

I couldn't believe it.

No negotiation. No demands. No seemingly endless back and forth. No ifs, ands, or buts.

Nestrom was not renewing my contract?

There was a heavy silence in the room, as I sat there stunned. I looked over at Paul, who stared at his shoes.

Ellen, however, did return my glance. And suddenly, she wasn't stone any longer. Her mouth twitched into a very smug yet very slight smile.

'Well,' I finally uttered, 'that wasn't what I was expecting to discuss.'

'I know, it must be quite a blow,' Barbara said, in her best faux-compassionate tone. Did they have some kind of HR acting school? If so, her training was really, really bad. I didn't buy her empathy for a second. 'It'll take you some time to digest,' she went on. 'And we're willing to work with you to make this transition as easy and as painless as possible.'

That was funny. Because right then I was gearing up to make this as difficult and excruciatingly painful as possible for her.

I took a deep breath. 'When?' I asked.

'The term goes through July,' she answered. 'And I don't see any reason why you can't stay through then.'

Oh, how generous! I thought. They would deign to honor the term of my previous contract.

Then I asked the question that I most wanted an answer for. 'Why?' I looked right at Ellen when I asked. But Ellen turned to Barbara. Yet another recruit to do her dirty work, I thought. Ellen wouldn't get her hands dirty even to wipe her own ass.

'Well,' Barbara started uncomfortably. I enjoyed watching her squirm. 'It seems that your vision and Nestrom's vision for the magazine have diverged for quite some time now,' she said.

That was the truth; I'll give her that. I half expected her to add, 'Plus, Ellen doesn't like you. She has always wanted to have her own magazine with her own name on it, and she hates that you did it first. So, there!'

But no such language exited her mouth. Ellen, however, finally did speak. 'I think this is best for everyone all around,' she said, trying her best to sound all sincere. 'I wish you the best, Jill, I really do. You're going to go on from here. But *Jill* isn't the same magazine you started any longer.'

Another truth. Yes, *Jill* was nothing like the magazine Paul and I dreamt up all those years ago. It had grown into its spoiled, annoying stepsister.

'We need a fresh, new vision to keep up with the times, which means we need a fresh, new editor-in-chief,' she went on.

There was really nothing more for me to say, then. I wasn't going to fight it. I had done all the fighting that I could. And truth be told, I was actually a little relieved that the decision to cut the cord from *Jill* had been made for me. I could now stop agonizing about it. It was a little freeing, actually.

'Would it be too much to ask for you to rename it?' I asked, knowing full well what the answer would be.

'Yes,' Barbara answered, point blank. 'We own the name *Jill*, and we're not about to rebrand it.'

'Then my name stays on the masthead as founder,' I said. Might as well remind them, as long as the magazine continued to exist, exactly who the Jill behind the *Jill* once was.

Barbara looked at Ellen, who nodded. 'Not a problem,' Barbara said.

'We'll get into the details of your exit package in a few minutes,' she went on. 'But I'd like to talk first about how we're going to present your departure. We're happy to work with you here. We all want to put the best possible face on this, and I'm sure you agree.'

'Okay,' I said. Then I sat silent. I was going to let her do the talking from now on, and I was interested in what her idea of 'the best possible face' would be.

'In light of recent events, I suppose the best spin is to say you are stepping down to focus on your health. No one will question that,' she said, giving me another one of her loathsome smiles.

'No. Absolutely not,' I said, shooting a dagger glare at Ellen, and a 'what the hell?!' look at Paul, whose eyes hadn't moved from his shoes since the second he sat down. It was amazing how goddamn mute he could be when he wanted to. This time, at least, he shifted uncomfortably in his chair.

'I don't understand,' Barbara said, looking at me over the top of her Armani glasses.

I started to boil over. 'Well, understand this – you are not using my personal business as an excuse for pushing me out. I'm offended – no, disgusted – by the mere suggestion.' I thought of Casey right then, who had it right all along. Why didn't I listen to her and prepare myself for this? I really didn't think they'd have the balls.

Barbara appeared shocked at my words. And she looked like she didn't have a planned response. Flustered, she shot Ellen a helpless look. That's right, I thought. Why don't you help her out and fight your own battles for once?

'Well, then. How about we say that you are stepping down to focus on starting a family?' Ellen said, thinking she was being quite the problem solver.

I snapped. 'Didn't you hear what I just said?' I had no need to be civil to the woman any longer. 'Or is that headband of yours too tight?' I couldn't believe the last part actually came out of my mouth. I mentally high-fived myself.

Ellen's jaw dropped. 'There's no need to get nasty,' she hissed, like a snake.

'Using my personal life as an excuse for pushing me out is downright nasty. And I won't cop to it. End of story.'

'Ladies,' Barbara stepped in, 'let's settle down, now. Jill, can you tell us what you feel an acceptable reason for your stepping down might be?'

I thought hard for a minute. An acceptable reason . . . hmmmm . . .

Would Ellen's envy be acceptable?

How about her stupidity? Or her loathing of me?

'Actually, no, I can't,' I replied. I was too angry, too sad, and too tired to pay these Nestrom games anymore. I was being fired from my own goddamn magazine. I had created it from nothing, spent years of my time and passion developing it, and watched it grow into the first and only legitimate alternative magazine that 800,000 young women read and loved every month. Fuck them. Legally, they could destroy it if they wanted to, but I was done – D-O-N-E – participating.

'No,' I said again, 'I really can't think of one reason that anyone with an ounce of business sense would believe.'

Ellen, the supposed businesswoman, glared at me. 'Wanderlust,' she said. 'We'll say you have wanderlust to try new things.'

It was as good – or lame – of a reason as any. And even though I would never, ever use a word like *wanderlust*, I agreed.

We then spent the next thirty minutes discussing the world's stingiest exit package: three months' pay for nine years of blood, sweat, and tears. When I protested, I was met with veiled threats.

'Certainly you want to keep the door open to work for Nestrom in the future,' Barbara said.

While I was tempted to say, 'No, thank you,' my common sense and my brain were clicking, despite my shock and the surreal situation. Nestrom was such a giant that there was a good possibility that even if I ended up at a completely different publisher, it could eventually be swallowed up by it, much the same way *Jill* was. And even though I wasn't sure of what my next move was going to be, I knew better than to burn those bridges if any plan I came up with included staying in the magazine game. I hated that Nestrom had me between a rock and a hard place.

We went on to talk about a nondisparagement agreement, which was mandatory if I wanted to get anything out of Nestrom. Again, I had no choice but to sign it, though I wished I could tell the whole world how heartless and greedy the Nestrom machine really was.

After agreeing to pretty much all of their demands, the details were left for our attorneys to bang out.

I let out a deep breath when I left Barbara's office. As I stood waiting for the elevators, I was surprised at the numbness I felt right then. I was expecting a rush of emotion – *something*. But I felt nothing.

Until Paul gingerly stepped out of Barbara's office and came to wait with me in the vestibule.

'Hey,' he said guiltily, before offering a hug.

I shrugged him off. 'He speaks!' I said. 'A miracle! I thought someone had cut out your voice box!'

'I guess I deserve that,' he said, once again looking down at his shoes.

I frantically pressed the elevator button. How was it that these things were so slow even in the newest, sleekest office towers?

'Look, you are so much better off,' Paul went on. Now, suddenly, he wouldn't stop talking. 'You can do anything you want once you're out of here. You're Jill White. People know you. People *want* to know you. I have to cling onto this job for my dear life. I'm nobody.'

'Oh, poor, poor baby,' I responded. I wasn't handing my pity party over to Paul – no way.

That didn't put Paul off. He just kept talking. 'You know how T.J. is. He's so fickle. Ellen and Myra are two of the very few who know how to handle him, for some reason. He'll be calling you in a couple of years to discuss another project, mark my words.'

That actually wasn't out of the question, I knew. Editors came and went so quickly here – kicked out, brought back, in and out of favor like a Democratic presidential candidate. But if I could help it I wouldn't willingly work for the man ever again.

'Hey, just say you'll forgive me one of these days,' Paul pressed, trying his best.

I had no patience left. But I did have a soft spot for him. 'One of these days,' I said.

The elevator came. I deferred to Paul, not wanting to ride down with him, just wanting to be alone. 'I'll catch the next one,' I said as he nodded, then stepped in the elevator, giving me a sad salute as the doors slid closed.

I pressed the 'down' button and waited another thirty seconds before another one came. I walked in, and just as the doors were sliding closed, a pale hand came out of nowhere and caused it to open. Ellen stepped in, seeming shocked that I was in there, too.

I stared at her, steely eyed.

'I'm sorry this didn't work out for you,' she had the nerve to say. 'I want you to know that I fought for you, but T.J. is just impossible –'

Fought for me? I had had it with her lies and her conniving. I couldn't keep my rage inside. I let it out, barely noticing the poor wide-eyed intern near the elevator buttons who looked like she wished she were invisible. 'Fought against me is more like it!' I fumed. 'Every step of the way! You made it your business to take something that meant something to me and hundreds of thousands of others and destroy it. How does it feel? How does it feel to ruin someone's dream?'

Ellen didn't even have a chance to respond. I stormed out

behind the frightened intern at the next stop, even though it wasn't my floor.

The only person I told before the official announcement was made was Casey, who burst into tears on the spot.

'You can't be surprised,' I said. 'You warned me.'

'I'm not surprised,' she answered, sniffling. 'But I was holding out hope.'

'Stop crying,' I told her, to make her laugh and to prevent myself from joining in. It had the adverse effect.

'I'm quitting as soon as the announcement comes out,' she said.

That's my girl! I thought, giving her a hug. But as much as I selfishly wanted Casey to march out the door right behind me, she had a family, and I wanted her to get every extra cent out of Nestrom that she possibly could. 'Don't quit. That's what they're hoping you'll do so they won't have to offer you a package. Hang in there and wait to get fired, which you eventually will. They won't want anyone so ensconced in my camp to linger, that's for sure.'

'What if I end up working for the new editor-in-chief, even for a little while?' Casey said hopelessly. 'I know I'll hate it and I'm not sure how long I'll be able to take it.'

'That will suck but I guarantee it won't be that long,' I said. 'She'll look at you as leftover baggage and she'll want to bring in her own people, I promise. Plus, it wouldn't hurt to have an inside woman to get all the good gossip from during transition time,' I chided. 'But when the time does come I'll do everything in my power to get you a great job.' And I would, though selfishly, I wanted Casey to come along with me wherever I ended up. I couldn't ask her to wait, though.

After we both calmed down, I called a staff meeting and made the announcement.

'I'm leaving *Jill*,' I said, 'to pursue other opportunities.'

To say they were shocked would be an understatement. Sven put his head in his hands and then wouldn't stop shaking his head. I knew he felt especially abandoned. Rosario's jaw practically hit the floor. Even Ruggles, Kyra the photo editor's dog, let out a little whimper. Mindy out and out lost it, collapsing into sobs.

I tried with all my might to hold back my own tears as I paid the proper lip service. 'It was a hard decision to make, but it's time for me to do new things. No one likes a mossy stone. I just started to feel a little stifled . . . and I need to move on.' I was such a bad liar, and everyone knew that.

'Tell us the real reason, Jill,' Sven said, clearly angry. 'How could this happen? What's going to happen to *Jill* magazine without Jill for Christ's sake?!'

'*Jill* will go on,' I assured everyone. 'It's just a new era for it. And for me. Thank you all for your incredible contributions, but more important, for your support and friendship during my era with *Jill*. And do me a favor, y'all, will ya?' My Southern accent only crept in when I was losing complete emotional control, and my face was now wet with parting tears. 'Take good care of her for me.'

The meeting turned into a giant hug session. And while we were bawling in the conference room like a bunch of babies, the halls of Nestrom echoed with a collective gasp as this memo hit every electronic in-box in the company:

To: Distribution@nestrom.com
From: Ellen Cutter@nestrom.com
Re: Jill White
It is with great sadness that I announce that legendary founder of *Jill,* Jill White, is stepping down as editor-in-chief effective August 1. 'The years I've spent editing *Jill* have been among the best of my life, but I have wanderlust to do new things,' Jill told me yesterday.
When *Jill* was founded nine years ago, it became an instant trendsetter among women's magazines. *Jill* the magazine, and its founder, have been among the most recognizable cultural icons of the last decade. It has been my pleasure to see them both grow and flourish since Nestrom purchased the magazine in 2001.
Jill is happy to be leaving *Jill* on solid footing. Though ad sales have not seen a significant change in the last year, newsstand is up 17 percent from last year, with a circulation base of 800,000 – quite an increase from the 400,000 of its founding. We will be looking for a new voice to carry over the essence of *Jill* and take it into a new era. A successor will be named shortly. In the meantime, please take the time to wish Jill the best in her new ventures. I know she will continue to be a success in whatever she chooses to do, and that is exactly what makes this farewell so bittersweet.
Ellen

My stomach turned when I read it. Ellen is sad and my farewell is bittersweet? Phony bitch.

My emotions were raw and my phone was ringing off its

hook, so I beat it out of Nestrom that day immediately thereafter. As luck would have it, I ended up in the elevator with Myra Chernoff. *Great,* I thought, *now here's* her *moment to gloat.* I nearly pressed the 'door open' button and walked back out to catch the next elevator, but I just didn't have the energy.

Myra looked over at me. *Here it comes*, I thought.

'Best of luck,' she then said, as she reached out and touched my arm in a sympathetic gesture. 'Now go show 'em up.'

I smiled. It was the first time I'd done so in about three days. How ironic that Myra would be the one to put a smile on my face. 'Thanks, Myra,' I said. 'That means a lot to me.' And it did.

'You're welcome,' she muttered, before we lapsed back to our usual stiff, hostile silence.

I went home, unplugged the phone, and collapsed into Josh's arms for the rest of the day.

I eventually did have to deal with the press, and I kept my promise to Nestrom and maintained an upbeat public face. 'It was the hardest decision I've had to make in my life, and it was very, very sad,' became my sound bite. 'I do feel like I am abandoning a great staff, and a legion of readers, but stagnation has never been my thing. But I do want to thank my staff and my readers for their loyalty, which really has been amazing over these years.' I'd inevitably end the statement with a tear in my eye. Sometimes it was just for effect, sometimes because what I was saying was really sinking in.

Reporters always wanted to know what my connection to the magazine would be once I stepped down. I wanted to tell them that my connection would be nothing more than running for the exit, screaming, and not turning back. But I'd put on my best fakey-fake smile and blather on how my name would continue to be on the masthead, and that I'd perhaps appear as a contributor from time to time.

'How long had you been considering leaving?' was another question I was often asked.

'I had offers that I'd been considering for months and months,' I always answered. 'And now I need to take the time to focus on them and decide which path to take next.'

Endless speculation went on about who my successor would be, and the press loved nothing more than to speculate what might be next for me. A magazine for older women named after my middle name perhaps? That was their favorite. Before I even thought about sussing out what *was* out there for me, the opportunities came rolling in with such force I had to actually hire an agent to field them all. There were book deals, talk shows, radio shows – even a satellite network that offered me my own channel. There were competitive publishers hungry for me to start another magazine, Lynn Stein among them, and there was the book publisher who wanted to give me my own imprint. There was the morning show that wanted to bring me on as a producer in order to bring in a wider, younger audience, and there was more than one network pitching me reality shows. It all made my head spin. Mostly, it made me feel confident that I was going to end up just fine and that I really didn't have anything to worry about.

But one thing happened that reassured me more than anything. One morning, I picked up the *Wall Street Journal* and found this headline leading the media column:

50% OF ADVERTISERS PULL FROM JILL AFTER FOUNDER WHITE STEPS DOWN

I felt a rush of different emotions reading that. Vindication, for one. But pride, most of all. It proved that I was essential to that magazine after all. Not any editor-in-chief could run *Jill*, simply because not every editor-in-chief *was* Jill. I think Nestrom finally realized this, too, and that accounted for its taking way too long to decide on my replacement.

Successor or no successor, I gave new meaning to the term *figurehead* over the next few months by checking in less and less. And that was necessary because I had to be weaned off of *Jill*, like a baby from its bottle. As time went on, the idea of never being there again became easier and easier to take.

Mindy was the first one to resign after I left, surprisingly. She was leaving to start her own business, a line of children's rainwear. I was happy for her to pursue something more than her current thankless job.

My mother was the second person to resign, even though she was just a book reviewer, and I must say I balked a little at her not making more haste. I told her that I wouldn't be upset if she stayed, though, knowing that she could use the money. But Mom just laughed. 'There's no way I'd want my good name associated with that sinking ship,' she said.

Thanks, Mom.

Rumor had it that people who were there since *Jill*'s inception were either angling to leave or heading for the chopping block. No matter what the circumstances, I stood behind every last one of them, and I vowed to help anyone who wanted out get a new job.

Before I knew it, the day came for me to pack up my office. On that day, I sat down and flipped through the very first issue of *Jill*, with Rory Bellmore on the cover, for nostalgia's sake. I was still proud of all I had accomplished with it, and no one would be able to take that away. I had, I hoped, gotten a new message out there to women everywhere, and no one would be able to change that, either.

I also read a few last letters from readers. Some were angry, accusing me of leaving them in the lurch. Others were very supportive, saying they were glad I was leaving, given the new direction of the magazine. They thought I was doing the right thing instead of selling out.

That's exactly why I loved my readers – they were so smart.

After I taped up my last box, said my last good-bye, shut out the light, and braved my last group of PETA protestors, I stepped out of the Nestrom building with a new mission: to take a lot of time off before I got involved in anything else.

Because I had to cleanse myself of *Jill*, first, before I could even think of taking on another project.

The first thing I did was go on a long spa weekend with Sarah, up at an old inn in Connecticut. We did nothing but get massages, take yoga classes, eat, read, relax, and drink bottle upon bottle of champagne to celebrate the publication of Sarah's first book, along with the publication of my last issue.

Then Josh and I spent a lot of time volunteering. We did

something new every week. One week it would be helping out at a soup kitchen; the next week it would be walking dogs from the animal shelter; the following week it would be sprucing up Tompkins Square Park; then it might be helping out at a nursing home. It was a great way to help me stop feeling sorry for myself, which I was certainly prone to doing from time to time.

After some time, I felt I got *Jill* out of my system, and it was one of the hardest things I had ever had to do in my life. At first, it was like reliving the same horror I felt when I saw that dog tearing up my Bay doll. But just like when I was a little girl, I knew that I had no choice but to move on. I knew that life would eventually go on, even though I would never forget about Bay the doll, or Bay the person. The same now had to happen with *Jill*.

I would never forget her. But it was due time to let go of her.

15

She's Totally Jill!

— Fashionista, October 2005

It was fun to sit back and watch the rumor mill run wild with the speculation of my replacement. 'How many people named Jill are actually qualified for the job?' was one of the tired, running jokes of the media press. But it would eventually cause the members of the press to reflect: 'How much of *Jill* was Jill?' and then they'd have to ponder how the magazine would fare without its founder.

The names being tossed around for the job ranged from the obvious to the ridiculous. Any higher-up at any women's magazine had her name mentioned as a contender, it seemed. Some obvious choices included editors who had once worked for me at *Cheeky* and who were now at other publications.

The ridiculous rumor was that Nestrom was going to bring in a celebrity to become the new face of *Jill* – a la Oprah or Rosie or Martha. Finding a celebrity willing to helm a magazine that doesn't have *her* name on it was preposterous enough; plus, being an editor-in-chief wasn't like receiving an honorary degree from a college. It was work. A lot of work. Definitely too much work for a full-time celebrity; and not a position for someone who didn't already know how to run a magazine.

And with advertisers dropping out of *Jill* left and right since my departure, I started to think that no one would be dumb enough to take my job. But someone was. Nestrom's pick turned out to be Bryce Bradford, who held the top position at *Jeune Fille*, the teen spin-off of the women's fashion monthly *Femme*. Bryce worked for Ellen as an associate editor at *Charisma* some time ago, and it was a well-known fact that she was desperate to get out of the teen market and step up into the world of women. It was also known that she was chomping at the bit for all the perks that came with it – front row seats at couture shows in Paris and Milan, invites to premieres – all the things about the position that had ceased to impress me long ago. I didn't actually know how friendly she and Ellen were, but I knew Bryce – she had written a few stories for me back in the early days of *Jill* – and she wasn't very Stepfordish at all. But Bryce wasn't known for having a strong personality – or voice – which was surely appealing to Ellen. After dealing with me, Ellen probably wanted someone as malleable as possible in the position. That made me feel a little sorry for Bryce. She probably thought she had a real opportunity to make her mark; instead, she was more likely to be used as a puppet.

I had heard about Bryce's appointment through the grapevine. But the rest of the world found out through a series of the lamest ads this side of Peoria. They featured Bryce donning faded jeans and a flouncy Michael Kors blouse casually perched on a stool looking over her shoulder as if to say, 'Editor-in-chief? Moi?'

Even more painful than her trying so hard to appear so cool and approachable, however, was the tagline.

She's Totally Jill! it said, right under her photo.

I kid you not.

I found the ad to be very telling in a lot of ways. Ellen was always quick to point out that 'my personality didn't have to be so tied in with *Jill*'s.' So I thought that she would want the new editor-in-chief to be sort of a nonpersonality, one of those vague figures who wrote an editor's note at the front of the book and that's all. And while that had probably been their original plan, advertisers were obviously worried about the future of *Jill* without Jill, and readers were writing letters complaining about my departure. So this Bryce ad seemed to backpedal on Ellen's initial decision. Suddenly they were trying to inject personality into Bryce. Publicly anyway. I supposed any personality would do as long as privately the new editor-in-chief let Ellen feel like she was completely in charge.

Saying that Bryce was 'totally *Jill*' also attempted to assure the readership that the magazine wouldn't be all that different from before, just in case readers were thinking of not renewing their subscriptions. How sorely disappointed they were sure to be.

I also took it as a strange and blatant attempt to separate me and, in a way, my name from the magazine. They seemed to be shouting, 'Jill White doesn't have to be the only *Jill* girl! Anybody can be a *Jill* girl! *Jill* is a concept, not a person!' Maybe they thought that by pointing out how totally *Jill* everybody else was, the world would forget about the real Jill.

Ironically, during my time off, I was rediscovering just who the real Jill was. I didn't spend a whole lot of time caring about *Jill* at all and had pretty much broken all ties. I did, however, keep in touch with Casey. It wasn't until I left *Jill* that I realized how much I valued our friendship, and just how much I missed having her around.

We liked to meet for early morning coffee every so often and gossip. 'The bloodbath has begun,' she told me one early Friday morning, as we settled into our cappuccinos.

'Who?' I asked nervously.

'Rosario, for one,' Casey answered.

'Ouch,' I said, because I knew how much Rosario loved her job. 'But she'll be okay. She's scrappy.'

'I'm not too worried about her,' Casey agreed.

By Casey's expression, I knew she was holding back bigger news. 'What else? Who else?' I was literally at the edge of my seat.

'Brace yourself,' Casey warned. 'It's a good one.'

'Firing?' I pressed.

'A quitting,' she answered.

'Who? Who?!' This type of gossip was the only thing about *Jill* I cared about anymore.

Casey slowly sipped her cappuccino, silently, just to make my anticipation more excruciating.

'C'mon, tell me already!' The suspense was killing me and the caffeine wasn't helping matters.

'Sven,' she finally said.

I gasped. 'No!' As much as Sven was one of my good

soldiers, I knew he had a hefty salary, and I also knew about his penchant for the good life. I thought he'd put up with anything to keep it all intact and I never would have expected him to walk out. Something pretty major had to have set him off. 'What the hell happened?'

Casey laughed. 'It was the craziest, most random thing. He just lost it. Bryce, Roger, and Ellen were constantly second-guessing him.' I knew Sven hated that, and he worked best when he was given a very long leash.

'Well, he made concession after concession for them,' she went on.

'Sounds familiar,' I interrupted.

'He even sucked it up when they started putting bursts on the cover,' she said. '"This isn't some Topps baseball card!" I heard him scream one time. But he did as he was told.'

'Then what happened? What threw him over the edge?' I was dying for Casey to get to the juicy stuff.

'He lost it over a coverline.'

I laughed. 'Go on.'

'Bryce had been changing them all last minute, punching them up to be all rhyming and alliterative. So one day, he gets this copy. Get ready for this one,' she said, pausing.

She was killing me. I just gave her a pointed look to go on.

She did. '"Tressing for Success".'

'Ew,' I said, grimacing.

'Exactly,' Casey said, pausing again to sip her cappuccino. 'So Sven comes marching into your – I mean, Bryce's – office and he hollers, "I just can't do it! I cannot work with anyone who uses the word *tressing!* It's over! I'm done! And I quit!"'

'Get out!' At first I couldn't believe it. But when I thought about it, I could picture it. Sven had quite a temper and he could be pushed only so far. 'I'm so proud of him!'

'Yeah,' Casey said. 'So anyhow, Bryce said she wanted to meet with me this afternoon. I think I'm getting the guillotine just in time for the weekend.' She didn't seem to be the least bit sad.

'Have you been looking?' I asked. 'How can I help?'

'I have been looking,' Casey said. 'And there's this position working at an investment bank . . .'

'An investment bank?' I echoed. I thought Casey was way too creative and lively to be working at an investment bank. I couldn't picture her putting up with a bunch of egomaniac traders.

'I know, I know – yawn,' she said, noting my horror. 'But it's located less than a fifteen-minute commute from home. I can spend more time with my family . . . I think I'd like to try it out and see how it goes. And it might be a nice change not to care so much about the kind of product I'm helping put out. It has the potential to make my life much simpler.'

'Then go for it,' I said. 'There's something to be said for quality of life. I'll just miss our coffee catch-ups.'

'I'll make special trips,' she promised. 'And, Jill? I want you to know that I know I'll never have a boss like you again,' she said, her eyes brimming with tears.

Casey's prediction of getting fired that day held true. And despite my warnings, she, too, was shocked at the stingy package she was offered. Still, she was happy to finally be done with *Jill*.

Over the next few months, the industry couldn't stop gossiping about *Jill's* revolving door and its bleak state of business affairs. Ad pages, which started to improve just before my stepping down, dropped another 15 percent, which meant that they had dropped a total of 65 percent from the time of my departure. Because of this, Roger Reynolds was canned just as abruptly as he was hired. Poor guy was the scapegoat for damage done way before his arrival.

The deathwatch for *Jill* was on. As much as that news should have given me glee, I was ambivalent about the possibility of it folding. I didn't want my name on something that had become a cheesy rag, but at the same time, I couldn't help but want it to live on forever, and become a classic. I thought it might have a few bad periods, yet a few new winds, kind of like *Saturday Night Live* through the decades. Though SNL had its times of brilliance and dreadfulness, the show is still an archetype, and no one will ever forget the original Not Ready for Primetime Players. A part of me hoped for the same for *Jill*. Even though it was morphing into something embarrassing, I dreamt that someday somebody would swoop in, make it great again, and redeem my good name.

Interestingly, as *Jill* started to lose focus, personality, and popularity, I was going through a personal renaissance. Instead of being a boss or an icon or a Nestrom drone, I relished being a friend, a daughter, and a wife, and I delighted in being on the sidelines for a while. Life became like walking around a foreign city. Sometimes I even felt completely anonymous, full of discovery and possibility. I loved it.

I especially took pleasure in returning the support given to me by the two most important people in my life: Sarah and Josh.

Sarah's children's book was released to great reviews. It made a lot of recommended reading lists across the country and her illustrations garnered her a major award. Shortly thereafter, the book ended up as number three on *The New York Times Children's Bestseller List*. To celebrate her success, I decided to throw her a giant surprise book party.

I splurged, renting a beautiful event space – a sprawling penthouse loft in Tribeca – and inviting everyone Sarah knew and loved: family, old friends, new friends, neighbors, people she worked with at the publisher. (Taso was a great accomplice for he photocopied her entire address book for me.) I hired a great dj; Jean Georges Vongerichten catered the food, with passed hors d'oeuvres and a top-shelf bar; and blow ups of her cover, and of the best-seller list, adorned the walls.

The best part was seeing Sarah's face when she walked into the room; I thought she might faint from the shock. The second best part was sharing in her glory as everyone congratulated her on her success. Sarah looked so beautiful that night, her thick, dark hair falling in waves around her beaming face. And it was satisfying to see Sarah receive all of the attention and praise she deserved. I loved making Sarah feel like queen for the night.

I thought back on our friendship as I watched her that night. I remembered the years in college, how silly we sometimes were, and how she saved me from ditching my college career for Richard Ruiz. I reflected on our time living together in New York – all the fun we made though we didn't have two nickels to rub together. I felt remorse when I recalled the years we grew apart, when I was too busy and selfinvolved to connect with her. And I reveled in the fact that our friendship now was stronger than it had ever been. Sarah was like my sister, always looking out for me, always full of good advice. I'll never take her friendship for granted again.

My relationship with Josh was also undergoing a rejuvenation. We took a long-overdue honeymoon to Bali, where we renewed our vows on the beach, and spent days hiking in the rice paddies and swimming in the azure ocean. At home, I spent entire days shopping and learning to cook dinner for us in an actual oven, rather than the microwave. And he, too, achieved a landmark in his career. Josh's current production of 'Between Rivers,' one of his most well-received dramas, won an Obie award, and talks started about bringing it to Broadway.

So life was good. Everyone around me was flourishing. And I was too happy to cheerlead for the two people who always helped me stay on track, even when I'd be heading for a major derailment. During the years when I didn't know where *Jill* ended and where Jill began, they showed me the way and forced me to stay true to myself, something I know I couldn't have done on my own. A good lesson to learn in my middle age, if perhaps a little late. It would be one of the first things I'd teach my child.

Yes, child.

A bit of a miracle occurred. At the age of forty, with one fallopian tube and without a battery of hormones, I somehow became pregnant. I couldn't help but feel slightly stressed out about it, unwilling for another crushing disappointment, but the prognosis was great, according to my doctors. The egg had implanted correctly this time, I was healthy, and everything looked good.

Even I could feel it. Something was very different and something felt very right about this pregnancy.

The fact that I was expecting facilitated the need for me to make some kind of career decision, so I signed on to start my own channel on the satellite radio network. It was too good of an opportunity to pass up. I would be responsible for programming the channel, along with having my own talk show. It seemed like the perfect situation: a forum for talk without all of the bullshit of being on camera. I also had an idea for a show that would feature emerging independent bands. And despite all of my freedom, it felt good to be going back to work.

On the day I signed the contract, I decided to walk home from my attorney's office, even though it was one of those dreary, late-spring New York afternoons. I felt keyed up, and what better way to use that energy than to walk to the Village from midtown. I forgot an umbrella, however. So of course the skies opened up and it started to pour.

I ducked into the lobby of an office building, waiting for the storm to pass. While anxiously standing in the vestibule, I spotted a newsstand on the opposite side of the corridor. I saw four unmistakable letters jumping out at me from the collection of magazines: J-I-L-L, spelled out in fuchsia Day-Glo.

It beckoned me, and I couldn't resist. So I walked over to the newsstand and picked it up.

There on the cover was a plastic-looking Katy Hanson, the cheesy reality show winner cum pop star.

Laughing, he did so. 'Oh, baby Buddha,' he said reverently, 'bring Daddy a great big movie deal.' He kissed my belly once more, then sprang out of bed. 'What time is Serena picking you up?' he asked for the third time since I had awoken thirty minutes ago.

I supposed his excitement about the meeting caused him to be a little forgetful. 'Eleven-thirty, like every week,' I answered. 'Remember it because that's the third and last time I'm answering that question.'

He anxiously checked his watch. 'I just want to know how long I'm going to have to pine for your return,' he said.

I tossed a pillow at him and hauled my bulk out of bed. 'What time is your meeting?'

He tossed the pillow back at me. 'Uh . . . two-thirty,' he said. 'But I have a lot I need to do before then.'

I could tell he had a lot on his mind as he fidgeted around, checking his cell phone, looking at his watch, and pacing from room to room. 'Are you going to be ready when she gets here?' he called from the kitchen.

I laughed. He was projecting all of his anxiety onto my day, too. 'Of course I'll be ready,' I called back. 'It doesn't take a whole lot to prepare for "bend "n" birth." '

'Bend 'n' birth' is what Serena and I jokingly called our weekly pre-natal yoga lesson. Serena was about two months behind me, and as a birthday gift she secured private classes for us while she filmed a movie in New York. And Josh knew my weekly routine – all I had to do was put on my yoga sweats, slip on flip-flops, grab my mat and I was ready to go. All of a sudden, he was stressing out about it.

The buzzer rang. 'She's here!' he called.

'We have time,' I said, looking at the clock. 'Tell her to come up.'

Was that an exasperated sigh I heard? I couldn't wait for this meeting of his to be over so Josh could go back to being his old, relaxed self.

I readied myself as Serena came up. She was a bundle of energy, too, bounding into the loft, ready to take on the yoga world.

'Still no bump? You're incredible,' I said. She was barely showing, and I was jealous of her still-lithe figure. As much as I loved being pregnant, I couldn't wait to get my old shape back.

But she had no time for chitchat today, and she, too, was rushing me out the door. 'Ready?' she prodded. 'Let's go. I have a zillion questions for Philippe today.'

'All right, all right, I'm going!' I said. 'You ever feel like everybody is on one schedule, and you're on another?'

'Let's go,' she said, plaintively opening the door, and quickly running out of patience.

We briskly walked to the studio, then had a nice, relaxing hour and a half class. Afterward, Serena was the sluggish one, asking Philippe for extra help, packing up her mat like she was in slow motion, stopping at the Jamba Juice for a smoothie, and poking her nose in what seemed like every boutique in the Village as we worked our way back to the loft. Usually, we just parted ways after class, but today Serena said she wanted to come over and hang out with me for a while. I was happy to have her over, as Josh would be out and I had nothing in particular to do.

We talked a lot of baby talk on the way home. It was great

having a friend who was pregnant at the same time so I didn't feel guilty about that making up most of my conversation. 'How am I going to do this?' I fretted, having one of my frequent moments of mommy-to-be panic. 'I don't have the first clue about raising a child. Maybe I'm too old. Maybe I'm too set in my ways. Maybe teaching parenting to me is like teaching an old dog . . .'

Serena laughed it off. 'You're going to be a great mom; don't worry,' she said. 'You'll be surprised how easily it will come to you. And when you have moments when you don't know what to do, just call me. Or call Sarah. You have a million people who are happy to give you advice.'

That calmed me down for the moment. But I started to feel all anxious again as we rode the elevator up to the loft. I realized it was because of Serena, who suddenly became all full of nervous energy again. What was with the world today? I wondered. I would need another yoga class to relax if she kept that up.

I did my best to keep my serenity as I pulled out my keys and opened the door – only to be startled by a chorus of screaming voices.

'Surprise!' they shouted, nearly sending me into labor.

Now it all made sense. Today was the day of my baby shower.

I stood there, stunned, in the doorway. I wasn't expecting a shower, thinking maybe I was too old for one. But seeing all my favorite faces there, I was glad that no one else agreed.

I looked around the loft. In two and a half hours, Josh had whisked in twenty people, decorated it all in pink, blue, and yellow; and snuck in caterers. He walked over and threw his arms around me. 'Well, come in,' he said. 'Enjoy your hen party. I have my meeting to attend and then some male bonding to do afterward.'

'You're amazing,' I said, returning a giant hug.

'Believe me, I had a lot of help,' he said, before giving me a kiss and shouting a good-bye to the apartment full of women.

When he left, I was finally able to concentrate on exactly who was in the room with me.

'Mom!' I said, as she grabbed me in an embrace. 'Where have you been hiding?'

'I spent last night with my friend,' she said. I knew which 'friend' she was referring to: a new man in her life, an architect she met at a lecture. It seemed like it was getting serious. The fact that she had finally started divorce proceedings tipped me off to that. 'I'm hoping you can meet him later on or tomorrow?' she whispered.

I told her that I'd love to. It was about time she moved on and I was really happy for her.

Sarah, of course, was there, and I had a sneaking suspicion that she and Serena were Josh's accomplices all along. After all, I had asked Sarah just a few weeks ago to be the child's godmother. Not that I was religious, or that there would be a christening or anything. But I wanted Sarah to know that she was without a doubt the person I would want caring for my child should anything – God forbid – happen to Josh and me.

'I wanted to get you a subscription to *Sweetie Pie*, but I'm afraid it folded before I even got a chance,' Casey joked when I greeted her. We both laughed, relishing the quick demise of Liz Alexander's new magazine for 'upscale moms.' It was so great to see her – we hadn't gotten together in a while, though we often chatted on the phone, especially since there was a lot of good industry gossip going around lately.

Turns out the Stepford Twins went down together. It was recently announced that *Jill* was finally being put out of its glossy misery, and along with it, T.J. finally cut Ellen loose. In my opinion, T.J. just couldn't tolerate all the negative press surrounding my 'resignation' and the media's subsequent questioning business savvy. After all, *Jill* and brand new *Sweetie Pie* tanked at the same time. In the end, both advertisers and readers concluded that *Jill* really did need Jill, or at least a Jill-like hand to guide it. As for *Sweetie Pie*, the critics had a field day. Liz obviously had no idea what parents in America wanted to read. The debut issue featured a fur-clad baby on the cover and coverlines like 'Seeing Belize with Your Newborn' and 'Giving Your Toddler the Academic Edge.' So, in the end, it wasn't the critics who did it in; it was the fact that there was simply no market for such a snobby, out-of-touch magazine, and it folded after only that first issue. And I guess it was then that T.J. finally saw how much Ellen was costing Nestrom. Or perhaps he just couldn't tolerate the bad press she had been generating. Whatever the case, I tried my best not to wish her ill. I had come to believe in karma, and I just wanted Ellen Cutter to stay far away from anything I was involved in. And that's exactly what went through my mind when I received a phone call from her, coincidentally – or not – just after the announcement of my new satellite radio gig.

'Just wanted to congratulate you, Jill,' she said in her syrupy way, like we were good old friends or something. 'And keep me in mind if you hear of anything that might be right for me.'

Sure, I thought. I knew of something just perfect for her. It's called early retirement. No reason anybody else in the world should be subjected to her reign of incompetence.

But today I wasn't going to dwell on Jill the magazine. In fact, seeing all these people I loved so much, I didn't want to dwell on Jill at all. 'Casey, so tell me how the new job is going.'

Casey told me that things were going quite well in her new position at the investment bank. I was glad – and sorry – to hear it. Glad because Casey deserved to be happy. Sorry because I had hoped to bring her back to work for me. I started to think of ways to woo her . . . perhaps a nicely paying part-time gig would do it. I made a mental note to discuss it with her next week.

'I can't wait another minute for you to open this,' Casey said suddenly, handing me a small, wrapped box. 'Open it now,' she demanded.

I did. Inside were matching mother/baby T-shirts with a photo of *Jill*'s first cover emblazoned on the front of each. 'In memoriam,' Casey said. 'And so you and your kid will never forget.'

'How could I ever forget?' I said, and I meant it. I thought about all of the people responsible for putting it together, and where they were now. The *Jill* experience, for the most part, led to better things for those involved.

Sven, for example, was now the art director at a top men's magazine, where he got to shoot more scantily clad women than he ever dreamed possible. Mindy's children's rainwear really took off; I often spotted the cute, brightly colored ponchos and boots in a number of boutiques around town. Rosario was working as a dj full-time, which was where her heart had always been. Paul had been promoted at Nestrom, back in T.J.'s favor since Ellen's departure.

And Liz Alexander had yet to be heard from again . . . Although whenever and wherever Ellen landed, Liz was sure to follow.

I thanked Casey and put the T-shirts back in the box. It was time to stop dwelling on the past and to think of all of the exciting new things I had coming. 'So, what do you guys think?' I asked as we settled into lunch. 'Boy or girl?'

Everyone put in their two-cents for a noisy minute before Sarah said, 'I have a fail-safe way to tell. It's never been wrong in my family.'

'Let's do it, then!' I urged.

'All I need is your wedding ring,' Sarah instructed. 'And some string. Then we're ready for the experiment.'

I slipped my band off my finger, then waddled into the kitchen to grab some string.

'Sit down, but stick out your belly,' Sarah then ordered, taking me by the hand and leading me to the couch. Everyone gathered around me as I jutted out my belly – not hard to do at this point.

Sarah looped my ring through about a foot of string, then tied the two loose ends together. She then dangled the ring over my belly before swinging it like a pendulum. It continued to swing back and forth for a few seconds before it settled into circular motions.

'Aha!' Sarah said. 'There's our answer!'

'What is it?' I implored.

Sarah stopped the ring. 'Well, according to trusty Greek superstition, you're having a girl!'

Mom shrieked. The others clapped. I laughed. Of course I was going to be happy with a living, breathing baby of either sex, especially after all I had been through the last couple of years. And regardless of its sex, I had a few life lessons I wanted to pass on to this child.

First, *try to understand your parents*, I thought, as I looked over at my mom. *They're only human and they are entitled to make mistakes*.

I thought about the hard times at Hillander followed by my blossoming at Bennington. *Brave the bad; good times will follow in spades*.

I remembered my first day at *Cheeky* and the early years of *Jill. Follow your dreams and surround yourself with your passions, and passionate people, no matter what*.

And finally, I looked around at the group of amazing women who had loved and supported me when so many others – those worst kind of women – had tried their hardest to make me lose faith in myself. *Be proud of who you are, no matter who tries to convince you otherwise*.

That's all I wanted my child to come away with. I hoped he or she was smart. And I hoped to give him or her every opportunity in the world. I'd also be sure that she or he understood how to be humble. If my child's feet ever stopped touching the ground, a visit to Grandma or Grandpa would surely remedy that.

But I was jumping the gun. The child would need nothing but unconditional love for a while, and I was certainly ready to give that. And I was going to be a well-prepared mom – my friends were certainly seeing to that. I turned my mind away from my parenting philosophies to open gifts.

There were a lot of useful things, like a BabyBjörn carrier, a bassinet, all manner of cute onesies, baby books, crib toys, and picture frames. As I looked around at the faces of my loved ones, I thought, *If this baby will come to know people like this, then he or she will be truly blessed.*

After the gifts, there was cake, and we finally finished with the baby talk, for a while. I mentioned putting the finishing touches on the radio channel, which was going to be called *Girlie*.

'I like it,' Casey said approvingly.

I did, too. I was still at a loss for the name of my talk show, however. 'Anyone have any great ideas?' I asked the group.

'Why not resurrect *Jill*?' Sarah said. 'Now that the magazine is dead, the name is up for grabs.'

'No way,' I said. 'I'm not giving my name to anything ever again. I've learned that lesson the hard way.'

'Not anything? Ever?' Serena pressed.

'C'mon!' Sarah urged.

'Well, it is a perfectly fine name,' I answered.

'It's a beautiful name!' Mom chimed in.

'Well, if Sarah's right about the sex, I guess I could make just one exception,' I relented, touching my belly. 'Maybe as her middle name,' I considered, realizing, for the first time, that the era of my most important creation was about to begin.

LORELEI MATHIAS

Step on it, Cupid

Amelie's life is arranged just how she likes it. Well, most of the time.

She has a brilliant job she adores, a great social life and a love life she can take or leave. So it's a shock when she realises that everyone she knows seems to be happily coupled up. Is it time she thought about settling down?

Assigned a nightmarish project in work – writing the ad campaign for Britain's biggest speed-dating company – she is forced into doing lots of market research, very much against her will. But with her best mate Duncan, her annoying boss Joshua and her ex-boyfriend Jack all causing havoc in her life, maybe a speed-dating romance could be her salvation?

Charming, engrossing and very romantic, *Step on it, Cupid* is a modern spin on the oldest story of them all – how to fall in love . . .

978 0 7553 3272 4

little black dress

SWAN ADAMSON

My Three Husbands

What's a girl to do when husbands just keep lining up?

Meet Venus Gilroy: twenty-five, carefree, irresistible, and with a nasty habit of getting hitched to the wrong guy.

Husband No 1: would have been a winner, if it hadn't been for the forgery and embezzlement charges.

Husband No 2: sometimes a girl has to realise – meeting a husband in a strip bar will never end well.

Husband No 3: is the real deal. Isn't he? Surely sexy, rugged, *principled* Tremaynne is finally the right one for Venus?

With her insane mother, not to mention her two gay dads, plus porn-video-store-owner boss, all weighing in with advice, it's time for Venus to learn for herself – how you know that Mr Right . . . doesn't turn out to be Mr Wrong.

978 0 7553 3364 6

little black dress

Now you can buy any of these other **Little Black Dress** titles from your bookshop or *direct from the publisher*.

FREE P&P AND UK DELIVERY
(Overseas and Ireland £3.50 per book)

Decent Exposure	Phillipa Ashley	£4.99
The Men's Guide to the Women's Bathroom	Jo Barrett	£4.99
How to Sleep with a Movie Star	Kristin Harmel	£4.99
Pick Me Up	Zoë Rice	£4.99
The Balance Thing	Margaret Dumas	£4.99
The Kept Woman	Susan Donovan	£4.99
I'm in No Mood for Love	Rachel Gibson	£4.99
Sex, Lies and Online Dating	Rachel Gibson	£4.99
Daisy's Back in Town	Rachel Gibson	£4.99
Spirit Willing, Flesh Weak	Julie Cohen	£4.99
Blue Christmas	Mary-Kay Andrews	£4.99
The Bachelorette Party	Karen McCullah Lutz	£4.99
My Three Husbands	Swan Adamson	£4.99
He Loves Lucy	Susan Donovan	£4.99
Mounting Desire	Nina Killham	£4.99
She'll Take It	Mary Carter	£4.99
Step on it, Cupid	Lorelei Mathias	£4.99

TO ORDER SIMPLY CALL THIS NUMBER

01235 400 414

or visit our website: www.headline.co.uk

Prices and availability subject to change without notice.